THEORETICAL MAGIC

THE FLOODMOUTH FILES
BOOK 1

T.M. BAUMGARTNER

ONE

Plastic tablecloths fluttered in the ocean breeze, threatening to steal hats and napkins. But all attention was fixed on the magic user starting his act on the Little Bites Cafe patio. Even the sunburned families coming back from the river tour slowed to watch.

Since the mage had commandeered the table next to mine, I had the best view in the square.

Like most businesses in the area, this cafe catered to tourists — if anyone I knew saw me there, I'd never hear the end of it. But Delia had chosen the venue, and if an actual vampire wasn't embarrassed, I wouldn't be either... though it was entirely possible she had no idea what it was like. My mentor may have looked at a map and picked the cafe closest to my workplace for our late-morning meeting.

The patio's speakers coughed to life as the mage spoke. "Welcome to Floodmouth, home of vampires, magic, and..." The man's baritone deepened as he raised his lavalier microphone closer to his lips and whispered seductively, "reliable public transportation."

The tourists giggled. Twisting in my seat, I scanned for any sign of Delia. I was ready to abandon the table if she looked bothered, but as kitschy as the place was, the mage's spells looked intriguing so I hoped we stayed.

Though he looked twenty and had alabaster skin and jet black hair, the hair and skin were due to a cosmetic charm, and his choice of comfortable loafers made me revise his age up a decade or two. After a few seconds, the wave of laughter died down. He grinned and poured scarlet ink into a silver chalice, the movements neat and practiced. "My name... is Master Vlad."

Secondhand embarrassment made me revisit my wish to stay. There were no vampire mages. *Everyone* knew the vampire council didn't transform humans who could work magic. Or... maybe not everyone, given the excited murmurs around me. Yes, the second vampire plague had been the focus of my PhD dissertation, so *maybe* I was a little more informed about the subject than the average person, but still. Some days I despaired.

The mage continued his patter as he poured black ink into another chalice, and I studied the incomplete spells on the plastic mat "Master Vlad" had unrolled on his table. His persona might be a sham, but he had some interesting magic. A Drake containment shell circled the perimeter, and at the center was a modified fluid movement spell. A dozen plastic chips stood in a neat stack next to the grease pencil at his right hand. Nothing I could see was particularly tricky, but it also wasn't beginner-level. At a guess, he'd trained on the east coast; the extra loop on the isolation barrier was a New York thing.

Blue ink went into a third chalice. "Today, we're going to see a little history made real." From the flair of the entertainer's movements, his act had been honed to perfection over time, as expected for an artist at a premier tourist spot. But I was fairly certain he'd never performed outdoors in Floodmouth — the corners of the mat had been weighted down with stones painted an arterial crimson. The rocks were a great idea; the color was *not*, though I had to give the guy credit for leaning into the bit.

A woman's voice interrupted my analysis. "Jen, my dear, how are you? No trouble getting away for a few moments?" With the grace of a dancer, Delia Tarragona slipped into the seat across from me. As with all vampires, age had been kind to her. I'd never been gauche enough to ask, but she was probably in her seventies. If I looked that good in forty years, I'd be elated. Given her strong features and a stubborn jaw, Delia may never have been a classical beauty, but I'd bet everything I owned that she'd never been overlooked.

These days, she had pure white hair cut into short curls that framed her long face. The only sign she was a vampire was the faint aura surrounding her. It was magic, but of a different sort than "Master Vlad" harnessed, the energy focused internally to keep her body healthy instead of wasted on gaudy displays. Delia's vampire aura was more subtle than most, but since the majority of people here couldn't see magical energy at all, she sat unnoticed among them.

I smiled and waved her concern away. "Everyone is in Seattle for an emergency summit."

Her eyes twinkled. "That must be a relief."

Delia was my mentor, so I suppressed my sigh. Somebody had to stay behind in Floodmouth to do any work that cropped up. As the most junior magical evidence analyst, I'd been picked. Theoretically, I *could* have gone to Seattle, because one coworker, Hamilton, refused to travel by public teleportation spell, so he had stayed as well. But my boss didn't suggest I go in his place and I didn't bring it up. Learning everything about a series of vampire deaths would have been fine. Spending a week crammed into meeting rooms with a supervisor who criticized my every move? Not so much.

It was nice to have a week without my boss noting every coffee refill and phone call. But I was still trying to impress Delia with my professionalism, so I merely smiled and said, "How are you?"

"Excellent. Before you ask, I'm still working on getting funding for the analyst position, so no news there, unfortunately. But I have a meeting with two of the board members later this week, and I think I can talk them around." She lifted the laminated menu. "What's good here?"

"People seem to like their cake pops." Possibly because cake pops were easy to eat while on the move. Or maybe because they were the cheapest thing on the menu. Either way, the seagulls had perfected the art of swooping in and stealing the treat before the tourists blinked.

Delia was silent as she studied the menu — just long enough for me to wonder how offensive the vampire-themed puns and stereotypes really were. Then her lips quirked up. "I need to get out more often."

This was a disaster. "Sorry. Why don't we find some-place else? There's a decent coffee cart around the corner." I should have offered to come to her, either before work or after.

"Nonsense. A bit of silliness is exactly what I need." She flagged down the server, a young woman with the unbothered facade of a university student who was only there for the paycheck. "I'll have the Blood Spatter

Surprise and a plain coffee. What will you have, Jen? My treat."

"Scarlet Pops and a coffee, please."

Once the server had left, Delia leaned forward. "Still having trouble with your supervisor?"

When I'd finally decided to leave academia last year, Delia's plan to hire me to develop spells for public applications had fallen through at the last minute, for reasons neither of us understood. In the aftermath, she'd become my mentor and friend and suggested I apply for my current position at the Federal Bureau of Magic Enforcement. We both agreed my resume would be stronger if I stayed at the FBME for at least a year, but I relied on her for practical tips to stay sane in that environment.

"Your suggestion to copy her on any direct requests helped," I admitted. "Occasionally, she replies that she doesn't need to micromanage my workload, but at least she's stopped complaining that I'm taking too long on my cases."

"That's progress. It may just take some time for the two of you to work out the best way to communicate. And that's on her, since she's the one in charge," she added. "How is it going with the rest of the team?"

I shrugged. "I'm the newest hire." Not just that — I was the only one who hadn't transferred in at a higher grade from another federal organization. The hierarchy of agencies was ill-defined and added complexity to the power dynamics, but everyone agreed I was at the bottom of the pile.

Next to us on the mage's table, a three-dimensional tableau was forming above the plastic mat, the scene loosely based on the jailbreak of the infamous outlaw Katie Tucker. Cerulean streamed out to form the Flood River and next to it, amber ink sketched the seven-story Italianate building of

The Vault — current home of the Federal Bureau of Magic Enforcement. The animation used a variant on Tsu flow mechanics that I'd never seen before.

The tour boats and water buses of the modern river had been replaced by a lone rowboat on the banks, which I chalked up to artistic license. In 1905, traffic on the Flood would have been heavy, since Floodmouth had been one of the most active ports on the Pacific and the river had been used to bring goods inland to the rest of California.

As an extra touch, the mage populated the scene with models of people, basing the features on cafe patrons. Each time he drew on a plastic chip and imbued it with magic, another table chattered excitedly as someone recognized themself. So far he had five members of Katie Tucker's gang in place on the roof of The Vault, ready to invade and free their leader. A small child darted across the patio to drop a bill in the mage's open case.

I wondered who "Master Vlad" would model Katie Tucker after. Probably whoever he thought might give him the largest tip.

Delia looked faintly amused by the show, but she stuck to the topic. "You may be the newest, but you're also the only one with an advanced degree, correct? I suspect they're intimidated. And concerned about their own advancement."

The idea of anyone being intimidated by *me* was ludicrous. "I'm the only one who can't do magic." Being able to *perform* magic wasn't technically necessary when documenting spells, but I had no illusions that I was on a promotional fast track.

Before Delia could respond, the server came back with our order. My cake pops were coated in white chocolate that had been dyed red. Though the texture looked nothing like blood, the color was pretty close. They were served in a magically cooled cloche with the Little Bite's logo, addressing two problems: melting chocolate and seagull attacks.

Delia's "Blood Spatter Surprise" turned out to be a vanilla cupcake with a raspberry cream center and raspberry syrup flung over the buttercream frosting. Suppressing a smile, she began eating with a fork and knife. "That may be an advantage in certain situations. Traveling to other cities, for instance. Not all places are as welcoming to magic users as Floodmouth."

I wasn't cut out for life anywhere else. I loved my crazy city, with its magic, vampires, and yes, reliable public transportation.

In Floodmouth, we still got tourists thinking vampires had fangs (they didn't), sucked blood (no, again), and were burned by light, holy water, or garlic (wrong on all three counts). There *was* a grain of truth in there. Vampires fed on human energy and that required a break in the skin, but it was done with sterile instruments in a highly regulated environment, and nobody was permanently harmed. Vampires didn't *need* to eat food, but they *could* eat anything they liked, including garlic. Sunlight wasn't a problem.

But Floodmouth never let the truth get in the way of a good story. Case in point: we were seated in a cafe full of people dying to see a real live vampire, and everyone was watching the show and ignoring Delia. Even *I* owned a hoodie stamped "Bloodmouth U" with tiny fangs dripping blood, a souvenir of a night out in Booksellers Row when I'd forgotten to bring a jacket.

The breeze picked up and I reached out with one hand to keep the entertainer's plastic mat anchored to the table, then pulled my hand back when "Master Vlad" narrowed his eyes at me. Did he think I was going to yank the mat away? Explaining would interrupt his show, so I folded my hands in my lap and hoped for the best.

With a theatrical wave of his arms, "Master Vlad" directed attention back to the scene in front of him. "It had just struck noon and all was quiet..." Magic flowed from his fingers to the final plastic chip as he set the spell. The unchanging tableau sprang to life as tiny waves bobbed on the surface of the river and the people on shore ran toward The Vault. Black ink billowed from the third floor and a sturdy woman leapt from the roof toward the river, her wrists and ankles still shackled.

Maybe I shouldn't have been surprised to see Delia's face on Katie Tucker since the vampire had all the subtle trappings of wealth, but seeing a vampire's face on the most famous magic user in Floodmouth's history made me blink. Delia let out a delighted laugh.

My phone buzzed with a text from Hamilton. *SA Salt came looking for you. I stalled, but you should get back here.* Crap. Supervisory Agent Salt was in charge of the FBME agents — all vampires — on the sixth floor. I didn't work for her. We'd never interacted. How did she even know my name? And why wasn't she in Seattle with the rest of the FBME vampires?

Delia leaned forward. "Do you need to leave?"

"Sorry," I said.

Delia waved my apology away as we stood. "Entirely my fault for asking to meet during working hours. Do you like opera? I have an extra ticket for Tuesday. *La Bohème.* It's Attilio Pagano's farewell tour, and having heard him in person will be something to tell your grandchildren. But no pressure — I know opera isn't everyone's cup of tea."

"I've never been," I admitted. With a wary glance at the

circling gulls, I wrapped the remaining cake pop in a napkin and shoved it in my pocket.

"Well, I won't put you on the spot, but if you'd like to go, send me a message. I'd be delighted to have you along." Her attention was diverted by Katie Tucker's flight across the Flood River, accompanied by her gang. Tiny vampire figures fired guns at the fleeing criminals, only to be driven back by spells. It was a scene worthy of a movie and bore zero resemblance to eyewitness accounts, which mentioned more subterfuge and sabotage and less cinematic spectacle.

Delia smiled again as she saw a version of herself throwing fireballs, and detoured to leave a large bill in the mage's open case. "Master Vlad" winked at her. Then he froze, as he finally noticed the vampire magic. His smile took on a pained rictus. But Delia turned and joined me, giving every indication she'd enjoyed the show.

As we reached the edge of the patio, a cluster of circling gulls dove to grab the stones holding down the plastic mat. They quickly realized the weights weren't cake pops and dropped them as they flew away, but the damage had been done. The ocean breeze flipped up a corner of the mat and suddenly the Drake containment shell inverted, splattering ink on everyone with a front row seat.

Shouting tourists leapt to their feet and wiped at their clothes and skin in dismay, smearing black, red, and blue ink with Little Bites branded paper napkins.

Delia looked at me. "*That's* what you were trying to prevent."

"Yeah..." I shrugged. "A Drake shield is great for demonstrations when it's set up on a solid base. But it's prone to inversion if the base isn't planar. And the seagulls around here really like those cake pops." My phone buzzed again. "Thanks again for the coffee and cake."

"My pleasure." Delia glanced back at the cafe patio, where "Master Vlad" was surreptitiously packing his case while the manager and servers rushed between patrons. "This was delightful. I really must get out more often."

I jogged back to work, leaving Delia sipping her coffee and watching the spectacle.

TWO

The Vault had seven stories, but strong wards were easier to protect below ground, so the magical evidence technicians lived in our own little basement world. Above us, the first two floors held the bureau's civilian administrators, mostly human, who dealt with timesheets and all the HR violations. On the third floor, there were temporary holding cells and offices for visiting law enforcement. The fourth floor held the armory. One floor up, the humans crazy enough to be on the entry override teams had offices, though they seemed to spend most of their free time running up and down the stairs and bragging about how much they could deadlift. Needless to say, the humans of the fifth floor were easily distinguished from those who worked in the basement.

Finally, on the top two floors, the FBME agents had offices. As far as I knew, they were all vampires, but I'd never gone up there to check. Vampires were less affected by most spells, so it made sense for the bureau to hire them. On the flip side, humans who wanted to be federal operatives gravitated toward other agencies, where vampires often weren't welcome.

There was no sign of Supervisory Agent Salt as I hurried down to the basement, and only Hamilton was visible when I opened the fire doors. Because we documented spells used for everything from terrorism to illegal surveillance, the basement workspace was structurally reinforced and had spells dividing the room to stop the spread of magic. I shared a section in the back corner with Hamilton. Given my own popularity, our proximity told me everything I needed to know about Hamilton's career progression. He wasn't bad at his work, but his personality quirks meant he'd never get promoted.

I made it to my workspace, feeling vaguely guilty about having been caught elsewhere — which was ridiculous, since I was an adult, and my job paid me for results, not to sit in one place. Across the aisle, Hamilton didn't look up from the lockbox he was working on. He'd been getting shocked intermittently all morning, but so far he'd refused my help.

"Thanks for the heads up," I said as I unlocked my desk drawer and removed the head-knock charm I'd been documenting.

"It's never good when upstairs comes looking."

"Think I should go find Salt? Or just wait?"

"If she didn't message you directly, I'd wait. Maybe you'll get lucky and something else will distract her." Then he yelped, muttered an obscene threat under his breath, and followed it up with a snarled, "And your mother, too!" It skirted HR rules about creating a hostile workplace. In the Federal Bureau of Magical Enforcement, nothing was real unless it was documented, and it would be hard to fire someone for the things he yelled. Not that I would complain anyhow, but we worked with more than one person whose method of climbing the ladder was to clear out nearby rungs.

Leaning one elbow on my desk, I said, "You ready for some help?"

He looked over and held up the back of his hand, all fingers pointing toward the ceiling. "Read between the lines, Perkins."

We grinned at each other.

Jason Hamilton wasn't a bad guy, even if he did have a few quirks. A skeletally thin white man in his forties, he ran ultramarathons in his free time and believed — or claimed to believe, anyhow — a vast array of conspiracy theories.

Hamilton went back to torturing himself, and I focused on my report. *The triple knot forming the power circle was first described by Doyle et al in Annals of Magic, 1948. Though once commonly used in North America, a survey of mages in 2010 showed most prefer the so-called Helicate Twist, aside from those trained at the University of Guelph.* I made a note to add the proper citation. Knowing that whoever had made this thing had trained in Canada might help the FBME agents find this mage. It was only through luck that the charm hadn't killed someone. Having the citations would help build the case if it went to court.

But even as I wrote up my findings, part of me worried about why Salt had wanted to talk to me. Finally, I locked the charm back in the drawer and stood up. "I can't deal with this. I'm going to find Salt."

Hamilton snorted without looking up. "It's your funeral." Then he grunted as the box shocked him again.

"That's it. I'm afraid to leave you alone with this thing." I walked to his workbench, flipped the latch on the lockbox, and lifted the lid. "Tada!"

Hamilton stared at the lockbox and then at me. "What the...? How did you do that?"

Flipping the lid closed, I centered the box between us. "Okay, so you see the anti-vampire ward here," I said, pointing to the runes on a band around the center. That would keep any vampire from coming within arm's length.

"Right."

"And then this section here is the shielding keeping the box hidden." This lockbox would tend to be ignored unless someone specifically looked for it — or it was in the magic-dampening Vault. The search team that found it had either known it was there or had done a thorough grid search of the room where it had been stored.

"Agreed."

Under the shielding spell was a tangle of spell knots I'd seen when Hamilton had pulled the lockbox from evidence. At first glance, they looked like decorative swirls, just like the other fake runes — it was a common tactic because it slowed down half-trained mages. Better to waste hours researching spells that didn't exist than risk losing a hand by triggering an unfamiliar exploding charm.

But I'd seen these specific swirls before. One of the primary sources I'd dug up when writing my doctoral dissertation was a group of scrolls held in a cask with both the anti-vampire runes and this spell protecting it. I'd spent two weeks analyzing the spells and then hadn't needed any of it for my dissertation, but no learning is wasted.

I ran my fingers along the swirls. "This reacts to the presence of any external magic." With a quick grin, I added, "It converts it into a pulse to the nerves, and the strength is related to the power of the external magic."

As the morning had progressed, Hamilton had tried a series of spells with increasing power to get into the chest. I hadn't been kidding when I'd said I was worried about leaving him alone. If he'd kept going for another hour, he would have thrown something stronger at it in frustration, and it would have knocked him into the wall.

"So you figured it out this morning and let me shock myself for three hours?" He laughed and shook his head. "I'm proud of you. That's cold."

"I thought maybe you had a different method of getting around it," I lied. "You know me, always bowing down to your greater experience."

"Brat." He reached forward and hissed as it shocked his finger again. "Hang on. Why did it do that?" Then he answered his own question. "Because I have my personal wards up." He closed his eyes and dropped his wards When he opened them again, he reached forward and flipped the lid open. "Nice!"

Personal wards weren't a problem for me, of course. Though I could see spells, design new ones, and disable traps, I was a magical dud. In academia, that wasn't a big problem; theory was the important part and there were plenty of mages around to cast a spell. But out in industry, nobody cared about the theory — they just wanted results. I had standard anti-theft and anti-corrosion wards on my bicycle, but I didn't bother wearing cosmetic charms at work.

We leaned forward to see what the spell had been protecting. Inside the lockbox were bundles of cash and a spiral-bound logbook. "Huh. If you show up tomorrow in fancy clothes and some bling, I'll know what happened."

"As if these clothes aren't as fancy as they get," he responded, offended. He rubbed his tie, a garish nightmare of blotches in a pattern he claimed warded off surveillance. With anyone else, I'd assume the tie was a joke, but I could never tell with Hamilton. "I might buy another of these beauties, though."

Stealing evidence would be harder than getting a second job to earn the money directly. The Vault was warded against that sort of thing. "It's not one-of-a-kind? That's the best evidence that a demon portal really did open in Eugene in 1964."

"Of course it did," he said with sincerity. He grinned and flipped the lid closed and open again. "Don't tell anyone about this. I want to get McPherson when she gets back."

"Just keep an eye on her," I called back as I walked toward the exit. "I'm not sure how much power it can reflect before it fizzles."

"Yeah, yeah, it's all fun and games until someone loses an eye."

I ran into SA Salt — almost literally — in the lobby when the elevator doors opened and she stepped out. Selina Salt had been an Olympic shot-putter, and she still had the same physique, though it was softened by her carefully tailored suits. Rumor had it she'd once dangled two mages over a four-story drop, one in each arm, to keep them from running away or attacking her while she was waiting for backup to arrive. Sure, she was a vampire, but that didn't give her extra speed or strength — it just changed the source of her energy.

Salt kept a hand on the elevator door to hold it open. "Local PD just sent over a search warrant for us to serve, and it expires at midnight. The rest of the entry override specialists are dealing with task force issues in Seattle. I need you to grab your gear and meet Agent Bowers down here in ten minutes."

"But..." My brain stalled. I was an evidence technician. We sat underground in The Vault and typed up our reports. We *never* served search warrants. "I'm not..."

Cutting me off with her free hand, Salt demanded, "You certified in entry override, did you not?"

Ah.

Technically... yes.

Vampire agents were a little harder to kill and immune to most magic. But they had one big disadvantage — if a private residence had anti-vampire warding, which was perfectly legal, the agents physically couldn't enter, even with a search warrant.

That was where the entry override teams came in. Humans would enter, disable the anti-vampire ward, and allow the vampire agents entry.

Never expecting to actually use the skill, I'd taken the classes and passed the exam last month. It gave me a bump in pay that I desperately needed, but more importantly, I found out what kind of magic the entry teams were likely to deploy. I'd been curious about the magical residue left on some items I'd cataloged.

I'd never expected to actually use the information out in the field. I didn't know one end of a gun from another, and my self-defense training consisted of strategically elbowing my big sister when we were kids and we both wanted the last slice of pizza. Sending me to enter a residence was ludicrous. I couldn't even cast spells to defend myself.

"Yes, but..." My words stumbled to a halt under her glare. She already knew every reason I could give for why this was a terrible idea. If I refused, I'd have to give back the money I'd been getting — if I didn't get fired outright.

"Ten minutes," she repeated. Then she turned, went

back into the elevator, and stabbed the button. "I have to get back to Seattle."

The doors closed before I could think of anything to say.

THREE

It took more than ten minutes. First, I had to print out my cheat sheet and equipment checklist. As I took the elevator to the fourth floor to check out a radio, bracers, and vest, I skimmed my notes.

"Identify myself as law enforcement," I mumbled. "Check for traps in front of the door, open the door, check for traps inside the door, and then find and disable the wards." Each part had multiple steps. Checking for traps in front of the door involved lying on the ground to search for raised concrete where runes might be embedded, and I had my doubts that the regular entry crew followed all these procedures. It would take twenty minutes to get to the door, and I couldn't see the entry team agents waiting that long. They couldn't even stand in line for coffee at the coffee cart across the street without complaining.

And why did it have to be with Agent Bowers? Even I, nearly completely insulated from the Bureau gossip, had heard of Bowers. He'd been there about the same amount of time as I had, but while I'd been keeping my head down and trying to fit in, he'd solved two high-profile cases and been trotted out for a press conference with the mayor. Granted, he'd looked supremely irritated the entire time he'd been in front of the cameras, but he was someone who was clearly *going places*. Given his reputation as a humorless automaton with no patience for inefficiency, this assignment could be nothing but an unmitigated disaster. And why was Bowers even here and not in Seattle?

It all made me wish I'd followed Delia's advice to keep applying for other jobs.

The elevator dinged and let me out into a nearly empty, airy room with marble floors. So this was the armory. Down in the basement, we had yellow fluorescent lights and carpet that had last been replaced in 1973 after the anti-vampire activists had been ejected from the building. Above ground, it was easier to remember the building had been created in the grand Italianate style. The Flood River sparkled in the sunlight. Tall windows, arches, and natural lighting — with this sort of environment, working with the agents might be worth it.

Then I looked at the equipment list, which included a bullet-resistant vest, warded bracers, and optional riot helmet. Actually, maybe I was fine staying down in the basement.

Aside from the procedures to stay safe, there was a whole sequence of things we were supposed to do to keep everything legal; with a warrant, we didn't have to be let in by the owner or renter, but if we damaged the door, we had to fill out a bunch of forms. Everything was probably second nature for anyone who had done a few of these. Normally, there were at least two people on the entry override team, so I *should* have been going with another entry override specialist, someone with some experience who could watch to make sure I didn't violate any laws.

But everyone else with the certification was gone and I wasn't about to argue with Supervisory Agent Salt.

The equipment counter had two inches of glass-clad polycarbonate, with some serious wards embedded between the layers, courtesy of the 1973 building takeover. The first thing the rioters had done was rush to the fourth floor and ransack the armory. They'd also stolen radios so they could listen in on the plans to retake the building. Many, many things had changed after that. In the current configuration, there was a sliding hatch allowing items to be passed in and out, and a round metal grill to allow sound through when the hatch was shut.

The hatch was currently closed, and the lone occupant of the room beyond was turned away, feet up on a shelf, watching a movie on his phone. He was a white vampire in his mid-thirties, with short brown hair and a belly hanging over his belt.

Leaning toward the metal grate, I cleared my throat. "Excuse me."

Without sitting up, he reached over and opened the hatch, then raised an eyebrow. "Yes?"

I knew what he saw — a white human woman in her thirties with mousy brown hair who looked like she should be grading papers at a college instead of wandering the halls of the Federal Bureau of Magic Enforcement. Raising my lanyard to show my ID card, I said, "I need to check out a radio, bracers, and vest." When he didn't move, I added, "I don't think I'll need the riot helmet."

His feet dropped to the floor. "For what?"

"Entry team for a search warrant." The training hadn't covered what we were supposed to say to get the armory sergeant to take us seriously.

He stared at me for a long five seconds. "We don't give

entry gear to evidence technicians," he said with finality. Then he shut the hatch, secure in the knowledge that I couldn't do anything about his job performance and he was sitting behind a barrier I'd never make it through.

With everyone in Seattle, this guy was enjoying a paid vacation. More power to him, but the only thing worse than being unprepared to serve on an entry team was being unprepared and *unequipped*. The movie's soundtrack resumed, and he leaned back in his chair and stared at the tiny screen.

I wondered what I was supposed to do now. Maybe call Hamilton and see if he knew the guy behind the counter? Somehow track down Salt and whine like a child because the guy in charge of the armory was being mean to me? Quit my job?

Maybe I could just go back to my workspace in the basement and pretend I'd never been assigned to this thing.

No. I was an adult. I'd successfully defended my dissertation in front of multiple faculty who thought the magical theory department should be defunded. I had a job, paid taxes, and did all the other boring adult things. I would step up there and *make* him take me seriously. Somehow.

Before I could act on my plan, the elevator dinged again and Agent Simon Bowers stepped out. In some ways, the vampire looked the same as he had during the mayor's press conference, including the air of irritation. But whereas he'd looked resigned to listening and answering questions then, now he was a bundle of concentrated energy in an expensive suit.

He was a tall man in his early thirties, with brown hair and light brown skin that could either have been what he was born with or the result of his latest vacation. With his angular features, it could have gone either way, though he definitely had that "yacht in the Caribbean" sort of look. He also had an air about him that said he was too good for this place. To be fair, the amount he'd spent on his suit and shoes would cover my rent for six months, and I'd never seen any other agents in bespoke suits, so maybe he really *was* too good for this place. Even his gear bag looked like it had just been dry cleaned.

He was definitely annoyed and not bothering to hide it. "Perkins?"

"Yes." I held up my lanyard in case he wanted proof, mostly because I still had it in my hand.

My response made him look even more annoyed. "So why are you up here instead of down in the lobby?" He saw the notes in my other hand, with neat bullet points and important phrases bolded, and blinked. "You're up here trying to remember what to do?"

"No." I mean, yes, I was, but that wasn't the hold-up, and given the tension in his jaw, I was glad. "They won't check out entry gear to evidence technicians."

"You're an evidence technician."

"With entry override certification, yes." I waited, figuring there were even odds he would throw up his hands and find Salt so he could track down someone qualified to do the job, or take on the armory officer. I hoped it was the former. Forget great views and marble floors. I would sit in the basement working on my reports until the end of the day without taking breaks if it would get me out of this.

Some people ran toward danger, but I've always felt it was better for everyone if I stayed out of the way and let the heroes do their thing.

Bowers turned on his heel and marched over to the still-closed hatch. "Taylor, she needs entry gear." It was an order, with no greeting to soften the words. Either this guy was rude to everyone, or these two had a history.

And just like that, a radio, vest, and bracers were pushed through the hatch, along with a clipboard for me to sign. From the look the armory officer gave me, I was betting he and Bowers were not friends. I hoped I never needed to come back up here again.

Once I'd collected the gear, we took the elevator down to the main lobby in silence. The vest was surprisingly heavy, and it took me a bit to tighten the velcro straps so it rode high enough that I could bend at the waist. The bracers were made of some sort of stiff fabric with dozens of spelled metal plates riveted on, and they smelled of disinfectant and rust. Stretching from the crook of my elbow to my wrist, they were meant to offer minor protection against a variety of attacks so the wearer could stay alive long enough to respond. But they'd been made for someone with much larger arms than mine. Even with the buckles pulled as tight as they would go, they still slid around every time I moved, and I had to raise my hands to get them to slide down far enough so I could bend my wrist. Next to the elegantly dressed man at my side, I looked like a low budget cosplayer.

Great. This was going absolutely great.

Just having the extra protection brought home how dangerous this could be. I felt like an idiot and gave serious consideration to whether paying the rent was *really* that important.

Outside, the glare made me squint until I dug out my sunglasses. The nice weather had brought the tourists, and we had to push through knots of people blocking the sidewalk as they read their travel guides.

Bowers ignored the flirtatious glances cast his way, his

face an unmoving mask of impatience. I was used to the crowds, but normally I could walk by unnoticed. Wearing the vest and bracers, I got puzzled glances.

Even those who couldn't see magic clearly could tell I wasn't a vampire. The everyday signs of cumulative damage, from sun-caused freckles to puffy eyes from my late night effort to find my father's current address, showed on my face. It wasn't that vampires didn't age — vampirism was no path to immortality — but the magic that sustained a vampire dealt with the minor annoyances. Eventually, their bodies grew old enough that they couldn't take in life power fast enough to counteract the damage, but until that happened, they remained healthy.

As far as I was concerned, that was the only attractive thing about vampirism.

A water taxi waited for us at the Third Street dock, though it would have been nearly as quick to catch the next water bus. The pilot was a stout woman with pale skin, green eyes, and copper hair, with a sun-block charm looped around her neck. Her face lit up when she saw Bowers coming. "Good to see you, Simon! Your mother says the mayor wants to give you an award. Congratulations!" Bowers must have made a face, because she laughed in a good-natured way, as if she'd been expecting that response. When I hopped to the deck after him, she held out her hand and smiled warmly. "Alice Donlan."

"Jen Perkins."

Alice had already reversed away from the dock by the time I sat down. Bowers took a seat on the next bench, not so far away that it would look like he was avoiding me, but too far for idle conversation. Maybe he was too good for me, too, but it felt more like he just didn't like to waste time with small talk when he was working. In a way, being impersonally ignored was a relief after dealing with the petty power plays in the basement.

The smell of the water competed with other odors as we traveled upriver. A tour boat gave off the sweet scent of fresh caramel popcorn, and we passed one pontoon with a gasoline engine.

Twelve years ago, when I'd first started spending more time on the river, most of the boats had fuel motors. But the cost of magic power had come down and Floodmouth had enacted strict regulations. These days, you could row on the Flood without risking carbon monoxide poisoning, though you still had to worry about being run down by someone in a hurry.

Alice was a competent pilot, traveling quickly but giving the other watercraft enough room that our wake wouldn't affect them. With her in charge, I relaxed enough to examine the wards on the boat. Water resistance for the cushions, a bit of extra strength on the hull, and one spell to keep the windscreen clear. It was a far cry from the cheap water taxis my friends and I took home if we stayed out late.

A bit of magic on the deck near the gate took me thirty seconds to work out, mostly because it was fading. There was a triple loop in a wave with a bounding ring to conserve energy, which could alter momentum in the area. Finally, I saw the jagged edge of a Heikatsu plane just above the deck. It was rare to see that triple loop used by mages outside the Iberian peninsula, but I'd never seen a Heikatsu plane incorporated by anyone who hadn't studied in Japan. The result was a neat little anti-slip spell, catching anyone sliding on the deck. I hadn't seen its like before.

Keeping one hand on the rail, I went forward to stand near Alice. "Who did your anti-skid spell?" I asked, gesturing toward the gate.

She glanced over, then turned her attention back to the scatter of paddleboats ignoring the rules of precedence in front of us. "My child's father. What do you think?"

A year ago, I would have wangled an invitation so I could find out his influences. But what would I do with that information now? There were no papers to write at the Federal Bureau of Magic Enforcement. "It's a nice bit of work. Starting to degrade a bit, though, so you might want to have him recast it."

Alice guided the boat to the Coopers Road dock. "Thanks for the warning. He's not out for another three years, but his brother might be able to help." She let the boat glide forward until it just barely kissed the dock, then grabbed a line and hauled on it to keep the boat in place. "Here you are. Call me when you're ready to return and I'll meet you here."

"Thanks, Alice." Bowers leapt to the dock with no effort and strode away.

I climbed up more slowly, hampered by the vest and the bracers that kept sliding down over my hands, making it difficult to hold on to the rail. "Nice to meet you."

Alice swung the gate closed after I'd reached the dock. "Stay safe, now."

Before I could respond, she had zipped away, and Bowers was standing on the sidewalk, waiting impatiently for me to catch up.

FOUR

The apartment was on the fifth floor of a postmodernist block formed of glass and steel, complete with a walkway tube that looked like a hamster habitat zigzagging its way up the front of the tower. As we walked in the main entrance, I wondered how they kept people from skateboarding or biking down what was essentially a seven story ramp. If this building had been in the Warehouse District where I lived, they would have outlawed the tube as a public health hazard. But dignity and money went hand in hand, so maybe it was never a problem here.

"Mohammed Murphy," Bowers said as we crossed the immaculate lobby to the elevators. "Goes by Mo on all his documentation. Arrested last week for smuggling some sort of endangered bird. He took a swing at the officers with a boat oar and then tried to run, so he's been sitting in jail all this time."

His voice was almost hypnotic, warm and confident, and it made me like him a little better. It also made me wonder if it was enhanced by a spell, and I missed part of what he was saying as I searched for any sign of magic.

Nothing. He just really had a great voice. When I tuned back in, Bowers had finished explaining that the police had obtained a warrant to search for anything relevant to Mo's smuggling business or other illegal enterprises — which covered a whole lot of ground when I thought about it.

At some point, the police had noticed spelled amulets on the animals. That put serving the warrant squarely in FBME territory, but there had been some mix-up about transferring the paperwork. Both sides were pointing fingers at each other, but the upshot was that Bowers was on his own with an evidence technician because everyone else was in Seattle setting up a task force and the warrant was only valid until midnight.

Honestly, I didn't need to know anything about Mo, but it was better than standing in silence as the elevator whisked us upward. The fifth floor landing had a door to the hamster tube, and I decided going that route on the way down would be my reward for dealing with all this.

Mo lived at the end of the hall farthest from the exterior walkway, which gave him a clear view of the river. There were only a few residences per floor, each about four thousand square feet. My apartment would fit in the hallway with room to spare. And I had a roommate. "Smuggling must pay pretty well," I said as Bowers took a set of keys out of an evidence bag.

"Hm? Oh, the building. He inherited the apartment from his parents." While I'd been goggling at the wealth on display, Bowers hadn't even noticed. Which meant he was used to such things. That fit with the suit and the shoes, but though FBME agents were paid more than evidence technicians, they didn't make *this* much. No, he had money from somewhere else.

While I contemplated that, Bowers knocked on the

door. "FBME," he called. "We have a warrant to search the premises."

Vampires could sense humans within a 20-foot radius — it had something to do with their sensitivity to energy — but this apartment was large enough that someone could be inside without Bowers knowing. He knocked again, then picked through the keys on the keyring.

As he slid the key into the deadbolt, I suddenly remembered there were things I was supposed to do before it was safe to open the door. "Wait!"

Bowers froze.

Smoothing out the cheat sheet I'd shoved in my pocket, I skimmed the procedure. There probably wasn't much point looking for runes in front of the door. For one thing, they would be under the carpet, and there was no way to look without cutting out a section. For another, Bowers was already standing there; if there had been a spell triggered by proximity, it would have gone off by now.

"Why do I get the feeling you've never done this before?" Even with disbelief threaded through, his voice was still beautiful.

"Give me a sec," I said, skimming over the rest.

"I just need you to go inside and disable the anti-vampire ward. It should take you thirty seconds, tops."

"And the longer you distract me, the longer it will take." I shoved the paper back in my pocket. "Okay, we should be good to open the door." Maybe this apartment wouldn't have an anti-vampire ward at all, and I could just leave him here and go back to work.

He unlocked the door without another word and pushed it open with the knob. His hand stopped short at the boundary, so the door slowly eased open. Bowers pushed his palm against the air, gaining a quarter inch before he yanked his hand back and shook it, as if it stung. He moved to the side and waited.

"Thirty seconds?" I asked.

"They say it's always right next to the door."

The vampire knew more about my job here than I did. I poked the air with one finger, ready to snatch it back if I felt anything, but my hand went through without resistance. It really was too much to hope that the door was warded against everyone and we could just leave.

The rest of the procedures I had on my cheat sheet boiled down to "find the spell and disable it." That was something I could do. Understanding spells took years of study and creating spells took innate talent, but breaking spells could be done by any idiot with water, salt, flames, or a bit of force.

Pulling out the shaker of salt I'd liberated from the break room, I crossed over the threshold. Mo's apartment had a wall of windows on two sides, so I didn't need to flip on the lights when I entered. Everything looked vaguely familiar, which was odd. I definitely would have remembered if I'd been in this building before. The living room had a leather couch that would have fit fifteen people, but there were no signs anyone had ever used it. The air smelled stale — nobody had been inside while Mo had been in prison. At least he didn't have a cat who'd been waiting all this time for someone to feed it.

Right next to the door, Bowers had said. I searched, but I didn't see anything anchoring a spell. If it was on the wall under a layer of paint, we might be here all day. A small table near the door held a carved wooden bowl, the kind interior decorators put in their catalogs for holding keys and mail, as if it wouldn't immediately fill up with everything else that had no specific place.

"He bought the full set of furnishings from the furniture store," I muttered as I looked around again. *That* was why it looked so familiar. I passed this exact layout on the corner of Thirty-second and Brown every day on my way to work. The only thing original was a mosaic set into the wall depicting Katie Tucker's last ride. This one was expertly done, but the artist had changed the river from blue to red, making it look as if the boats floated on a tide of blood. It was an odd image to embed in this beige and white apartment.

From out in the hallway, Bowers called, "Problem?"

"No." If Mo didn't mind living in a generic showroom, who was I to say he was doing it wrong? Trix and I ate breakfast on a table we'd scavenged from the street and refurbished with tubes of glitter acrylic paint her ex-boyfriend had left behind.

The carved bowl didn't have anything in or under it, and neither did the table. So much for Bowers's certainty that the ward would be right inside the door. Moving past the mega-couch, I checked the glass-topped coffee table. Yep, it even had the pyramid of wooden balls from the furniture store. There were a few rings from glasses someone hadn't put a coaster under, but no sign of the spell anchor.

I chose the kitchen next because it had a line of sight to the front door. Something beeped as I walked past the refrigerator and I stopped. Five seconds later, it beeped again. "Uh, I may have a problem here."

"What?"

The beeps sped up, in the way they did when a home security system was about to call the cops. Or a bomb was about to go off in a thriller movie while the hero tries to decide which wire to cut. But this wasn't a standard security system, and I didn't think it would just sound an alarm.

Screw it. I hadn't signed up for this. I sprinted for the door.

Just before I reached the hallway, I hit an invisible barrier so strong that I rebounded, landing flat on my back on the floor. Blinking at the ceiling in confusion, I tried to figure out how I'd ended up there.

"Perkins! Get up!" Bowers was agitated. "You need to disable that thing."

The beeps became a solid wall of noise. Then there was silence.

I raised my head. Nothing happened. Bowers was still standing in the hallway, looking like he would rush in and beat the alarm to death if he could just get past the anti-vampire ward. And between us, I could see another ward, one that hadn't been there before.

I couldn't get out until I took that one down.

"This doesn't normally happen, does it?"

He ignored my question. "Get up and find that thing right now."

As I climbed to my feet, I examined the new spell. Since it had been triggered in one location and affected only this door, it was easier to trace. "Kitchen cabinet," I said aloud as I followed the line of magic back to the kitchen. It was probably where they had set the anti-vampire ward, too. By having the second one show up, they'd actually made the place less secure.

A loud screech from the bedroom interrupted my thoughts. That had been something big and bird-like. "What was *that*?"

The answer to my question trotted into the living room and screeched again. It was almost as tall as me and had wings. At first, I thought it was some sort of deformed pelican. Then it opened its tapered jaw, and I saw a row of short, sharp teeth.

That was a *pterodactyl*, my brain informed me in disbelief, even as I was running away. I rounded the couch, but it hopped over. With a speed that I could never match, it darted forward and grabbed my leg in its jaws and clamped down. Its teeth went through my khakis, through my skin, and down to the bone. I screamed.

As much as I'd like to say my response was logical and carefully determined, the truth was that my instincts kicked in and I performed the same "Get it off me!" maneuver I would have done if a wasp had come near me. It wouldn't have done anything at all if the bracers hadn't slipped down over my hands and hit the pterodactyl. Its flesh shriveled where the bracer made contact, black oily smoke rising between us.

The pterodactyl released my leg and jumped back, circling the couch warily. I could make out the imprint of the bracer on one cheek. My heart pounded in my ears as I scrambled to keep furniture between us.

Bowers yelled, "Destroy the ward and let me in to help!" But even though I knew knocking out the ward was the only way to survive, I was too frightened to turn away from this dinosaur.

(Though pterodactyls were technically not dinosaurs, as one of my grad school friends was fond of telling people, since they lacked the hole in their hip bones and the crest on their upper arm bone. Even as I was fighting for my life, my brain was stuck on pedantic distinctions. Also, Amar was going to be so upset he wasn't here right now when I told him about it later.)

I limped as I rotated to keep the pterodactyl in front of

me. Now that it wasn't chewing on my leg, I could see that it was magically animated. Probably that should have been obvious, since pterodactyls had been extinct for tens of millions of years. All the magic tied back to something in the kitchen cabinet, except now there was a no-longer-extinct not-dinosaur blocking my access.

But I had a weapon that I knew worked. The pterodactyl was wary of the bracers now, which gave me a chance to limp sideways around the couch, keeping the glass wall close to my back. The creature feinted. I almost fell down when I jumped to avoid it.

"Keep it away from your throat," Bowers said, the first useful thing he'd offered since... well, since I'd met him. He was right. Contact with the bracers would make it let go if it grabbed my leg again, but if it grabbed my throat, I'd be dead before I could react.

Another step closer to the kitchen. It cocked its head, as if thinking about my motives. Then it screeched, a sound which paralyzed me long enough for it to rush forward, jaws agape, aiming for my face. I caught a whiff of smoke and rotting flesh.

Though I tried to knock it aside, my reactions were too slow and my hand ended up in its mouth — which worked even better than I'd planned. The back of its throat bubbled where it touched the bracer. It tried to back away, but its teeth caught on my shirt and I went with it.

By that time, I'd realized this was the best position to be in, and I clamped its head to me with my other forearm. Flesh sizzled, I screamed, the pterodactyl roared, and then all at once, its head popped and I was showered with gobbets of putrid flesh.

I stood, shaking, as noxious fluid mixed with my blood and dripped onto the floor. When had I signed up for *this*?

FIVE

My involuntary daydream about nice, safe academia —
where I never had to deal with extinct animals trying to
literally kill me, that I'd stupidly left just so I could pay off
my loans and afford to eat something other than ramen
every once in a while — came to a halt two seconds later
when what Bowers was saying finally got through to me.

"... break the ward so I can help you if another one of
those things shows up."

Right. Another one. *That* was a valid reason for me to
move. I staggered into the kitchen, leaving a trail of carnage
behind me.

First, I needed to clean off my hands so I didn't accidentally modify another spell by dripping pterodactyl fluids
onto it. The kitchen sink had a touchless faucet, one of
those ones that sensed when anything was close. I'd never
considered how useful those might be, but it kept me from
leaving smears of blood and charred flesh on the chrome as I
washed my hands. Despite my best efforts, one bracer
slipped down into the water, but the spells held.

Mo would have fun cleaning up when he came home,

but it served him right. What kind of person creates a ptero-dactyl to protect against strangers coming into their apart-ment? That was overkill. Half the time, Trix and I didn't bother locking our doors.

A three-ring binder with activated spells rested in the long, thin cupboard that had been meant to store cutting boards. I flipped through until I found the laminated card tucked in the back pocket. Brown stains obscured the lines, but I could make out the caster's sigil on the bottom left and a neat line drawing of a pterodactyl in the upper right. There would have been pterodactyl DNA mixed in with the ink used to draw the spell — at first glance, I could make out a proximity sensor, a timer, a protection ring entwined with a blood-made-flesh fractal and a containment rune. That last bit was either sloppy or malicious — containing the pterodactyl was important, but that rune had also kept me from escaping. The whole thing was inert now, which was good because my own blood oozed onto it. Wrapping the towel around my bleeding biceps, I flipped back to the front.

The first page held a standard anti-vampire spell, drawn on some sort of treated cardboard. The page after that was nearly illegible — the power circle activating it had faded down to nothing. There would be no surprises coming from that.

The last two pages held commercial anti-noise and anti-rodent spells, which made me side-eye the apartment. If a place *this* expensive had rats and noisy neighbors, I didn't feel so bad about mine.

Secure in the knowledge that no more creatures were likely to attack me, I flipped back to the anti-vampire spell. The page wouldn't tear, but salt or flame would break the spell. Naturally, the kitchen had an induction stove, so I couldn't just burn the paper. I'd dropped my purloined salt shaker when I'd bounced off the containment spell. No problem. Even people who ate takeout for every meal had salt in their kitchen. Mo had granulated iodized salt and a box of kosher crystals.

I dumped a handful of kosher salt into my palm and stopped. Vampires didn't drink blood, but they absorbed energy released through breaks in the skin.

Letting a vampire into the room when I was bleeding all over the floor might not be a great idea. To some degree, vampires couldn't help themselves, and I had enough going on with blood loss and fighting off infection from the crud congealing on my clothes. Having a vampire drain energy wouldn't kill me, but it would lengthen my recovery. There was a reason vampires weren't allowed to work as paramedics or doctors.

When I walked back to the front door, Bowers had switched from shouting commands to pacing impatiently. I waited until he stopped and looked at me. "I found his home-spell book and nothing else is going to attack me. Before I neutralize the anti-vampire spell, do you have a first-aid kit in your bag?"

"I wouldn't —" He snarled in frustration, then dug open his bag. The pouch he tossed to me was heavy. "Wash the wounds under running water first. I can... Never mind." He shoved his hands in his pockets.

The gauze and tape weren't spelled, which seemed odd — even the cheapest first aid kits had anti-infection spells embedded into their components. Then I remembered the kit had been meant for a vampire. Most magic didn't work on them, and complications were unlikely anyhow. The bandages were probably to keep Bowers from bleeding on his fancy suits while he waited to heal.

My trousers were a total loss. Even if I could get the bloodstains out, the fabric was ripped in patches from knee to ankle. There was no point in taking off my clothes to save them, so I cut the cloth to make my calf easier to access. My leg was a mess as well, but the pterodactyl had missed the major blood vessels. I'd be able to walk into urgent care and wait in line with everyone else who wasn't actively dying.

Ten minutes later, I was patched up enough to feel secure about letting a vampire through the front door. It could have been worse. Aside from my chewed-on calf, there was a long laceration on my upper arm where the bracer hadn't protected me, and a couple holes on my cheek. But I could still move all my fingers and I hadn't lost an eye. With the right healing spells, I wouldn't even end up with scars. Makeup would cover the worst of it by Sunday, so I wouldn't have to answer awkward questions at my sister's fifteen-year memorial service.

Hopefully, the Bureau would replace my ruined clothes. If not, I'd be wearing the same slacks every day until my birthday in three months. My mom was always good at buying practical gifts.

I poured kosher salt onto the cardstock with the anti-vampire ward and ground the crystals into the page until the lines were severed. There was a fizzle under my palm and two seconds later, Bowers was standing in the kitchen.

"How badly are you hurt?"

"I'll live." Maybe my battle with death had impressed him enough that we could develop some sort of rapport.

"Right, but do you need to go to the hospital now, or can it wait?"

Oh. Not rapport or empathy. Legally, there had to be at least two people in the room for a search. If I left for the hospital, he'd have to get another agent out here, and there wasn't anyone left. "Let's do this."

We started in the living room, Bowers on one side and me on the other until we'd finished our part and switched. After that, we continued to the kitchen, the front bathroom, the home theater, the guest suite, the office, the main bathroom, and the main bedroom. Since I had zero experience searching, I probably could have just sat down and watched while the vampire worked, but he didn't say anything. Out of the corner of my eye, I watched how he examined each item and tried to emulate him, taking everything out of spaces before feeling around the extents with my fingers. He *had* to have seen me using him as a guide, but he only added, "Don't forget to knock on surfaces to see if they're hollow. We get some people trying to be clever with false bottoms and secret drawers."

Neither of us found a damn thing.

I had a brief flicker of hope when I found a tiny fire safe under Mo's bed, but that dimmed when I realized he'd written the combination below the keypad. It held his birth certificate, passport, and a few other documents, but nothing of any interest to us. His phone and laptop had already been seized when he'd been arrested.

All my adrenaline had faded by the time we reached the end, and I sat on the floor with my back against the wall watching Bowers take out each dresser door and examine it. "I don't get it. Why risk a murder-by-magical-means charge when you're not even hiding anything?"

The pterodactyl spell was all kinds of illegal, and Mo would probably get at least three extra years in prison for having it enabled. If it had killed me, he would have spent the rest of his life behind bars. We had multiple laws detailing mandatory minimum sentences for things like that. Nobody in their right mind would keep that sort of spell in their home, so those laws let the politicians appear tough on crime without alienating their donor base.

Bowers grunted and slid the drawer back in. "We might be missing it."

A clump of goo was drying on my shirt. I said, "If there's something here, I can't find it."

"Or it might not be here anymore. It's been a week. He might have had a friend come over and move everything."

If he had, Mo's friends did him no favors. Leaving that pterodactyl protection spell active had been a major misstep. Still, my short tenure at the FBME had taught me that criminal masterminds were only found in fiction. Real-life criminals were just as stupid as everyone else.

Bowers finished with the dresser and stood. "I give up. Let's get you to the hospital."

I climbed to my feet, a process that took ten seconds since I was exhausted. "I'm not spending five hours in the ER for someone to give me a few bandages and a healing spell. The urgent care on Fifteenth Street will be fine."

He gave me a look of barely concealed horror. "Half the doctors there are practicing on provisional licenses, and the DA's office will want documentation. We'll go to Flood-mouth General. I know people — it'll be quick."

Floodmouth General had a riverfront entrance, so at least I wouldn't need to get on the subway looking like this. I had questions about why a vampire FBME agent would have connections there. Most hospitals only allowed vampires in when escorted, unless they were being treated for major trauma. But I was too tired to argue about it.

I was also too tired to suggest walking down the hamster tunnel ramp on the front of the building, which was just icing on the cake of this miserable experience. I'd been chewed on by a pterodactyl and ruined an outfit, and all we had to show for it was the notebook of home spells and a new hole in the wall out in the hallway that neither of us mentioned. From the look of it, Bowers had tried to get around the ward on the door by tunneling through the wall. It was a nice effort, but any competent ward covered walls and windows as well. Occasionally, I'd run across one where the caster had ignored the ceiling or floor, but that was just one more reason not to buy cut-rate spells on Booksellers Row.

The elevator seemed miles away as I trudged grumpily away from the apartment. If there was any justice in the universe, Mo would have a severe rodent infestation by the time he got out of prison.

SIX

The water taxi waited for us at Coopers Road dock. Alice took one look at me and wrapped a blanket around my shoulders. It was thick and woolen and had a heating spell on it and was possibly the most comfortable thing I'd ever touched. I really hoped it was self-cleaning, because I was still covered in pterodactyl gore, but I was too exhausted to work out the spells on it.

"We'll have you there before you know it," she told me, and then proceeded to break multiple laws to prove it, though she did slow down so as not to swamp a family in a canoe.

Bowers spent the journey pacing along the rail, as if that would make the boat faster. Getting the only available entry override non-agent banged up on her first outing was probably going to be a paperwork nightmare for him. Maybe that was why he was so gloomy. But better gloomy than irritated at me, so I didn't complain.

When the boat glided to a gentle stop at the hospital dock, a man in green scrubs and a white coat waited with a gurney. He had short brown hair, light brown skin, and the energy of someone who thought biking across every bridge on the way to work, followed by an hour of lifting weights, was exhilarating. His ID badge read Dr. Jose Aguilar, and someone had crossed out his first name and written "Che" with a red marker. "Simon! It's good to see you, man!"

Bowers actually smiled briefly. "Hey, Che. Thanks for this."

"Not a problem." Then the doctor jumped into the boat and helped me up, keeping hold of one arm as if he was worried I might fall over.

I handed the blanket to Alice. "Thank you so much. I'll pay to get it cleaned." There had to be some way to get reimbursed for that.

She smiled and took my other arm. "Don't worry about it. I'll send the bill to the FBME. It's included in my contract with them. You just concentrate on getting well."

Dr. Aguilar practically lifted me onto the dock. "Have a seat," he said, patting the gurney. "I'm Che and I'll be your doctor today. And you are?"

"Jen Perkins." Behind me, I heard Alice's boat pulling away, leaving the dock free for the next emergency. Bowers was still on board. I tried not to feel abandoned, since the hospital wouldn't want a vampire standing around inside, but this still felt like the wrong place to be. "Look, I know Bowers said we had to come here, but I'd be fine going to urgent care."

Che laughed. "You're here now. Relax." And then he jogged inside the building, pushing me and the gurney in front of him. Various people in scrubs looked up as we entered, but quickly went back to what they were doing. Not an emergency, their expressions said, just Dr. Aguilar trying to burn off extra energy.

We ended up in a curtain-lined alcove where he

removed the bandages, starting with my face. "Simon didn't put these on," he stated.

"No," I agreed. "I hadn't disabled the anti-vampire ward yet. Thought it was better to patch myself up first."

Che sighed. "Such a waste of talent."

My questioning noise turned into a hiss as he pulled the tape off my arm and the bandage stuck to the wound.

"Sorry about that." He poured saline into a waiting bowl and soaked the wound. "Simon used to work here," he said, answering my unasked question even as he prodded the flesh. "He'd just finished his surgical residency before he changed."

"He... What?" It made no sense. Everyone knew vampires weren't welcome in hospitals. Nobody would bother spending all that time and money getting a medical degree when they would have to throw it all away the moment the vampire council approved the application.

Che moved on to the bandage on my leg and winced in sympathy when he saw what lay beneath. "Why does it look like you got attacked by an alligator?"

"Pterodactyl."

His hands stilled and he looked up. "You got attacked by a dinosaur? Damn! Magic enforcement gets some *serious* shit."

I couldn't help myself. "Technically, pterosaurs aren't dinosaurs. They branched off at a different point." Then I heard my words. "Sorry. I have this friend who's really into this stuff."

He gave me a broad smile and went back to cleaning my leg. "Are you kidding? This is great. My five-year-old nephew tells me everything there is to know about dinosaurs every Monday when we have our big family breakfast. Now I can say, 'Yeah, but did you know pterosaurs aren't even dinosaurs' and he'll stop treating me like the village idiot for a few minutes."

"Take him to the Seventh Street Museum and ask for Amar at the paleontology exhibit. Then stand back and let them babble at each other for a few hours." Aiming a fixated child at a friend might be a little mean, but Amar owed me for all the times I'd listened to him talk about his favorite subject.

"I may just do that." He frowned at my leg, then pulled off the dirty gloves and rummaged in a drawer before donning clean gloves. "How did you end up getting chomped by a pterodactyl while Simon didn't even get his clothes dirty? He doesn't stand back and watch other people take risks."

So I told him about the anti-vampire ward, and inadvertently ending up on an entry override team of one, and how I'd just done the training so I'd get a few extra bucks every month. In the meantime, he slathered on a cream that had the most powerful anti-microbial spell I'd ever seen. I broke off my complaint about how I'd been tricked into leaving the basement. "Holy crap, there are three power circles in that little tube." At the rate Che was using expensive supplies, I was going to have to leave one of my kidneys behind as a down-payment and then disappear without a forwarding address.

"Nothing but the best for Simon's partner."

Honesty made me correct him. "You know I just met him a few hours ago, right? On Monday, the real teams will be back and I'll never leave the basement again."

"Sure. But right now, you're the closest thing he has to a partner and Simon needs people around him who aren't part of that..." He shook his head. "Let's just say I stopped by one day and I wasn't impressed by the people he worked with." He angled the lamp so he could examine the bite mark on my cheek, and I closed my eyes to avoid the light while he taped my skin back together.

"He hadn't planned on becoming a vampire," I said, working it out from Che's earlier comment. "What happened?"

"If I were his doctor, I wouldn't be able to tell you, but lucky for you, I'm his friend, not his physician. And I'm only telling you this to help you understand that he's... Well, this wasn't the life he'd planned." He placed something solid on my cheek which made my skin tingle. "He'd already finished his residency by the time he got the diagnosis. Fabry Disease. It's a lysosomal storage disease. Progressive."

"There's no treatment?" My cheek had gone numb.

"No. It progresses pretty slowly, but he was already having days when he couldn't use his hands. Not great if you've just spent years training to be a surgeon."

He didn't need to tell me that vampirism was perfect for slowly progressing diseases. Bowers might have to feed a touch more, but the magic would keep his illness in check and probably reverse any damage that had occurred before he changed.

When Che angled the light away from my face to work on my arm, I opened my eyes again. "How long ago was this?"

"Since his diagnosis? A couple years. He tried to ignore it for a while, but he had to face facts pretty quickly."

That might explain why Bowers had been the one to stay behind; the other agents had seniority. But the timeline didn't work. "I thought it took years to get the council to even *look* at an application. How'd he apply and get changed so quickly?"

"Ah. That's a story I'll let him tell you. Have to leave

him some secrets. I just want you to cut him some slack if you can. It's hard to have a career that you love one day and then find out you can never do that again."

"Tell me about it," I said with feeling.

"Yeah?"

"Four years as a postdoc and I finally had to admit my career in academia was never going to happen. So now I have a bunch of debt and a job where I get attacked by pterodactyls."

"Could be worse," he said.

"I guess?" My voice rose at the end when I couldn't think of anything.

"You could have gotten attacked by a dinosaur." He grinned and continued putting my arm back together.

In another fifteen minutes, he slid his chair back and stripped off his gloves. "Tada! Good as new. Or it will be soon." He flipped off the light. "Leave the bandages on for another hour and don't get them wet. After that, you can do whatever you want. If you notice any redness, swelling, or pain after tomorrow, come in as soon as possible. I'm serious about that. We don't normally treat pterodactyl bites, so there could be unexpected complications."

I slid off the gurney to stand on the floor. "Thank you."

"You're welcome. You're cleared to go back to regular duties tomorrow, and I'll send all the paperwork over as soon as I can. Tell Simon he owes me a beer. And I mean it this time."

SEVEN

Hamilton was appropriately horrified when I arrived back at my workspace in the basement. "What happened to you?"

"Pterodactyl." Nobody on the crowded water bus had wanted to stand near me. At least I'd been able to change into my workout clothes when I got back to The Vault. My outfit might not look very professional, but it was better than the ripped and gore-splattered clothes I'd tossed in the trash. The officer in the armory had stared at the charred and splattered bracers when I'd returned them. I hadn't even wiped them off because the training slides had been very clear about not doing any sort of cleaning or mainte-nance on checked out equipment. "You don't happen to know what sort of form the entry override team is supposed to file, do you?"

There was no point in asking if there *was* a form, because the first thing I'd learned about working at the FBME was that there was a required form for everything.

"Not a clue, but they probably mentioned it in that training you were stupid enough to take." He checked the time. "Worry about it tomorrow."

"Yeah." But I sent Bowers a message, because the alternative was asking Supervisory Agent Salt and she was scarier. *What kind of form do I need to file? Also, Che says you owe him a beer and he means it this time.*

Then I filed my report on the head-knock charm, because I wanted to feel like I'd accomplished at least one thing during the day. Finally, I went to the bathroom and peeled the bandages off my face, hoping I'd be able to cover up the worst of the bruising with the minimal makeup I carried with me.

To my surprise, my face had healed. Not just patched up in a "people won't faint when they see it, though they'll have questions" way, but healed in a "nobody will know anything happened if you don't tell them" way. Che had used the expensive bandages on me and I really *was* going to need to donate a kidney when the bill arrived. Except I hadn't signed anything at all when I was there. Maybe I'd be able to slither out of paying on a technicality. Or maybe Che was being helpful because he thought I'd be a positive influence on his favorite depressed vampire.

Bowers hadn't replied to my message by the time I left, so I locked up my computer with a clean conscience and went off to have drinks with friends.

MY FRIEND AMAR — the paleontologist I'd cheerfully thrown to Che, though he didn't know it yet — owned a studio apartment in the Butcher District, four blocks from the ocean and an equal distance from the river. He claimed it had been willed to him by a distant relative. If it had been mine, I would have sold the place and retired, but Amar liked living in the area. He had access to a rooftop terrace, his neighbors didn't mind if he invited over a herd of poor academics, and his place was easy to get to from anywhere in the city, so more often than not, we congregated at Amar's place.

The Butcher District had originally been just what it claimed, an area of butchers and meat-packing plants. But as increasing silt in the harbor shifted trade down the coast to San Francisco, the area became known as a haven for vampires when they went public in 1925. These days, the vampire clubs were highly regulated and most of the bars catered to tourists, but it stayed busy until dawn.

Amar had the third floor of what had originally been a brick townhouse, and I trudged up the narrow stairs after he buzzed me in. When he answered the door, I handed him the bottle of red I'd picked up at the wine shop near work. "You are going to be so jealous when you hear about my day."

"Am I?" He was a tall man in his thirties, with black hair, dark brown skin, and a nose that would have been long and thin if it hadn't veered off to the left. Ask him any question concerning the Mesozoic Era and he could talk for hours; anything more recent than that was a lost cause. After that time he'd nearly ended up in Australia instead of Austria, Trix and I checked over his itinerary any time he traveled outside of Floodmouth. Amar was not the person you wanted on your trivia night team, unless the subject was dinosaurs. "I think I can still win the contest of who was stuck in the basement with the worst lighting."

I followed him into the living room where three people were already making a serious dent in the pizza, bread, and pitcher of margaritas. Amar's margaritas were both legendary and the reason I'd left my bike at work and taken public transportation. The door to the balcony was open, and we could hear drunken people calling to each other from the street below. On the leather couch that had come with the apartment, Trix eyed me over her glass. "Why are you wearing different clothes than the ones you left home in?"

Leave it to Trix to notice every detail. Trix was my roommate, a white woman with a round face, green hair, and black eyes that could pin you in place while she discussed the history of conflict between vampires and magic users in renaissance Europe. She was fairly sound, if a little less obsessive, about other time periods as well, which I'd found helpful when writing my dissertation. Trix had nearly as much student loan debt as I did, which explained why we still shared an apartment in the Ware-house District even though she was a full-time lecturer at the university and translated texts from French, German, and Latin for private clients on the side. Even now, she had a stack of papers in her lap.

Next to her, Paul had a bottle of beer and a roll covered in a thick layer of hazelnut spread. With his receding blond hair, pale skin, and wire-framed glasses, Paul couldn't have looked more German if he tried. The Birkenstock sandals and thick woolen socks were a given. He'd come to America as an undergrad to study engineering, promptly switched to art history, and stayed. He was currently working on the fourth rewrite of his dissertation, the first three having been nearly complete when he decided to add one more thing, which then changed the entire argument. I figured we were getting close to another breakthrough and the start of number five.

The fifth member of our usual group was Petra, who was flopped sideways on the recliner. She was a short Black woman with dark skin and a shaved head. Petra had two states: vibrating with energy, and sloth-like languor. She was the person to text if you were up in the middle of the night and bored, because she had an ongoing experiment with flatworms that required data collection every six hours. For three years, she'd gotten by with catnaps and caffeine. So far, she'd gotten eleven papers out of the flatworms, and she'd just barely scratched the surface. Petra had tried to explain the experiment to me once, but it had been four in the morning and I didn't understand half of the words she used.

Amar poured me a margarita and pulled over another chair from the kitchen table. "Alright. Make me jealous."

"*I* got attacked by a pterodactyl today."

Of course, nobody would let me leave it at that, so I explained about entry override teams and everything that had happened at the apartment. Just for Paul, I described the mosaic on the living room wall — he kept threatening to write a paper on the mythology around Katie Tucker as depicted in the art of Floodmouth, and this would be my contribution. I was vague about the area of town we were in and left out the owner's name, so I figured I wasn't telling any agency secrets.

Predictably, Trix was concerned for my safety — she'd been worried about me applying to the Bureau in the first place — and Amar was disappointed I hadn't taken a picture of the pterodactyl before I'd let it explode. Paul asked detailed questions about the art, and Petra fell asleep while the others were taking turns grilling me. Petra would have her own questions later, probably about the biology of a creature magically created millions of years after it went extinct. I could expect a series of texts on my phone when I woke up tomorrow.

They all had questions about Bowers. Nobody asked

why I'd taken the training for the override team if I had no plans to actually use it. Knowledge was knowledge, and a monthly stipend was a no-brainer.

"But what kind of texture did the skin have?" Holding the bottle of wine between his knees, Amar wrestled with the cork. He didn't own a corkscrew, so he had twisted a wood screw almost all the way in and was now yanking on it with pliers. Since the screw was shorter than the cork, the top half of the cork was about to break off, like it always did. According to him, a few flakes of cork in the glass never hurt anyone.

Had I touched the pterodactyl's skin? My memories revolved around the sound it made and the terror I felt. Plus my view of a huge jaw full of teeth heading straight for my eye. "I don't know."

"Are they going to pay for therapy?" Trix looked me over. "And your medical bills? Though you look better than I would have imagined."

I explained about the trip to Floodmouth General and Che's use of healing spells I'd never be able to afford. "If I never filled out any forms, can they legally charge me for all that?"

That got me a round of shrugs. If any of us had the slightest talent for money management or legal contracts, we never would have gone to grad school.

"If that's not an on-the-job injury," Trix ventured, "I don't know what is."

"But what kind of pupils did it have? Vertical or round?" Amar interrupted. As expected, the top half of the cork had ripped off. He inserted one handle of the pliers and jammed the remaining cork down into the bottle. "Who's ready for wine?"

"I didn't get a great look at its eyes while it was trying to eat me."

Paul set down his empty beer bottle. "Bier auf Wein, lass das sein; Wein auf Bier, rat' ich dir."

"Oh god, he's speaking German now," Trix said. "Next comes the singing."

"You adore my singing," Paul said, accepting a glass of wine from Amar and using his fingertip to fish out a bit of cork. "My question is, did you find what you were looking for?"

It was an odd question coming from Paul, who cared nothing about magic spells or law enforcement. "No."

"A-ha! I thought so!"

"Because...?" I shook my head at Amar, who had waved the bottle at me, since I still had half a tumbler of margarita left.

"Do you have a photo of your mosaic?"

"No. Bowers might." The vampire had done a walk-through and taken video before we'd searched, mostly so we had documentation of what was present before we started. It would be attached to the case file, but I didn't have access.

"Then you must invite him over." Paul had a way of making proclamations that sounded like he had reached the last step of a three-page proof.

"Ooh, good idea!" Trix said. "We want to meet the new partner."

"Did *he* take pictures of the pterodactyl?"

I blinked a few times and let out a long breath. "Not my partner, I think he was too busy yelling to take pictures of the dinosaur, and why do you need to see pictures of the stupid mosaic?"

Amar shook his head and cast me a disappointed look. "I know you called it a dinosaur just to hurt me."

"Because," Paul said, ignoring the others, "I know a forger. Well, no, he's not a forger. He copies famous paintings, but he makes them not exact."

"Okay." I was regretting having told Paul anything about the mosaic. Like most of my friends, he could be a little obsessive, and he would keep asking questions I didn't have answers for.

Paul held up a finger. "Ah, but *why* he makes these copies is to hide the opening for a safe built into the wall."

I stared at him. "What?"

"Maybe safe is not the correct word. A hidden cabinet. Very thin. But one must know it is there and how to get in." He shrugged. "But perhaps this is just a mosaic. I cannot say without looking at it."

Resting my glass on one knee, I messaged Bowers. *Do you have a picture of the mosaic in the living room? We may have missed something.*

My phone rang before I could put it in my pocket. Bowers didn't bother with a greeting. "What did we miss?"

I moved onto the balcony, partially so I could hear him better, but mostly so there was a chance he wouldn't hear my friends talking about him. "My friend Paul says there's a guy who makes forgeries with safes behind them. If you send me a picture, I'll show it to him."

In the living room, Amar yelled, "Ask him if he has any pictures of the pterodactyl."

Bowers was silent for a moment. Then he asked, "Where *are* you?"

"I'm at a friend's apartment in the Butcher District. But you can just send me the photo..."

"I'm in the area. What cross streets?"

I gave him directions and he hung up. It made some sense that he would be nearby. The Butcher District was famous for its vampire clubs, places vampires could go to feed from willing humans. Those clubs ran the gamut from bars that refunded the cover charge for anyone willing to lose a little blood at the end of the evening, to expensive salons with a roster of employees scheduled to come in once a week. In the nicest places, potential donors had to be pleasant and hold intelligent conversations; they recruited heavily at the university. I'd even considered signing up once or twice when money was tight, but I'd always found an excuse not to.

When I went back inside, Trix brightened. "Do we get to meet him?"

"You're making it weird. He's just someone I work with."

"Do we have to call him by his last name?"

That took me aback. Everybody at work always used surnames. I'd gotten so used to it that I didn't even notice anymore. "You can call him whatever you want." I lifted my hand when Amar opened his mouth. "I don't know if he has a picture of the pterodactyl. You can ask him when he gets here."

Paul finished his wine and poured another glass. "Will I get a consultant's fee?"

"No clue."

Paul shrugged, the topic forgotten now that he'd passed on his information. "Did I tell you I found the diary of a rival of Johann Durst? It is astounding. I may have to rewrite the opening arguments in my dissertation."

And thus was the next rewrite started. Trix thought Paul's dissertation advisor intentionally brought in new material any time it looked like Paul might finish, since Paul's nearly free labor would be gone if he ever defended his PhD. But I was pretty sure any intentional sabotage was being done by Paul himself. He didn't know what he wanted to do after he finished at university, and the easiest way to solve that problem was to make sure he never did.

We'd heard five minutes of the new argument — to wit, Johann Durst's color choices had been heavily influenced by the paints he was able to steal from his bitter rival — when the door chime sounded. Amar buzzed the caller up and then sprinted past me to open the door while Trix and Paul laughed.

To my surprise, Bowers wasn't alone. Che stood next to him with a cheesecake from The Blood Sugar Cafe, a bakery around the corner. He handed it to Amar. "Hi, I'm Che."

"He's the doctor who patched me up today," I explained, then dragged all three of them toward the living room before Amar could pepper Bowers with questions while he was still standing on the doorstep. I quickly introduced everyone. Bowers smiled politely at everyone, even Petra, who was still asleep on the recliner, but it was obvious he just wanted to get the information and leave. Che glanced down to make sure Petra was breathing, then accepted a glass of red wine.

"Paul's the one who knows about art," I said, gesturing toward him.

Paul stood. "Do you have a photograph?" He and Bowers moved to the edge of the room and looked at the vampire's phone. Meanwhile, Che slid onto the couch, apparently quite happy to stay and socialize. A string of fire-crackers went off in the street.

Squinting at the phone, Paul said, "Oh, yes, this looks like one of the Tiger's works. The secret is to examine what is different. Here, that is the river. There will be a button or lever there that will open the cabinet."

I glanced at the time. If the warrant expired at

midnight, we needed to go back to the apartment tonight. But I was going to have some cheesecake first. I sat down and served myself a slice.

Che grinned, clearly having understood my thought process. "He can wait another ten minutes." Then he and Amar started talking about the museum and I enjoyed my cheesecake.

Trix leaned forward and dropped her voice. "Were you able to get in touch with your dad today?"

"No." He hadn't returned my phone calls, and my mother had asked me if he would be going to the memorial — twice — which was her subtle way of saying she really wanted him there. I'd found his current address, and I'd intended to take off work a little early and go to his house, but then the whole pterodactyl thing had happened. "I'll go by tomorrow."

"Let me know if you want company."

I nodded my thanks. This Sunday my mother was holding the fifteen-year memorial for my sister and it was important to her. I'd mostly made my peace with Julie's disappearance, but my mom still struggled. Not having a body to bury made my sister's death harder to accept.

My father had dealt with the loss by not acknowledging any of it. Within a year of the day Julie disappeared, he'd moved out and begun distancing himself from us. For the first few years, I got birthday and Christmas cards from him, accompanied by a crisp new hundred-dollar bill, but even that stopped when I turned eighteen.

I hadn't seen him in person in twelve or thirteen years and hadn't even spoken on the phone in seven. This memorial would be the last effort I'd make to keep in contact, and I was only doing it for my mom.

Trix leaned over again, and her voice went even quieter.

"So... is this guy single?"

An unexpected pain in my chest kept me from answering, just long enough to realize Trix was asking about Che, not Bowers. Clearly I was less sober than I thought if I was entertaining thoughts about my vampire not-a-partner. That was *not* a direction I was willing to go, for all sorts of reasons. "I don't know. You'll have to ask."

By the time I'd finished the last raspberry on the cheese-cake slice, Paul had told Bowers everything he knew about opening the panel, Amar had been disappointed by the lack of pterodactyl pictures, and Trix had begun quizzing the vampire on any connections who might have access to archival materials from her period of interest. It was time for us to go.

"Maybe I should go with you," Paul said, swallowing half his glass of wine in one gulp, which was probably the best way to drink that particular wine. "Just in case you can't get it open."

"Or me," Che added, a twinkle in his eye. As one of the few sober people, he found the whole situation hilarious. "Who knows what you're going to run into?"

"We should *all* go!" Trix shoved herself off the couch, got halfway to her feet, and then fell back again, acciden-tally landing closer to Che. "Give me a sec."

As amusing as it would be to invite the whole group along, Supervisory Agent Salt would fire us if we brought a bunch of inebriated friends when serving a search warrant. So I kept my leave-taking short and ushered Bowers out to the relative quiet of the street, where there were still crowds of people laughing and shouting, but they weren't laughing and shouting in a small room.

Time to find the secret Mo had been prepared to kill a total stranger to protect.

EIGHT

After the raucous energy of the Butcher District and a water bus packed with partiers, The Vault felt funereal, even more than it had during the daytime with everyone in Seattle. It would have been faster to stay on the water bus, but we'd had to come back to pick up the apartment keys.

And a set of bracers. For all we knew, there was another nasty spell protecting the contents behind the mosaic, and I wasn't too proud to admit it was the hardware that had saved me the first time.

We'd made it all the way to The Vault without talking. In the elevator on its way to the sixth floor, Bowers finally spoke. "Sorry about crashing your party like that."

"It wasn't really a party. We get together once a week for the Thursday Night Grant Writing Workshop." At his raised eyebrow, I shrugged. "We met in grad school and it's easier to tell your advisor that you're going to a class on writing effective grants than to admit you're having pizza and beer with your friends. At least with some advisors." My advisor had been reasonable about maintaining work-life balance, though she'd had other failings. In contrast,

Petra's advisor had encouraged her to run a multi-year project that had led to Petra bringing a tank of flatworms along when she'd traveled to Los Angeles for her grandmother's funeral.

The view of the city from the sixth floor was breathtaking at night, the different lighting styles making it easy to pick out the various districts, with the fog rolling in from the ocean casting a soft filter over it all.

Even as the newest agent, Bowers had a glass-walled office of his own, with a desk made from walnut holding a keyboard and monitor and a large travel mug with the agency's logo on it. Unlike the other offices we'd passed, there was nothing personal — no pictures, posters, or diplomas, not even the clutter that accumulates in an agency that stocked such terrible coffee that everyone had their own secret stash. Compared to this desk, my workspace told volumes about my lifestyle and personality, and I had the neatest area in the basement.

Bowers unlocked the safe embedded in his desk and pulled out the set of keys we'd used earlier in the day. Then it was down to the fourth floor, where he walked off and left me waiting for the armory officer to dig out a vest and bracers. This time, I'd declined the radio.

By the time Bowers returned, I was stowing my gear in my bag. "Looking for someone?"

"Thought some of the entry team might have returned for the night and they could take over."

I stopped messing with the bag's zipper and stood. It had been a long day and I was tired. That was the only excuse I had for getting so irritated. "Look, I know I'm not really on the entry override team, and I can't fight, and I can't even do magic, but since literally all you need is someone to be in the same room while you look for evidence, it's a little insulting that you're trying to ditch me now." I slung my duffel bag over my shoulder. "We're both here already. Let's go."

It was a good speech. Short and to the point. And if we hadn't needed to stand and wait for the elevator in awkward silence right afterward, it would have been perfect. If I'd had any idea where the stairs were, I'd have stormed off. But we'd taken the elevator up and I had only a vague idea of where the stairwells were, and it was possible the doors were alarmed. The only thing worse than standing in silence would have been stomping around in a huff before getting lost and having to return to the elevators.

Finally, the elevator came and we started the descent. Bowers cleared his throat and said mildly, "I didn't mean to be insulting. It's just that you never signed up for this and it seems unfair to put you in danger. Especially with no training."

My cheeks burned. But I'd put my foot in my mouth enough times to know that apologies only get harder the longer you wait, so I forced myself to take a deep breath and say, "I'm sorry. I misunderstood."

The silence after that was less awkward, but not in a way that achieved statistical significance.

We were standing on the dock waiting for the next water bus when he spoke again. "No magic? Really?"

Looking to the west, I could see a wall of fog beyond the next bridge. In another fifteen minutes, visibility would be down to just a few feet, and the water buses would have to drop their speed.

"Can't even make a spark." I thought about asking him the same, but luckily stopped myself before I opened my mouth. Of course he couldn't. He was a vampire. If he had any ability to do magic, the vampire council would never have approved his

application. And if one believed the texts I'd read for my doctor-
ate, he wouldn't have been sane if they had. More than one
history had warned about vampires with magic needing round-
the-clock care to keep from harming themselves and others.

Once again, I wondered how he'd been changed so
quickly, but it wasn't a question I could ask a virtual
stranger.

"Interesting."

"Why?" I looked over and held his gaze. A little belliger-
ent, maybe, but it was late and he already knew this was a
touchy subject.

"Perkins, you have a PhD in magic theory. It seems an
odd choice for someone who can't cast spells."

He had a point.

The water bus arrived before the fog and we found a
place near the bow, far enough away from other people that
we wouldn't be overheard. "You've been checking up on me,
Bowers." But I couldn't find it in myself to be upset about
that. He'd want to know how far he could trust me in the
field. Besides, Che had told me about him, so we were even.

"I like to know who I'm dealing with."

The cool river air blew some of my irritation away. "I've
always found magic theory fascinating. I was that kid who
knew all the librarians in the arcane room at Elisabeth K.
Tucker before I was ten." Some books on magic theory were
available in digital form, but others, the ones with some or
all of the spell cast in the vellum, had to be examined in
person. The Elisabeth K. Tucker Library over on 37th Street
was known for its collection of arcane books and objects.

"And it never bothered you that you couldn't cast any of
the spells?"

Of course it had bothered me. "I went through a phase

when I was pretty jealous of my older sister," I admitted. "But then we started working together to create things. It was fun." Julie had never been good at the theory, but if she'd studied spell casting, she would have been a real powerhouse.

"And what does she do now?"

"She died." I smiled briefly, the way I always did, to show that talking about it wasn't a big deal and the other person shouldn't feel bad for having brought it up. "It's okay." It was either a preemptive smile or dealing with awkward apologies. Though maybe Bowers wouldn't have bothered. Weirdly, that thought made me feel more comfortable around him. "It's been fifteen years.'"

He hummed an acknowledgment. "But then you went to college and majored in magic theory."

"In academia, you don't really need to spellcast. You just need to keep up a strong publishing schedule." I shrugged and moved over to the gate so we could get off at the next stop. "You didn't consider going into medical research?" After he became a vampire, I meant.

"Not my thing." He jumped to the dock, and we headed toward the glass and steel building that shone like a beacon in the night.

AS FAR AS I could tell, the exterior of Mo's apartment was just as we'd left it, with no anti-vampire ward on the door and no evidence that anyone else had gone in after us. Drywall chunks littered the carpet beneath the hole in the wall. Even so, I took a moment in the hallway to put on my gear. The bracers were either a new set or someone had spent a lot of time cleaning the old ones. They still didn't fit my forearms, though.

Nothing attacked us when we went through the door, other than the smell. Bits of blood and gore decorated the pale carpet of the living room, more than I remembered. "They're going to have to replace all that."

"Not our problem." Bowers looked around for a few minutes before he found the switch for the blinds. The vertical slats hummed smoothly into place, hiding the view but also making it impossible for anyone to see us from outside.

Then we faced the mosaic.

Even knowing it might hide something behind it, I couldn't see any joins or openings. The red of the river dominated the image in a way the dark blue of the original never had, making Katie Tucker's death at the hands of the city's vigilantes seem inevitable. Bowers moved forward, hands raised.

"Wait," I said, grabbing his arm to stop him. "Let me do it." The bracers protected against harmful magic, and we already knew Mo hadn't wanted vampires inside his apartment. It wasn't a leap to assume he might have another trap protecting his safe.

Bowers looked at me for a long moment, and I thought he was going to refuse. Then he stepped back, pulling his arm away from my hand. "Go ahead."

Moving forward, I ran my fingers over the tiles that made up the crimson river. "If another pterodactyl shows up," I murmured as I pressed tentatively at the edges, "make sure you take a picture for Amar."

"Of course."

Was that a hint of humor in his voice? Surely not. But before I could spend too much time thinking about it, the tile directly under Katie Tucker's feet shifted. "I think this may be it." I pressed harder and felt something click.

Bowers made a noise that might have been a growl. "Careful..."

The tile pushed back against my fingers and the entire mosaic swung open to reveal a shallow cabinet with three shelves. Each shelf held plastic bags of metallic bracelets and rings, all heavily spelled. Now that the safe was open, I could see the wards intended to hide the presence of magic, which explained how we had missed the cabinet despite passing next to it multiple times.

I was still looking when Bowers stepped up next to me, his shoulder brushing mine. He took a series of photos and then put his phone away. "Can you tell what they are?"

Common sense said I shouldn't touch a heavily spelled object without knowing what it did, and my short time as an evidence technician had taught me that people would create the most dangerous spells without caring about the consequences. But there were so many little bags that all the patterns overlapped. I used a pen to knock a bracelet to the floor, then crouched to look at it more closely.

It was a solid metal cuff with ten small links filling the gap to account for sizing. Designs that looked vaguely Incan were stamped into the metal, and a flat glass turtle was glued on top, a blob of epoxy visible on one side. From the weight and sheen, the bracelet was probably made of aluminum, and it looked like the cheap costume jewelry sold by street vendors or given away as free merchandising.

But nobody in their right mind put a spell this compli-cated on such a cheap piece of costume jewelry. For one thing, aluminum was fragile — if the edge caught on some-thing, the links would snap. For another, the metal was malleable and spells usually weren't. Bend this too far and any magic element that depended on a particular shape would do something unpredictable.

As for the spell itself, it was an odd mixture of sophistication and ignorance. "This is weird."

"How so?"

"It's..." I struggled to describe it, knowing Bowers didn't have a background in magic theory. "It's like someone with no training found an advanced spell book and got things to work. So parts of it are really complex." The bracelet had a Moebius loop power circle running around it, a neat design I'd never seen used in a wearable spell. "But other parts are just jammed together with no thought to the second-order effects."

Adding a collector cell directly under a bunch of glass would decrease the effectiveness. There might be valid reasons to do that anyhow, but this didn't look intentional. Instead, whoever had designed the spell had increased the size of the collector cell to the point of instability. Plus, I was pretty sure there were traces of blood in the casting, and blood magic was notoriously tricky in its effects on other spell elements.

"What does it do?"

That was always the real question, and one I spent most of my professional life answering. Or rather, it was one of a pair of questions: What was it *intended* to do? What does it *actually* do? Because for many spellcasters, those two answers weren't the same, and the report from a forensic magic technician like me might make a difference during sentencing.

I considered the bracelet. It gathered and stored life energy — the same thing vampires fed on, though it could also be used to power spells. That sort of power didn't come through skin easily, which was why vampires couldn't feed just by walking through a crowd. But as to how the spell incorporated blood magic... *That* wasn't something I encountered very often — I'd need to look up the tangle of lines in a reference book. "I'm not sure." Then I picked up the bag with my bare hand. "I'm fairly certain it won't do anything unless it's worn. It might just be something cosmetic, like making the stone glow. But if so, why make it this complicated?"

Bowers made a low note of agreement. "And why bother hiding them in a secret safe?"

I stood and pulled another bag from the shelf. It had different designs stamped into the metal and a glass shark instead of a turtle, but the spell was identical. "I'm missing something." It was late and I was tired. "Maybe it will be clearer after I've had some sleep."

THICK FOG BLANKETED the city when we entered the glass walkway leading down to the ground. I refused to give up my second chance to take the hamster tunnel along the front of the building, though I'd told Bowers he could take the elevator down and I'd meet him on the street. He came along without comment. Sound echoed oddly in the tunnel, inducing a bit of claustrophobia even though I could see out. On every level, we had to pass through a door to keep going down, probably due to fire regulations, though it would also keep people from cycling down the ramp. All in all, it was an interesting architectural addition, but I could see why it hadn't caught on.

With the fog making the river nearly unnavigable, we opted for the subway, which involved making a wide loop around the city and walking three blocks. By the time we reached The Vault, I missed the old days when I could sleep under my desk at the university and nobody would bat an eye.

As soon as we'd logged in the costume jewelry and I'd returned the bracers, I pulled my bicycle out of the storage room on the first floor. One of the best parts of living in Floodmouth was that even federal buildings were bicycle-friendly.

Bowers eyed the fog. "Are you going to be okay out there?"

"Are you going to send a pterodactyl after me?"

"No."

"Then I'll be fine." I stepped on the pedal and swung my leg over, gaining speed as I flew down the ramp to the bike path, but I was almost positive I'd seen the start of a smile.

NINE

I was laughing at Petra's texts when I arrived at work the next morning. She'd wanted to know if the pterodactyl would have been recreated with any intestinal parasites and if I could get her a sample of any feces — she was careful to specify she meant pterodactyl feces — or DNA that might have been left behind after my encounter. Those requests were followed by a terrible photo manipulation of the flatworms in one of her tanks, with their front ends replaced by tiny pterodactyl heads. The picture was both hilarious and terrifying and I was absolutely not going to help her get any pterodactyl DNA. Sleep deprivation could remove her guardrails.

Hamilton was already at his workstation, examining a pair of leather gloves that exuded hostile magic even at a distance. He glanced up as I was putting my bag away. "Told you it was a mistake to let the upstairs people know who you are. The big cheese has already been down here looking for you." At my questioning look, he added, "Supervisory Agent Salt. She wants to see you as soon as you get in."

"Crap."

He leaned over his workbench again. "It's been nice knowing you."

"I'll be back," I said, but I closed the drawer and headed for the elevator. I assumed SA Salt had an office on the sixth floor. If she didn't, at least I'd run into Bowers and he could tell me what this was all about. Surely Salt wouldn't bother making a trip to the basement just to tell me I hadn't filled out the proper forms yet.

I found both of them in Bowers's office. Bowers and I had spent most of the previous day together, but we hadn't yet developed our own wordless communication style; when I looked at him with raised eyebrows, I couldn't read anything in his steady gaze.

Salt pivoted to see who Bowers was looking at. "Ah, there you are. I heard you had a little incident yesterday. How are you feeling?"

"Fine." I opened my mouth to preemptively apologize for not having followed the after-action procedure — it must have been covered in the training, but I'd assumed I'd never need that section and I'd left the video running while responding to email — but she was already nodding and moving on.

"Excellent. After yesterday's success, I've temporarily transferred you to the entry override division, so there's no need for us to wait on the stack of warrants. You and Agent Bowers will be out in the field again today. If anyone is trying to sneak something past us while we're busy, let's teach them a lesson, alright?" This time, she didn't wait for me to respond, but turned back to Bowers. "I've sent you the information. Let me know if you run into trouble."

And then she was gone, striding down the hall so forcefully that anyone trying to stop her would bounce right off.

"Um," I said into the vacuum left by her presence. "What just happened?"

"That pterodactyl spell you disabled yesterday has killed three agents in the last year. HQ confirmed it was the same thing. You're the first one to survive, so now you're the expert. They're calling your method the Perkins Maneuver."

I stared at him in horror. "That was an accident."

"Keep your voice down. A commendation looks good on your record, and it will come with a bonus."

Hopefully, the bonus would pay to replace the clothes that had been destroyed. "This... I'm really not qualified to do this."

Bowers pulled out his bag and stood. "You have two choices. You could talk to Salt now before she goes back to Seattle and tell her she got it all wrong. That's probably career suicide, but if you don't mind staying at the same pay grade for the rest of your career in the basement, it's an option."

My loans waltzed through my thoughts. "What's choice number two?"

"We do the searches today and on Monday, when Patel is back, you talk to him. He's old school and he hates Salt interfering with his personnel decisions. I can almost guarantee he'll send you back to the basement and tell Salt you don't have the necessary training."

Jonah Patel was in charge of the entry override division; he was currently in Seattle with everyone else. "I *don't* have the necessary training."

"There you go then." He gestured me out of his office. "This should be an easy day. I promise, ninety-nine percent of the search warrants are drama free."

This time when we stopped at the fourth floor armory,

Taylor didn't say anything, just handed over the bracers and vest while I signed them out.

Outside, the fog still hadn't burned off, and it left the area with the hazy look of an oil painting by an artist trying to fudge the details. According to Bowers, the first address was in the Warehouse District, so we were heading back toward my apartment. It would have been faster to travel by bicycle, but since Bowers didn't have one, we took the subway.

"How can you live in Floodmouth and not have a bicycle?" The subway was crowded with morning commuters, but we'd carved out a little space at the end of a car, mostly by Bowers glaring at anyone who came close. I'm not sure if people backed off because he was a vampire or because he was wearing a jacket with the FBME logo on the chest; either way, it worked, and I wondered how I could create a spell that had that effect on others. If I could put it on a patch that worked for an hour, I could make millions, pay off my student loans, and retire. Then I wouldn't have to talk to Salt *or* Patel, which I decided was my new life goal.

"I just... never needed one. Besides, I'm not sure how seriously people would take an FBME agent who showed up on a bicycle."

I wanted to say, *You're a vampire with a badge. People will take you seriously if you show up on a unicycle with a clown nose.* But I refrained. From what Che had said the day before, Bowers wouldn't appreciate reminders he was a vampire. "I think we should get you a bicycle."

That got me a raised eyebrow before he went back to staring out the window. We rode in silence for the next ten minutes.

As we were walking up the stairs to ground level, I

asked something that had been bugging me. "Why aren't you in Seattle with everyone else?"

"I'm not allowed to leave Floodmouth until next month. Safety year." He slipped on a pair of sunglasses as we reached the sunlight. While we'd been underground, the wind had kicked up and blown the fog away, leaving a glare from the wet pavement.

That explained it. In the first year after transformation, the movements of new vampires were restricted since they were required to stay close to their support system. That allowed them to get accustomed to their new routines and the signs that meant they needed to feed.

I'd known Bowers was a new vampire, but I hadn't realized he was *that* new.

We were just a few blocks north of my apartment, but Bowers turned east and threaded his way through the vendors illegally set up on the sidewalk, selling everything from secondhand clothing to tarot readings. This close to the university, most of the inhabitants were students with little money. You could get a great meal for cheap if you didn't mind overlooking a few health code violations.

Somehow I doubted Bowers had ever eaten in this area.

In the Warehouse District, most of the original buildings had been pulled down to make room for apartments, but some had been left in place and converted to living space, with as many floors added as they could fit in the existing building. The address we were looking for was one of the latter. A battered couch with three people reading sat on the sidewalk next to the door. None of them looked up as we passed by.

We were looking for an apartment on the third floor, but first we had to find the stairs. The first floor was a maze of poorly framed drywall set up in random intervals. One apartment took up a quarter of the building, and then there were three doors so close together that the living space couldn't have possibly held anything larger than a twin bed and one chair. Everything smelled of burned toast, mold, and lemon-scented cleaner. It took me back to the place I'd lived during my final year as an undergrad — I'd been ecstatic when I'd met Trix and we moved into an actual apartment.

Bowers stopped abruptly when the hallway we were following ended without leading to the stairs. "This can't possibly be legal. The whole place is a fire hazard."

"Yeah, though they've got a decent fire and smoke dampening spell," I said, pointing at the ceiling. "That and a few bucks probably keep the inspectors off their case." They should have sprung for an anti-mold spell as well, but those were expensive this close to the waterfront.

We backtracked and tried another fork in the maze. Thankfully, this one led to the stairs, because my sinuses were clogging from the dust.

The ramshackle chaos of the first floor had not carried over to the third. It was all one living space, with an actual lock on the door. Bowers knocked, the sound echoing oddly. "Federal Bureau of Magic Enforcement," he called. "We have a warrant to search the premises."

We listened, but there was no sign of anyone in the apartment. "I don't think they're home," I said. That was good. I'd have a harder time pretending I knew what I was doing if someone other than Bowers was watching.

After another few minutes, Bowers removed a set of lock picks and opened the door. As it had the day before, his hand abruptly stopped at the entryway, leaving the door to slowly swing open. He looked at me. "Try not to get killed."

"Funny." I'd already pulled on the vest and bracers, so I took a deep breath and eased into the apartment, my heart pounding in my ears. Whoever had framed the living spaces on the first floor hadn't set foot in here — I could see the entire floor from the doorway. They hadn't even separated the bathroom from the rest of the living space. Aside from that and the excessively low ceiling, it was almost nice. But whoever had converted the building had crammed three floors into a space meant for two, so anyone over six feet had to stoop. In some areas, the air ducts made it even lower than that.

In my mind, pterodactyls were hiding behind the furniture and I had to lock my knees to keep from sprinting out the door. But despite my nerves, it took me less than ten seconds to find the anti-vampire ward taped to the wall next to the door. I ripped the corner to disrupt the power circle, and the ward disintegrated.

Bowers stepped inside before I could move out of the way. "All good?"

I nodded, not trusting my voice. He started the search without commenting, though it must have been clear as day how nervous I was.

Given the lack of places to hide things, our search didn't take long. Underneath the bed was a box holding inks, brushes, and a template for creating a libido-enhancement spell. It wouldn't be hard to find two or three stalls on this block with casters selling this sort of body art. They were legal if painted with the full consent of the recipient, but a quick mage could paint the pattern and infuse it with magic before an unwitting victim realized what was happening. Since the renter had been forbidden from practicing magic due to a previous conviction, the possession of the template was illegal.

We carefully bagged and documented everything we found, then went to the next location on the list.

On our way there, I received a text from Hamilton, who was back at The Vault, wading through one case after another. *Must be nice to see the sunlight.*

Hooking one arm around the subway car pole, I typed, *My tan is coming along nicely.*

That got me a raised middle finger emoji. We were almost to our stop and I'd just put my phone away when it buzzed again.

Are you messing with me?

That deserved a three character reply. *???*

Those bracelets you booked into evidence last night. None of them have any magic.

"What the..." I finished with a wordless exclamation.

Next to me, Bowers stiffened. "What's wrong?"

"I don't know yet." My fingers hit my phone with more force than I typically used. *Don't even joke about that.*

I'm not joking. These things have less magic than a null chest.

As Bowers and I climbed the stairs to ground level, I told him what Hamilton had said. "Diminished in power overnight, maybe, but I don't understand how they could have lost everything completely. Those things had already been untouched for ten days and none of them had failed."

We threaded our way through a cluster of slow-moving pedestrians as he thought. "Could they have been stored near something that nullified the spells?"

"I guess?" There were objects that could drain nearby spells quickly, but the FBME evidence storage had been designed to prevent that sort of tampering. "It would almost *have* to be deliberate."

Bowers moved out of the stream of traffic and stopped. "Is there anything you could do if we went back?"

"No." If the bracelets had no magic, nothing I did would change things.

"Then let's keep going. I'll let Salt know so she can open an investigation."

TEN

By lunchtime, we'd finished four locations. None of them had been protected by anything other than basic anti-vampire spells, and by the last one, my heart wasn't pounding when I went through the door. When Bowers had said it usually only took the entry override team thirty seconds to find and disable the anti-vampire wards, he'd been telling the truth.

We were one block away from Booksellers Row, on a tourist-clogged street with apothecaries and wholesale spell ingredient shops. Possibly not the best spot to find somewhere to eat, but I was starving and the smell of gyros made my stomach rumble. "Do you want anything?" I asked, handing my duffel bag to Bowers so I could dig out my wallet from my purse.

He raised his eyebrows and looked at me, as if trying to see if I was serious, then shook his head once. "No, thank you."

"What? Just because you don't have to doesn't mean.... Never mind." Vampires didn't need anything beyond the energy they took from their donors, but they could eat and drink like anyone else, and most enjoyed doing so. True, alcohol and other drugs did nothing — anything their body saw as a toxin was immediately neutralized by the magic that kept them alive — but that didn't mean they couldn't find pleasure in food and drink.

With a gyro, fries, and a soda carefully balanced in a cardboard box, I snagged a spot on a low wall and considered our location as I ate. Bowers stood nearby and watched the crowds walking by.

The address I had for my father was only two blocks away. I didn't particularly want to take Bowers with me, but I also didn't want to come back at the end of the day. It made sense to drop by there now. It was the middle of a workday, so with any luck, my father would be out, I could leave a note, and then I could truthfully tell my mother that I'd tried without actually having to talk to the man.

Waving the fries at Bowers, I said, "Are you sure you don't want one?"

To my surprise, he took one, inspected it, and then ate it in two bites. "Those are pretty terrible fries."

"Sure, but even terrible fries are worth eating." The gyro was better, with enough sauce that I had it all over my hands when I was finished, though I was careful not to get it on my last clean button-down shirt. Trix had offered to go thrifting with me on Saturday, and I prayed to the clothing gods we would find something wearable. The thin napkins were nearly useless, but five of them got the worst of it off my fingers. "Do you mind if we make a quick detour? I need to run an errand."

Two blocks away, we might have been in a completely different district. Rows of narrow brick two-story townhouses lined the streets, each built against the neighbors on either side, with gated front yards and what I suspected would be tiny back gardens with another row of townhouses mirrored on the other side. Unlike in Booksellers Row just a few blocks away, there were no tourists here, just some bicycle traffic and a woman pushing a stroller with two small children inside.

I checked the address again, and then let us into the orderly front garden of number twenty-five, where moss crowded the path to the front door. A battered red bicycle leaned against the short wall, unlocked but sporting an anti-theft ward that would make it inoperable if someone stole it. That was interesting.

The ward would be easy enough to disable, and any experienced bike thief would carry the kit to do so. It was the kind of spell Julie had put on our bikes, but I'd never have imagined my father would bother. Then again, what did I know about him, really? I hadn't spent much time with him since I was sixteen, and the year before *that* had been a nightmare of grief and false hope. Maybe he *was* the sort of person who would put a useless anti-theft ward on his bicycle.

The steps to the front porch were lined with colorful pots holding ferns and orchids. It was another odd note. My father had never been interested in plants or gardening when I'd known him. Had losing a child and then the rest of his family left a hole he'd filled with new hobbies?

Did I have the right house?

None of it mattered. All I had to do was knock on the door, wait thirty seconds to prove he wasn't home, and then leave a note. I'd be able to tell my mother I'd tried and I'd never have to think about him again.

When I raised a hand to the brass door knocker, I could feel the anti-vampire ward. Awkward, though not a surprise. From the day Julie had disappeared, my father had blamed everything on her obsession with vampires; when the infamous vampire serial killer Raiden Martin had been arrested, we'd *all* been surprised that my sister's remains weren't in his basement.

But Bowers would look up this address later, if he hadn't already, and quickly realize it was my father's house. Even standing behind me, he could probably feel the wards. Having a bigoted family member wouldn't help our relationship.

The clang of the knocker against the base echoed through the house. Before it had stopped, I'd pulled a page from my notebook. "Let me just leave a message and then we can go."

I was still trying to decide what to write when the door opened.

Julie peered out. "Can I help you?"

MY BACK HIT Bowers's chest before I realized I'd stepped back.

Then the sound of her voice pierced the haze of my thoughts. The pitch was higher than Julie's had ever been, with the lazy drawl I heard from my friends' kids. And Julie would be in her mid-thirties now. This girl was in that liminal age between the softness of childhood and the rebellion of the teenage years. There were other differences, too. Julie's eyes had been the blue-green of a stormy ocean; these were brown.

This wasn't Julie.

In the same instant I figured out who — what — she must be, she saw Bowers and her face lit up. With a furtive glance, she came out onto the porch and closed the door behind her. "You're a *vampire*. That's so metal. But my dad's going to buzz if he sees you."

My first attempt at speech came out as a croak, but the second was successful. "Is your dad here?"

"Yeah." The look she cast me was borderline resentful, as if I was getting in her way. "Why?"

"I need to talk to him."

The girl looked from me to the vampire in disbelief, then she gave a little smile with a hint of malice. It was an expression I remembered Julie using when she could see a disaster coming and had decided to sit back and watch it all happen.

The resemblance made my chest hurt.

"It's your funeral. Wait here," she commanded, then went back inside and closed the door.

The last part might have been intentionally rude, but it could just have been practical. After all, Bowers couldn't enter the house, and my sister — half-sister, I supposed — knew it.

Behind me, Bowers said quietly, "She didn't notice the resemblance." He'd clearly realized what was going on. Probably figured out who the girl was before I had. So there it was, all the family drama played out in front of him. Thank all that was holy that he didn't seem like the type to laugh about such things with the rest of the office.

Then the door opened and my father looked out, with my half-sister peeking past him. The last time I'd seen him, he'd been thirty pounds heavier from a diet of fast food, insomnia, and alcohol. Despite the hint of gray at his temples, he now looked ten years younger, a more relaxed and active version of himself. Then he recognized me and the blood drained from his face. He slipped outside and shut the door with his new daughter on the other side. "Jenny." He made a gesture with his arms, as if he was going to hug me.

I moved back so fast I would have fallen down the steps if Bowers hadn't stopped me. My voice shook. "Since you didn't answer my calls or email, I came by to let you know Julie's memorial is this Sunday. Mom would really like it if you came." I was speaking so fast he'd have a hard time understanding me. But I'd followed the script and now we could leave. A spark of anger flared. "Though maybe it's best if you don't bother."

"Jenny, it's not like that..."

I held up both hands, palms out to stop him. Then I turned and walked down the steps and out the gate, not running, but at a pace much faster than I could maintain for long. There was a buzzing in my ears. I stopped at the end of the block when black spots appeared in my vision and gulped air.

A hand pressed on my shoulder. I swung around, furious, fists up, ready to hit my father, the man who had claimed to be *so devastated* by Julie's death, and then had immediately fathered another child.

But it was Bowers. He left his hand on my shoulder. "Breathe."

I'd never been big on crying in public, though Julie's loss had cured me of any embarrassment on that score. But crying in front of my coworker was the last thing I wanted to do. I swallowed around a lump in my throat. "I don't want to talk about it."

And then I burst into tears.

To his credit, Bowers didn't seem particularly bothered. Maybe his experience as a doctor had left him immune to other people crying. He just guided me to a low stone wall and then sat down next to me and waited.

After a few minutes, I dug the tissues out of my bag, wiped my eyes, blew my nose, and decided I would *never* tell my mother what I'd found. Revising the scene in my head, I saw the door unanswered and my hand slipping a note into the mail slot.

"Sorry," I muttered, suddenly feeling sorry for the vampire waiting for me to get my shit together so we could do our jobs.

"No apology necessary. You didn't even throw the punch."

"I probably would have broken my hand if I had." I blew my nose again and got up to throw the tissue away.

"No, I would have ducked."

It was said so matter-of-factly that I snorted. So then I had to blow my nose again, but I felt better. "Where's the next address?"

He made a show of looking at his phone. "Just a few blocks from here." Walking at an easy pace, he led the way.

We headed back toward Booksellers Row, with its bustle and noise. Soon, we were dodging clumps of tourists as they stared at the street performers. There were at least two pickpockets working the crowd around a street mage juggling fire, but they saw Bowers and melted away into the crowd.

When we turned the corner, I asked, "How old do you think she was?"

He didn't even pretend not to know what I was asking, which gave him another good mark in my books. "I'm not great with kids' ages. Twelve or thirteen?" He glanced at me. "Younger than fourteen, I'm pretty sure."

Not that it made any real difference, but I was glad that meant my dad hadn't been cheating on my mom during that first horrible year after Julie's disappearance. I gritted my teeth as I thought about how many times my father had failed to tell me I had a little sister. Then I blew out a careful breath. My work colleague didn't deserve to have me dump all this on him.

Trix, though. Trix was going to hear *all* about it when I got home that evening.

The next address was a one-bedroom apartment above a row of shops. The units all had entrances from an exterior walkway above the rear of the businesses, with access to the second floor provided by a rickety steel ladder covered in peeling brown paint. There were five units, but only number three had a sign affixed. Logic said the door to the left would be number two. When I touched the lintel, I felt only the faintest glimmer of an anti-vampire ward. Whoever lived here had opted for a cheap street vendor's ward that probably only covered the door and a few inches on either side.

Anti-vampire sentiment was weird, especially in a place so dependent on tourism. Vampires had *never* fed from unwilling victims, even before the Accords were signed. As far as people being forced to transform, only ridiculous horror movies showed evil vampires stealing new recruits off the street. In reality, multiple vampires had to work together to transform a human, and that only happened after a formal application and years on the waiting list. Except for Bowers, who had somehow become a vampire in less than a year.

"There's nobody in there," Bowers said. Given the size of the apartment, his vampire senses would cover the entire place. But it was protocol, so he knocked and announced us. You never know who's going to be watching, and there was no reason not to follow the rules.

While we waited, I looked over the railing to the alley

below. Somewhere down there was a cart selling the caramel pretzels Booksellers Row was famous for — I could smell it. Before we left this street, I was getting the largest one I could find. Some people lost their appetite when stressed, but stress always made me crave carbs. After everything that had happened today, a huge pretzel laced with caramel and salt would be perfect.

We waited a full minute, but as expected, nobody answered the door. With lock picks in hand, Bowers tried the handle. It turned, and the door swung slowly open, releasing the stench of death.

ELEVEN

All thoughts of caramel pretzels left my head.

Bowers and I looked at each other. "They didn't cover this in class," I said. At least not the part when I'd been paying attention, I added silently. "What are we supposed to do?" I really hoped the answer involved closing the door and letting someone else take over.

"If this is connected to magic, the FBME has jurisdiction and we call in our people. If not, we leave everything as is and hand it off to the city police."

What he didn't point out was that the only way to make that determination was to go inside and look around. And since I was the only person who could get inside, it was up to me. This was the kind of thing that had made me choose a job in the corpse-free basement of The Vault. "Just for the record, this day massively sucks."

"The ward keeping me out is probably right by the door," Bowers said, his voice practical. "You don't need to go any farther."

The smell when I entered nearly drove me back out again, but I forced myself to stop thinking about vomiting and looked around the entryway. The door was on the right side of the apartment. To the left was a kitchenette, only partially separated from the narrow living room with a balcony at the end. The living room was covered with bits of drywall, as if the renter had remodeled without putting anything down to protect the cheap carpet. Two interior doors on the left presumably led to the bathroom and bedroom.

The kitchen had about one square foot of counter space, and it was piled high with bills and other mail. Nothing was taped to the wall and the cabinet only held an assortment of mismatched plastic containers and a frying pan with most of the coating scraped off. Given the shoddy workmanship of this anti-vampire ward, I was pretty sure it needed to be within a few feet of the door, which meant the ward was somewhere in the pile of mail, most of it addressed to *Occupant* but a few addressed to Joshua Baker. I didn't have to disable it; I just had to move it far enough away that it wasn't blocking the door.

Scooping up everything on the counter, I moved into the kitchen and dumped it down on the electric range. "Can you get in now?" The pile slid when I let go, and I reached to keep it contained. That was when I saw the bodies.

The nook was probably advertised as the dining area, but whoever rented the apartment had used it for a gaming console, large screen, and one of those chairs that provided haptic feedback from the game, so he could be jolted as virtual bombs exploded next to him. The screen still showed the front of a tank driving in circles over a desert scene, at least where dried blood on the monitor hadn't obscured the view.

A white man in his thirties, presumably the Joshua Baker who failed to pay his bills, lay slumped in the gaming chair, his long blond hair plastered down by dried blood. Every bit of exposed skin on his face, neck, and arms had been slashed, with the wounds overlapping, a frenzied attack with a knife or razor.

On the floor next to him was another dead man whose hair and clothes suggested he was about the same age or a little older. But I couldn't be sure, because his face had taken on the distinctive rictus of an emaciated vampire. He was covered in blood and had a knife in his hand. All the wounds seemed to be on the human.

The dead vampire looked exactly like the old photos taken of vamps who had been captured and chained, back before the Accords had been signed. Those vampires had starved to death. But this vampire had nearly flayed a human to absorb his energy — he shouldn't have been *able* to starve.

"I think the FBME has jurisdiction," I said. Then I nearly screamed at movement from the living room, but it was just Bowers. With the ward shifted to the side, he'd been able to get through the door and detour around the kitchen.

He took one look at the bodies and pulled out his phone. "This is what they've been seeing in Seattle," he informed me as he dialed a saved number. There was something funny about everyone else being in Seattle to get up to speed on the problem and the two of us finding a new case, but laughing now would only lead to hysterics.

Supervisory Agent Salt's voice was audible, swearing as Bowers described the scene. While he did that, I flipped through the stack on the range until I found the anti-vampire ward near the bottom. It was a scrawl on the back of a takeout menu, creating a 6-foot sphere which would have blocked the door and part of the walkway outside.

I ripped the corner to disable it and then dropped the paper on top of the rest of the stuff I'd moved. The CSI technicians were not going to be happy with how much stuff I'd touched, but that wasn't my problem. The ward had needed to be taken down for the FBME to process the scene.

Except... How had the vampire entered? The French doors leading to the balcony were still closed. If Joshua was the type of person who warded his apartment, I couldn't see him temporarily moving the protection so he could invite a vampire in to play video games. Besides, there wasn't a second console.

The significance of the bits of drywall on the floor hit me. I ducked around the kitchen cabinets to look at the living room wall. Sure enough, there was a gaping hole on the right side, the shared wall with apartment number three.

Bet Joshua really wished he hadn't cheaped out on that ward. I felt guilty for thinking that, but it was true.

Bowers hung up. "Salt's calling people back from Seattle, but we're probably stuck waiting here for a couple hours until we can hand the scene off to them."

The ward was disabled; my job here was done. Waiting around to hand off the scene could be accomplished from outside the apartment. I was almost out the door when Bowers called me back. "Perkins. Take a look at this bracelet."

Going back in there seemed like a terrible plan. "It can't wait until after the crime scene technicians are done? I've probably already contaminated everything more than enough." I could look at everything back in the safety of The Vault, where there wasn't blood spatter decorating the walls.

"And if the spells suddenly disappear like the last ones did?"

That was irritating enough to make me turn around. This time, I followed his path around the kitchen and stopped where his body blocked my view of most of the gore. Unfortunately, it didn't block the smell. "Would it screw things up if I opened the patio doors?"

"Leave them. What do you think of this?" He crouched and pointed at a silver metal bracelet on the carpet between the two men. From the way Joshua's arm was outstretched, I assumed he had dropped it.

Most of the blood had dripped down under the gaming chair, so I was able to find a clean spot to crouch next to Bowers. At first glance, the bracelet looked like it could have come from the same batch as the ones we'd found in Mo's apartment the night before, with stars and moons stamped onto the metal and a glass pendant of a stylized sun glued on top. The links that completed the circle had broken, probably when it was ripped off. But even from a foot away, the magic felt different.

If this bracelet had contained a Moebius loop power circle like the others, it should have been destroyed when the chain had failed. But the collector cell pulsed, feeding power to a combo of whorls and knots that were part of the blood magic I hadn't yet looked up. "I don't like this. Blood magic is almost never a good thing."

There were too many similarities with the other jewelry we'd found for them not to be related, but if the power circle was broken, this should be getting weaker, not stronger. I looked more closely, putting my head near the floor so I could see the edges better. At some point, the aluminum cuff had bent, giving a different construction to the segments of the spell.

This was why nobody put complicated spells on aluminum — it bent and warped too readily.

I stood and took a step back, happy to get a little more space between me and the corpses. "I think you're right. It's related. But I need to look some things up back at The Vault. Blood magic isn't my specialty, and this is some high-level shit." Glancing down, I considered what had happened to the evidence we'd collected the night before. "Do you want to bag it now and take charge of it? Or leave it for the crime scene techs to photograph and collect?"

Bowers didn't respond. When I looked over at him, he was staring at me. And not in a way that suggested his mind was elsewhere, but as if he was hungry and thinking about his next meal. His skin had paled, giving it the translucent edge only seen with severely injured vampires.

After two days in his company, I trusted Bowers. But we were standing next to the corpse of a vampire who had starved to death while literally draining the life from another human. Something was *very* wrong.

"Bowers," I said firmly, "I need you to move over to the other corner." When he continued staring at me, I lifted my forearm and knocked the bracer against his chest. It hadn't been meant as a weapon against vampires, but it disrupted all sorts of magic, and vampires had magic coursing through them.

Hitting a coworker like that was probably a fireable offense, but the hairs on the back of my neck were standing up. I was far more worried about my life than my job.

He blew out a startled breath, and I saw him come back to himself with a jolt.

"In the far corner," I repeated, and held my breath until he complied. His feet made a trail through the drywall dust, but I no longer cared about scene integrity. When his back hit the wall, I said, "Toss me a containment box."

We'd carried a bunch of small magical containment boxes with us all day to keep the evidence from our searches from contaminating each other. While I had no proof that the bracelet had caused one vampire to go into a killing frenzy and made another unstable, I wasn't taking any chances.

His hands shook as he unzipped his bag, and his throw sent it off to the side, but my years of softball came in handy and I snagged it before it went past. Using an envelope to scoop the bracelet off the floor — if this thing affected vampires so strongly, I wasn't touching it — I slid it into the mahogany box, and then closed and latched the lid. The wards on the box shimmered to show they were working.

I stood, so I could keep a wary eye on Bowers while I filled out the evidence details. "Did that help?"

He had his eyes closed, and his arms wrapped around his torso. His whole body shook. "I think so. You need to leave."

Leaving seemed like a great idea. Except he was near doors going to a balcony and a street full of people. With the bracers, I at least had a chance of fending him off long enough to make him think about what he was doing.

I needed help from someone who knew about vampires and how to stay safe. "Bowers, what club do you go to?"

He took a shuddering breath. "Silver Edge."

Even I'd heard of that one. It was where the rich and famous went to relax and feed. "Someday you'll have to tell me how you afford those fees on an FBME salary," I muttered, even as I was looking up contact details on my phone.

He choked out a laugh, and I kept my eyes on him as I called.

The call was picked up on the first ring by a woman with what I could only describe as a posh English accent. "Silver Edge. How may I help you today?" Her voice was warm and reassuring and I was ninety percent sure her accent was genuine.

"I have one of your members here. Bowers. Uh..." I had to think a bit to come up with his first name. "Simon Bowers. I think he's been exposed to some sort of artifact and he's... in distress. Do you have any sort of delivery service? Or can you talk me through how to get him to the nearest club safely?"

"Of course. Where are you now?" The sound of keyboard keys clattering came through the line, but the woman's voice kept its serene tone.

"Near Booksellers Row." I gave her the address.

More typing. "And your name?"

"Jen Perkins."

"Okay, Jen. My name is Amanda. I've dispatched a car that should be there in fifteen minutes. Have there been any injuries?"

By injuries, she was asking if Bowers had started slicing up bystanders like poor Joshua, whose body was just a few feet away. "No." I held the phone away from my mouth and said, "Fifteen minutes," to Bowers.

Not opening his eyes, he pulled his gun and tossed it in my direction. "Shoot me if I come near you."

"Don't be such a drama queen," I said, keeping my tone light. "You can handle fifteen minutes." But I darted forward and picked up his gun just the same. It was heavier than I'd expected. Moving the phone back into position, I whispered, "I'm assuming there's no safe way for me to feed him myself." Slicing up my skin wasn't something I particularly wanted to do, but better that than having him run wild in Booksellers Row.

"Only as a last resort," Amanda said firmly. "And I don't believe we'll need that today. Has the artifact been neutralized?"

Right. Because presumably they were sending vampires to handle Bowers in the car. "I think so." Could there be a second one? No. He'd stopped getting worse as soon as he'd moved away from the bracelet. "Yes."

"Excellent. I'll stay on the line with you until the car arrives."

Then, while I watched Bowers shiver in the corner, Amanda calmly asked me questions about myself and my job for the next ten minutes, as if we were at a cocktail party and she was delighted to have met me. When she asked about the best way to see the city, I told her all the different ways I'd traveled around during the public transportation strike the previous spring. Even as I recounted trying to steer a paddleboat with a missing rudder, I kept my eyes on the vampire across the room. It was a surreal conversation.

Finally, Amanda interrupted my anecdote about fending off sea lions while kayaking to say, "Jen, the car has arrived at your location, and I have three attendants coming up the stairs now. Can I ask you to open the door for them?"

"Uh..." Up to that point, I'd had some idea of convincing Bowers to walk out the door by himself so we didn't further contaminate the crime scene, but now it seemed like a bad idea to upset the precarious balance we'd achieved. "I'll be right there."

When I moved, Bowers opened his eyes, his nostrils flaring. His whole body tensed as if he was about to spring forward. I glared at him and held up a finger, which made the ill-fitting bracers slide toward my elbow. "Stay!"

For a second, I thought it wasn't going to work. If I ran, I might make it to the door in time... not something I wanted to test. And if I ran, he would lose himself in the chase.

But then a hint of outrage cut through the hunger and he pulled away, turning his back to me and resting his forehead on the wall. "Get out of here."

A tactical retreat was in order. I backed my way to the apartment door and fumbled it open to find two men and a woman on the other side, all of them vampires. In a coordinated move, the woman grabbed my upper arm and yanked me away from the door, and the men went inside.

The woman put herself between me and the apartment, but her intervention wasn't necessary. Thirty seconds later, Bowers walked out, propped up between the two male vampires. He staggered like he was drunk, and I could see the glow of a binding spell around him. They walked down the stairs and through the passageway to the street.

Once they were out of sight, the woman in front of me relaxed. She turned around and gave me the once-over. "You aren't injured?"

"No." Not physically, at least. I'd probably have nightmares about what we'd found in the apartment, but that wasn't what she was asking. Now that I was safe, I felt lightheaded. "What happens now?"

"They'll take him back to the club."

"And he'll be okay afterward?"

"By tomorrow, it will be like it never happened." She raised an eyebrow. "You're FBME?" A hint of doubt crept into her voice.

I'd have been giving me that look, too. "Evidence technician. I don't usually work in the field."

"That explains it." She tilted her head toward the apartment. "I'm assuming the FBME will handle the bodies?"

Half a second before asking her how she knew there were bodies — as if the smell wasn't enough of a clue — I realized she had an earpiece in. The real entry override team probably had them also, to go along with the radio I hadn't bothered to check out from the armory. "I guess?" I had no idea.

"Good." She straightened. "Is there anything else you need before I go?"

"No." Then I remembered Bowers's gun, the one I'd left on the counter inside. "Wait. Do you know anything about guns? I need to make sure this one is safe to carry around." Maybe I should have waited for the FBME team to arrive and had them take possession, but Bowers had given his gun to *me* and I was going to hang onto it until I could get it back to him.

AFTER THE SILVER Edge team had gone, I stood in the doorway with our equipment and the evidence we'd collected earlier — and Bowers's gun — and considered how I was going to lug it all back to The Vault.

But first, I needed to call Supervisory Agent Salt.

TWELVE

It took me another ten minutes to find Salt's number, and as the phone rang, I wished with all my might that she would let it go to voicemail. Naturally, she picked up. I explained what had happened, and she listened in icy silence. Around the second time I paused to check if the call had dropped, I realized I probably should have called her earlier, instead of chatting with Amanda about the best bike routes around the city.

Finally, Salt cut me off. "Get outside, close the door, and wait for the CSI team to arrive."

She hung up before I could respond. After a short internal argument, I went back inside and grabbed the mahogany containment box with its properly filled out evidence sleeve. This thing was dangerous enough to kill people and I couldn't trust that the crime scene technicians wouldn't open the box to look inside. There were vampires among the CSI techs. I wasn't going through *that* again, no matter how angry Salt was. Then I went back outside, shoved it into my duffel bag, and closed the door.

I was a professional. Waiting near two bodies wasn't

hard. Adults did things like this all the time. There was probably a bunch of forms I was supposed to be filling out, but I didn't know what they were, so I was just going to stand there and wait until I stopped twitching. I could use some alone time to process the events of the day anyhow.

Closing the door helped with the smell, though not completely. After a few minutes of wondering if one of the Silver Edge employees had opened the window, I realized the odor was coming from my clothes. I sat down with my back against the door, closed my eyes, and wondered how much mail carriers got paid.

A voice from my left startled me. "It's about time someone showed up to deal with that crazy vampire!"

I opened my eyes and looked to the side to see a middle-aged white woman in a purple caftan emblazoned with the message *Love is All*. She carried a huge macrame bag over one arm, and her hair was pulled back into a sloppy bun with silver hair sticks holding it in place. To my eye, she looked like the sort of person who made life decisions based on having her palm read. Then again, my path through life hadn't exactly been giving me stellar results lately. And *she* probably had less debt than I did. "Excuse me?"

"You're FBME, right? I called the cops this morning to say that vampire in three was going to hurt someone. They said they'd call you guys, though if I'd known it was going to be so long before someone took me seriously, I'd have gone to stay with friends. That FBME vampire that came by earlier spent less than two minutes inside. Then she came back out and said everything was fine and I should mind my own business. All those vampires are a menace."

Clearly, *Love is All* had a few gaps. "Why did you think your neighbor was going to hurt someone?"

"Because he started screaming and banging on the walls.

Made me glad I paid for an anti-vampire ward the minute he moved in. That sort of thing should be a tax write-off." She eyed me suspiciously. "They won't let him come back, will they?"

I blinked, picturing the death mask of the vampire inside the apartment. That vampire wasn't going anywhere other than the morgue.

She must have seen my confusion, because she added, "Sure, he looked quiet when they walked him out of here. But take my word for it — you can't ever trust them."

It took me longer than it should have to realize she'd seen Bowers leave and confused him for her dead vampire neighbor. In my defense, it had been a long freaking day. "The vampire in apartment three won't be back," I said with complete sincerity.

She harrumphed and headed down the stairs. "You'd better be right. It would be safer to just kill them all." And having blithely advocated for a war crime, she left.

Stuck in front of the apartment for at least the next hour, I tried distracting myself with games on my phone, but I gave up after a few minutes. My thoughts were a tangled mess of the personal, professional, and a mixture of the two.

Holy shit, my father had a whole other family that I knew nothing about, and I had a *sister*. If Bowers hadn't been impacted by the bracelet until he was right next to it, why had the vampire on the other side of a wall been so severely affected? And how had the FBME agent — if it really was an FBME agent, who stopped by earlier — not noticed a person-sized hole in the wall and two corpses in the apartment next door?

Assuming the neighbor wasn't lying or confused, a vampire from the agency had entered apartment three this morning and left everything as it was, including a bracelet that had come very close to sending Bowers on a killing spree.

Getting attacked twice in two days... Every data set had the occasional outlier. *Twice* felt like the start of a pattern. But if the attacks *had* been intentional, Bowers was the likely target. I was just a cog in the basement machine, easily replaced by someone like Hamilton. Bowers was a real agent, and he didn't strike me as someone who would give up on things easily. The pterodactyl spell had been triggered by a timer — Bowers would have been inside the apartment with me if I hadn't gotten distracted by the furniture and taken so long to find the anti-vampire ward. He was stronger and better at fighting than I was, but the bracers had been the thing that saved me, and he couldn't have worn those. Up to now, nobody had survived a pterodactyl attack. If Bowers had been inside, his death would have been written off as an unfortunate accident.

And today, if Bowers had lost control, he very likely would have killed me and possibly others. Completely draining the energy from Joshua hadn't been enough to save the vampire next door. So even if someone hadn't killed Bowers during his murderous rampage — a clear act of self-defense — he would never have worked for the FBME again.

If he'd killed me... I didn't think he would have lived long afterward. Bowers seemed especially conflicted about being a vampire, and a death on his conscience would tip him over the edge. How often had the looks I'd assumed were irritation at me really been self-loathing?

Laughter from the street startled me, and I shook my head to clear my mind. This was insane. Nobody was out to kill either of us. It had just been a couple of terrible coincidences. To arrange something like that would require someone high in the FBME calling the shots.

Except... The neighbor had referred to the vampire who came by earlier as "she". Supervisory Agent Salt had been one of very few vampire agents in town this morning.

By the time the crime scene techs arrived with two male agents I didn't recognize, I hadn't resolved anything. Instead of the suits that agents usually wore out in the field, these two were wearing black windbreakers with FBME in large white letters on the back over more casual clothes. I assumed they'd come straight from the task force meeting in Seattle.

I'd been expecting them to take a statement from me, but the taller vampire waved me off. "We have the scene. You can go."

So I went.

THIRTEEN

I don't know what I looked like as I lugged the two duffel bags on the subway, but I got almost as much space as Bowers and I had earlier in the morning. Maybe I didn't need to develop a spell that exuded the menace of an irritated FBME agent. Maybe I could just make one that transformed any person into a Woman Who Has Seen Some Shit. It seemed to work just as well.

Back at The Vault, I turned in all the evidence we'd collected in the morning. Filling out forms and making idle chit-chat with the guy at the evidence locker made everything seem almost normal.

But I kept the mahogany containment box with me.

What with the spells disappearing from the jewelry we'd logged into evidence last night and a female vampire showing up at the apartments earlier that morning, I was developing a severe case of "trust no one".

Technically, as long as I kept it under my control as a designated evidence technician, I wasn't violating any rules. I tried to keep that in mind as I rode the elevator to the fourth floor to turn in my vest and bracers.

After that, I went up to the sixth floor to drop off Bowers's duffle bag in his office. Unlike that morning, the floor was a hive of activity. Salt must have called everyone back from Seattle. I could hear her ordering people around, but with all the activity, it was easy to slip into Bowers's sterile office and leave his bag under his desk without anyone noticing me. His gun was in my bag, along with the containment box holding the bracelet.

My next stop was my desk in the basement, which was still as quiet as it had been all week. Hamilton looked up from the tiara he was examining when I came in to grab my spare set of workout clothes.

"They let you out on your own and suddenly Salt's calling everyone back from Seattle. What happened?"

"Dead bodies."

"No shit?"

"No shit." I tried to act unbothered. "Think they'll let me stay in the basement from now on?"

"At this rate, they may chain you to your workspace."

"Be right back." I grabbed my clothes and went off to the locker room to change, bringing the duffle bag with me. If I had to attest that the containment box hadn't left my possession, I wouldn't be lying.

I caught a glimpse of my face in the locker room mirror after I'd changed. All things considered, I looked less frazzled than I had any right to after this day. Maybe the people on the subway had been avoiding me because of the smell of death coming off my clothes. I shoved everything, including my shoes, into a plastic bag and made a mental note to air them out when I got home.

Hamilton laughed when he saw my t-shirt, shorts, and sneakers. "Taking office casual a little seriously today, are we?"

"Dead bodies," I reminded him.

"Right."

I set the duffle bag down on my chair and crossed the room to look at the tiara in front of him. "Getting ready for a night out?"

He snorted. "If I'm getting fancy, I'm going with a full crown, not this thing." He tapped the metal with his pencil. "Sold to some poor woman as a glamour aid to make her hair look better, and it caused brain damage."

Leaning across the workspace, I traced the clover leaf pattern as it traveled across the arc of the tiara. "It probably works on a straight barrette, but that intersection... They got sloppy tying off the knots."

Hamilton waved me away. "Stop helping. That was supposed to take me another two hours to figure out so I'd have something easy to work on after the weekend. Now I'm going to have to start something new."

I straightened. "So those bracelets you looked at this morning...?"

Kicking his chair back, he turned to face the table behind him. "Figured you'd want to see for yourself, so I left them out." He pulled a handful of evidence bags from a cardboard box. "Knock yourself out." He swiveled back to the tiara.

It was definitely the same jewelry that Bowers and I had logged in to the evidence room the night before — I recognized the patterns stamped into the aluminum and the glass pendants glued to the cuffs. But instead of the powerful magic that had forced me to separate one bracelet from the others to study it, these had absolutely nothing.

Picking up a bag, I stared at it, trying to find any trace of the spell. If nothing else, the Moebius loop power circle should still be visible. But no. There was *nothing* left.

Checking over my shoulder to make sure Hamilton was still busy with the tiara, I shook the bracelet out of the bag and licked the metal with the tip of my tongue.

Salt.

Someone had rubbed the jewelry in salt — or, more likely, soaked them in salt water — sometime after Bowers and I had dropped it off in The Vault. That had destroyed every trace of magic. With any other metal, a saltwater bath would have been obvious, but aluminum resisted corrosion.

I wiped the bracelet off on my shirt and dropped it back in the bag. "That's so weird. But you're right. They're completely blank now." I piled the bags back into the cardboard box, aiming for an air of casual disappointment. "There must have been some sort of timer or something that I missed. That's what I get for not staying and writing up the report last night."

Hamilton looked up from the tiara in consternation. "Perkins, the main benefit of a cushy government job is that you get to go home at the end of the day. Well, that and the coffee."

"Ha. I bet the private sector has much better coffee. But speaking of going home..." I slung the strap of my duffle bag over my shoulder. "I'm taking the rest of the afternoon off. If anyone comes looking for me, tell them it will have to wait until Monday."

"Will do." He was already concentrating on the tiara again.

I left.

Outside, the sun was still shining, which felt a little unreal because this day had been at least forty-eight hours long already. But a look at my phone told me it had just passed four-thirty.

Going home, taking a shower, and crawling into bed for

the next year was an appealing option, but I didn't think I could afford to do so. Eventually, someone would notice the missing bracelet from the crime scene — I'd told Salt about it when I'd called her after Bowers was taken away. I needed to talk this through with someone.

Normally, I would have sat on our couch and dumped it all on Trix. She was an excellent sounding board, and as a bonus, she knew I didn't imagine conspiracies everywhere. But Trix didn't know anything about the FBME.

Hamilton might be a good second choice, but... We were friendly, sure, but he wasn't actually a *friend*. Besides, he rather famously refused to pay attention to any FBME gossip or power plays, and that was the knowledge I needed.

He also hadn't noticed the bracelets had been soaked in salt water. Maybe it was just a sign that he'd done everything by the book, with the least effort possible — that *was* Hamilton's modus operandi, after all. It was why he would never be promoted out of the magic technician group in the basement. He'd also never be stupid enough to do the training for the entry override team, so I was beginning to think maybe he had the right idea. Show up, do your job, go home, and wait until you could retire with a full pension.

The only person at the Bureau that I was absolutely sure wasn't involved in a plot to kill Bowers was also the person who followed office politics enough to predict Jonah Patel's reaction to Salt assigning me to his group. Plus, I had his gun.

I rode my bike two blocks away from work — the vendor prices were twice as high next to The Vault because it was a popular tourist destination — and stopped to buy a giant cinnamon roll from the family-run bakery at the corner. The first sugary bite was heaven. Extra stress required extra carbs.

When I'd inhaled enough sugar to improve my outlook on life, I called Silver Edge. Amanda answered. "Jen, it's good to hear from you again."

Her warm greeting before I'd even identified myself threw me off, since I'd been expecting to need to explain why I was calling. This was easier. "Uh, hi. I was calling to check on... Simon." I'd almost called him by his last name, but that would have been weird. "Is it..." Wait, asking if it was safe to be around him was probably offensive. "Can I go there and talk to him?"

"Let me see if he's up to receiving visitors. May I put you on hold for just a moment?"

"Sure." I used the next two minutes to eat the rest of the cinnamon roll. My stomach protested, but it was just going to have to deal with it.

"Jen?" Amanda was back, breaking into the Chopin nocturne they were using as hold music. "Simon asked me to invite you to come by. Do you have transportation?"

Did vampires all forget about bicycles? Or no, this was probably just a rich people thing. "I'm fine. I'll be there in twenty minutes."

The bike path along the river smelled of the ocean and popcorn — a tour boat had just gone by. I joined the crowd of weekday commuters and students heading to weekend parties. Friday night in the Butcher District would be a zoo. It would be best to get out of there before it got dark and I had to dodge drunk people setting off cheap glitter spells. Not that the area around my apartment in the Warehouse District was much better, but at least there were fewer tourists and most people knew better than to walk in the bike lanes.

Four blocks from the ocean, I turned left, rode past Amar's building, and then past two more plazas and a park.

Silver Edge was housed in an eight-story glass and pink brick building constructed in the 1910s, when vampires were still a secret. Though I'd ridden past the building before, I'd never noticed the discreet brass plaque next to the door that said *Silver Edge Recreation Club*. I chained my bike to a light pole and hoped it would still be there when I came out again.

The front door was locked, but there was a button and a camera. "Yes?" A man said neutrally when I pressed the buzzer.

"Jennifer Perkins, to see Simon Bowers." His first name came more easily this time.

The door unlocked with a clunk that suggested sturdy bolts. Even though the last riots against vampires had happened over forty years before, Silver Edge was prepared. Or maybe they just wanted to make sure their clients never had to deal with the riffraff from the street.

The entryway was long and narrow and could have easily been defended by one person with a gun. Which was a fairly disturbing image. Shaking my head, I tried to get a grip on my paranoia. Just because I'd never been in a vampire club before didn't mean I needed to give my imagination free rein. A male vampire in an expensive suit opened the door at the far end. He was a white man in his thirties, with blond hair, tanned skin, and a pleasant expression even as he regarded the duffle bag with its FBME logo. "Would you care to check your belongings?"

"No, thanks." I went past him into a quiet lobby with hardwood floors, oriental carpets, leather couches, and a chandelier that kept the lighting just bright enough to read by but not so bright that it would highlight wrinkles. It felt like walking into a different universe with the wild energy of the Butcher District streets just a few feet away.

Two women, one human and the other a vampire, hunched over a chessboard in the corner. An older male vampire lounged on the sofa reading a newspaper with a glass of some amber liquid near his hand. Alcohol didn't do much for vampires — the magic quickly recognized it as a toxin and got rid of it — but some people still enjoyed the taste.

In my t-shirt and shorts, I was both underdressed and lacked that indefinable something in my posture that rich and influential people had. If there had been anywhere else to go, I would have turned around and left the building.

I'd started to ask the doorman where I'd find Bowers when an interior door opened and a stunning Black woman emerged, a wide smile on her face. "Jen! I'm Amanda. It's so good to meet you in person."

Human like most of the staff, Amanda was in her forties, with the smooth skin that cosmetics charms always promised and never delivered. Her curly hair was clipped short on the sides and left longer on the top. Just like the other employees, she wore a black suit with a crisp white shirt. The outfit cost more than anything in my wardrobe. Silver Edge clearly paid their people well.

Taking my elbow, she led me toward the back of the building where an elevator waited. "You," she said, "did an amazing job today, and everyone here is extremely grateful."

I glanced at her uncertainly, half convinced she was being sarcastic. With her accent and poise, I'd never know if she was. But she *seemed* sincere. "All I did was call you. You took care of the rest."

"Nonsense." When the elevator door opened, she stepped inside and pressed the button for the fifth floor. "You kept your nerve and helped Simon wait for aid to arrive. If you hadn't..." She shook her head, as if to dispel an image. "I'm glad he had you with him. Simon's one of my favorite people."

That was interesting. I'd worked enough service jobs to know that the staff often saw a completely different version of people. Usually, it was the worse side, like the woman who'd hosted a fundraiser for refugees. As part of the catering staff, I'd quickly learned to avoid her. Simon appeared to be that rare breed of person who intimidated his colleagues while being nice to the staff.

When the elevator dinged, Amanda said, "The fifth floor contains our medical wards. I'll give you a tour of the entire club later if you'd like. Do you want something to drink while you're visiting with Simon? Or I can have the chef whip something up for you?" She led the way along a short, carpeted hallway that might have been a private residence. It was a far cry from the ER at Floodmouth General.

Though I was tempted to come up with some difficult challenge, just because this would be the only time I'd have the opportunity, the cinnamon roll still lay heavily in my stomach. "No, thanks."

"If you change your mind, just pick up the house phone." She stopped at a closed door and knocked. "Simon? Your partner is here." Then she opened the door for me and left.

FOURTEEN

The room was small and cozy, with a leather couch, a glass-fronted bookcase, and a large television mounted to the wall. It presumably had a good Wi-Fi connection as well — everything someone would need to wile away the time when stuck in one place. The only discordant notes were the bare linoleum floor and a recliner with sturdy leather straps where someone's chest, waist, and wrists would be.

Bowers got up from the couch when I entered. He looked better — his skin had lost that translucent quality and he had clearly showered before changing into FBME sweat pants and a t-shirt — but there were lines around his eyes that hadn't been there that morning. The casualness of bare feet made him seem like a different person from the immaculately dressed man I saw at work. Still, in comparison, I felt grubby and out of my depth.

"You're looking good," I said, forcing the light tone that everyone used when visiting sick people in the hospital.

He cast me a withering stare. "Stop acting like I have a terminal illness. I'm fine. Have a seat. Do you want coffee or something to eat? They have a decent chef here."

"No, thanks." Deciding the recliner had too much of a bondage vibe going for me to relax in it, I sat on one end of the couch and pulled the duffle bag into my lap. "I brought you a present."

"You didn't have to..." He trailed off as I dug out his gun and the magazine that I'd stored in a spare evidence bag. "Thanks. I assumed you'd handed it off to the crime scene techs and I was never going to hear the end of it."

"I didn't improve the FBME's reputation when I had to ask one of the Silver Edge people to make it safe for transport," I warned him. "I didn't want to put it in the duffle bag and accidentally shoot someone on the subway."

He blinked. "We should go to the range so I can show you how to safely handle a weapon. Just in case."

Though my initial response was to refuse – Why would I need to know anything about guns when I was back in my real job? – I considered everything that had happened in the last two days. "Okay."

We lapsed into silence. On my part, I was trying to find the best way to say *Hey, I think someone is trying to kill you* without sounding like a complete idiot. His thoughts were apparently running in a different direction.

"I wanted to thank you," he said finally. "I know I've been treating you like you aren't qualified for the job, but you handled yourself like a pro in that apartment. If you hadn't, it would have been bad. Really bad."

I started, "Bowers." Then I stopped and started again. "Sorry, if you're going to be barefoot, I'm using your first name."

"Agreed," he said gravely.

"Okay. Simon," I said, stressing his name, "you couldn't find anyone *less* qualified to do the job I've been cosplaying for the last two days. You've been showing me how it works without being a condescending ass about it. And I think you're not giving yourself enough credit."

"For nearly losing control and killing you?"

"For keeping it together long enough for help to arrive," I corrected. "All those deaths in Seattle? You're the only one who's survived to say what happened."

He stared at me.

I waved a hand. "Look, can we put your emotional crisis to the side for a few minutes? We have bigger issues." I paused. "Wait. That came out wrong. I'm not saying your feelings aren't important."

Simon rolled his eyes. "Get on with it."

I took the exit he'd given me so I didn't dig the hole any deeper. "Can you think of any reason someone at work would be trying to sideline you?" Attempting to be as coherent as possible, I ran through my reasons for the question, from my suspicion that a trap had been set for him at Mo's apartment, to the deliberate sabotage of the evidence we'd gathered there, and ending with the neighbor's report of an FBME agent hours before we'd found the bodies along with the deadly bracelet.

He leaned back and considered my words. When I finished, he grimaced. "All that could just as easily have been aimed at you. You're the one who almost died both times."

"Yeah, but there would be no point in killing *me*. I don't run investigations — I just write reports for the artifacts they hand me. If I died, there are another fifteen people who would keep going."

He shook his head slowly. "Your lack of ego is amazing."

I sighed and flopped back on the couch. "If only my dissertation advisor had agreed with you."

With a throaty noise I suspected might be his version of a laugh, Simon said, "You have a reputation, you know. Even up on the sixth floor."

For a moment, I stared at him, horrified, convinced that my drunken ramblings at the departmental Christmas party had surfaced to kill *this* career as well. Then I remembered that nobody at the FBME would care what I'd said about the department chair at the university. "What?"

"The reports you write. People request you for their cases by name because the reports don't get torn apart on cross examination."

That was the first I'd heard of it. Though it might explain the unexpected hostility I'd encountered from a coworker a few weeks ago. I'd just assumed I'd run afoul of another unwritten rule about sending questions directly to the investigator. "Okay, but being good at my job and being worth killing are two different things. I still think it must be you."

"Or it's just coincidence."

I'd been afraid he might say that. "Soaking the evidence in salt water couldn't have been coincidence."

"No, but you didn't lick any last night *before* we logged them in, did you? Maybe it was a residue leftover from setting the spell. And, by the way, licking evidence is a really stupid thing to do. Who knows what you might have exposed yourself to?"

"I needed to know," I protested. "What about the FBME agent the neighbor saw? How do you explain that away?"

"Maybe she lied. Or maybe her vision isn't great, and she misidentified the person who came by. I'm not saying there *isn't* something going on, but a conspiracy within the FBME? Do you know how unlikely that is?"

He wouldn't like what I said next. After putting the duffle bag on the ground, I kicked off my shoes and brought my knees up, turning so I was facing him. "I kept the bracelet we found at Joshua's."

"You *what?*" He tilted the left side of his head toward me, as if he hoped he would hear different syllables if I repeated myself.

"I never logged it in. I've still got it with me."

His gaze locked on the duffle bag at my feet. "In there."

"Yes."

Simon closed his eyes. "Let's ignore the fact that you brought it *here*, the building with the highest concentration of vampires in the city. You just tampered with evidence. If any charges get filed for those deaths, they'll have to exclude the findings."

"It's been in my possession the entire time," I argued. "There would be no reason to exclude it." There would also likely be no case — both Joshua and the vampire who had killed him were dead.

He opened his eyes and looked at me for a long moment, all trace of our earlier rapprochement gone. Finally, he said, "I need to call Salt."

Well, feeling like I wasn't a complete failure had been fun while it lasted. He was probably right. I'd based my decision on faulty information.

Shoving my feet back into my shoes, I asked, "You want me to leave it here with you?" I dug through the duffle bag and pulled out the mahogany cube, still sealed in its evidence bag.

With his phone pressed against his ear, Simon held out his other hand and took it between two fingers. I stood and shouldered my duffle bag. "See you on Monday." Assuming I still had a job on Monday after Salt found out I'd been hanging onto evidence. And honestly, with the way things had gone the past two days, that might be just as well. Maybe I could go back to tutoring undergrads.

Between now and Monday, I still had to get through Julie's memorial service and avoid answering any questions my mother asked about my father. Screw the FBME. I didn't need the extra stress.

My sense of being out of place grew as I stood in the empty hallway waiting for the elevator. What had I been thinking, taking a job at the FBME? I'd never fit in there. I *certainly* didn't fit in here, at Silver Edge. Half an hour from now I would be lounging on our lumpy couch in my most comfortable sweatpants and it would be glorious.

The elevator dinged just as Simon called me. "Perkins! Wait!"

When I turned, I saw him standing in the open doorway, his feet still bare. The elevator door slid open behind me, but I didn't move.

He beckoned me toward him, and I realized he might not be *able* to leave the room. "You have to hear this."

For two seconds, I considered getting on the elevator and leaving. He wouldn't be able to stop me. Telling Trix about my day would go a long way in helping me process it.

But there hadn't been enough time for Bowers to tell Salt what I'd done and then wait for her to finish yelling about it.

I stayed where I was. "Why?" Maybe what I'd done was so serious she was sending someone over to take me into custody and Bowers was supposed to detain me until then. If so, my best bet was to run, unless I wanted to spend the next decade in federal prison. The FBME onboarding paperwork had made it very clear they didn't screw around when there was malfeasance.

But Simon looked worried and unsure of himself, not like someone who had the strength of the FBME behind him. "Someone attacked the CSI van on their way back to The Vault and torched all the evidence they'd collected. You might be right."

FIFTEEN

Back inside Simon's room, we sat on opposite ends of the couch and stared at the mahogany containment cube on the cushion between us. Simon slowly ran his fingertips over the leather of the couch next to his knee as he thought. Vampire or not, he still had the strong hands of a surgeon.

I forced my gaze back to the cube. "So what now?" It was the obvious question, but sometimes the obvious questions had to be asked. Simon hadn't told Salt we had the bracelet — as far as anyone knew, all the evidence from the crime scene had been destroyed. "There's no way to tell who can be trusted."

"So we don't trust anyone." He forestalled my next question with a quickly raised hand. "Just for now. If we can get more information, maybe we can get a better handle on who benefits. Then we can make better decisions."

He was so confident; it made me remember that investigating things was what *he* was good at.

Except we'd have to get more information without the resources of the FBME.

Normally, that would be a huge problem — not having

online access to the massive databases maintained by various government agencies made things more difficult. But in this case, the FBME didn't have what I needed, anyway.

I tapped the cube. "I'm almost positive there's blood magic incorporated into the spell. The university's arcane library has some references I need to study." I looked at my phone and added, "Tomorrow." The arcane wing kept standard business hours, which I'd found extremely annoying as a grad student.

As in all arcane libraries, the dangerous books and scrolls were examined in a null room, so I wouldn't need to worry that opening the box to look at the bracelet would affect nearby vampires. I'd just need to be sure there weren't any vampires in the room itself.

Simon nodded. "I'll work from the other end. Someone is manufacturing and distributing these things. If we can follow the supply chain back to the origin, we'll have a better idea of who might be involved. I'll visit Mo in jail tomorrow and get him to tell me where he got them."

"If he's smart, he won't say anything."

"Hopefully, I can convince him we'll ease up on the attempted murder charges if he helps."

"So you're going to lie?" For Mo to avoid an attempted murder-by-magical-means charge on the pterodactyl spell would require a prosecutor to sign off.

"No. There are a hundred ways to write up an incident report, and I haven't filed mine yet. If he has a decent lawyer, they should be able to help him understand that." A notification came up on his phone and he tapped to dismiss it. "Can we take a fifteen minute break? Amanda will take you to the restaurant for coffee or tea."

It took me a moment, but I realized that was his discreet

way of telling me it was time for him to have another meal and he didn't want me around while it happened. I'd already stood up when there was a quiet knock at the door.

"Come in." Simon's habitual irritated frown had returned, and I wondered again how much of that was discomfort that I'd misidentified.

Picking up the mahogany cube, I said, "I'll just take this with me," and shoved it into the duffle bag when he nodded.

There were three people at the door: Amanda, a young Indian man who looked like a university student, and a Latino vampire in his forties wearing the same tailored black suit that seemed to be the employee uniform.

As Amanda took my arm and drew me toward the elevator, I heard Simon say, "Hi, Vikram. Haven't seen you in a few weeks. How are things?" Then the door closed behind him and I didn't hear a reply.

AMANDA and I ended up at the restaurant on the second floor, where I had the best cup of coffee I'd ever had in my life. It was a nearly religious experience. After the first sip, I stopped and shook my head.

Ever attentive, Amanda said, "Is something wrong?"

"I'm never going to be able to drink the coffee at work again. How does... Simon handle it?" Then I answered my own question. "He never drinks the coffee there, does he?" I'd certainly never seen him with a mug in hand.

Amanda laughed. "I'll see if we can get a care package sent over for the two of you."

She probably would, too. Now I'd have to hope I kept my job at least long enough to receive it. I shoved the duffle bag further under my chair, and the plastic bag holding my clothes crinkled. "You must know this area pretty well."

"Of course. What do you need?"

"Is there a laundry service that could turn my clothes around this weekend?" With one outfit lost to the ptero-dactyl, I either had to get the one I'd been wearing today cleaned or show up on Monday smelling like a corpse. My plan to find another outfit at the thrift stores had gone up in smoke now that I needed to spend my Saturday researching in the arcane library.

"Leave them with me. I'll have them ready for you to pick up tomorrow morning." When she saw my expression, Amanda smiled. "Jen, handling dry cleaning is literally in my job description, along with about fifty other things."

"For members," I said.

"For members and guests," she clarified. She sipped her own coffee and eyed her cup. "You're right. I'm so used to it I'd forgotten how good the coffee is here." Then she looked me in the eye. "You don't seem to understand how much good will you accrued in the vampire community today."

"Because I called you? It wasn't entirely a selfless act, you know. I was the one who was going to get sliced up if it all went wrong."

"You called, and you *stayed with him.*" She leaned back in her chair. "I'm not a vampire — yet — but there's a stage they call the 'dangerous hunger', which every new vampire is taught to avoid. Have you heard of it?"

I nodded and followed it with a shrug. "What I know could be wrong." As with everything else related to vampires, popular fiction had seized upon the dangerous hunger as a plot device in everything from murder mysteries to rom-coms.

She acknowledged that with a tilt of her head. "They

don't exactly advertise it. The dangerous hunger is the reason new vampires can't leave their local area for a year. Because once it starts, it's nearly impossible for them to think of anything other than feeding. The more depleted they are, the stronger the pull." She took another sip of coffee. "What's happening in Seattle is a public relations nightmare for the vampire community. It would be even more disastrous if it happened here, given Floodmouth's history."

I'd only heard about *vampire* deaths in Seattle. Amanda's words suggested multiple *human* deaths had been covered up. Which... made sense if what had happened in Joshua's apartment today was related. Since I hadn't seen any headlines about rogue vampires on my way to Silver Edge, Joshua's death had also been kept quiet. The vampires were serious about damage control.

She continued. "But the important thing to remember is that the dangerous hunger is harder to resist with stress, loud noises, or quick movements." Amanda indicated the carpets and sound-dampened walls with one hand. "It isn't an accident that this building is furnished this way. Not that we often see the dangerous hunger here, but when it happens, staff are *very* careful not to make it worse."

She paused to smile and nod a greeting at a vampire couple who had walked in. Not knowing the protocol as a guest in a vampire club, I didn't look over until I heard a familiar voice.

"Jen Perkins? Is that you?" Delia Tarragona had nearly reached the table before I could get over my shock at seeing her. Which was stupid, because Silver Edge catered to Delia's demographic — rich, powerful, and older.

I hastily stood to hug her, noting that her vermillion silk blouse somehow remained uncreased, even at the end of the day. Had it really only been yesterday when we'd been having coffee at Little Bites? So much had happened in the last day that it felt like weeks ago.

Leaning away to look at me with her hands still on my shoulders, Delia cocked her head. "Don't tell me *you* were the one with poor Simon today! Jen, since when have you been doing fieldwork?"

"It's temporary."

"I should *hope* so." She let her hands drop. "It's one thing to put your head down and stay at a job to show you can stick with something, but it's quite another to stay somewhere that's putting you in danger. I'll call some people and see what's available." She held up a hand when I opened my mouth. "Not another word. You don't have to accept anything if you're happy where you are, but you should know your options."

Then she looked at Amanda and me. "And now I'll leave you two in peace." Tilting her head at the man waiting for her by a table across the room, she added, "Possible new investor. I need to convince him the foundation is the perfect place to leave his inheritance."

"Good luck," I offered.

"Thank you. I'll get in touch by next Friday with any leads." She smiled at us both, turned, and strode across the room.

After a moment when we both adjusted to the sudden change in energy, Amanda turned her attention back to me. "If you really are looking for another job... New hires here spend days learning everything to do and say. And there you are, running through it flawlessly, without any training. If you ever want to switch careers, I'd hire you in a heartbeat."

Delia was right — it was good to have options, even if I

had no plans to take Amanda up on her offer. "My one summer working retail made it clear that I was not suited for any customer-facing job," I admitted ruefully.

"That's a pity," she said lightly. "But you never know unless you ask."

"So even knowing you could kill someone if you lose control," I said, redirecting the conversation, "you still want to transform."

"What a diplomatic way of asking," she laughed. Then she sobered. "Ovarian cancer runs in my family. My grand-mother died at 52, my aunt at 56, and my mother at 55. And that was all after years of chemotherapy. There are disadvantages to being a vampire, but I might make it to a healthy seventy. Maybe even longer if I change before the mutations stack up. You've never considered it?"

"No." Even suggesting such a thing would send my mother into a panic. Both my parents had strong feelings about vampires after what had happened to Julie. "There are family issues."

"Ah," she said. "Family support is important."

Before I could agree, my phone buzzed. Trix had texted. *Che has a friend with access to the Trinity collection and he's taking me there for introductions. They even have a private teleporter!* That was followed by a string of excited emojis. Trix had been trying to get in to see the private collection at Trinity for *years*.

Another text came through. *Back on Sunday for the ceremony.* There was a two-second pause and then, *Should I be worried about the Men in Black watching our apartment?*

I froze, staring at my phone. It had never occurred to me that Trix would be dragged into this mess. We'd always joked about me working with the Men in Black — she thought FBME agents were nearby.

Amanda leaned forward. "Is there a problem?"

"Not sure." I texted back, *Have a good time at Trinity. I'll deal with the Men in Black. See you Sunday.*

We needed to fix this nightmare. And soon.

SIXTEEN

When I returned to Simon's room, Vikram and the vampire who'd escorted him in were just leaving. Vikram had a spelled bandage on one forearm and he looked a little tired, but he was still cheerful. "It was good to see you again, Simon. If you watch the second season, let me know what you think."

Simon was in the recliner, removing the strap around his waist, but someone else had unbuckled it first — he wouldn't have been able to reach behind him when it was fastened. "Medical wing rules," he grumbled, then sighed. "I needed this a few hours ago, so I guess I shouldn't complain."

I shrugged. "If you told me it was to keep you from flying, I wouldn't be able to prove you wrong. This is the first time I've been in a vampire club."

"That surprises me." As he walked over to the couch, I noticed that his stride was stronger and the lines in his face had lessened. If I hadn't been there when everything went wrong earlier today, I'd never have known anything was off. A little life energy from a guy like Vikram made a difference. "We get so many university students coming through here, I guess I just assumed everyone tried it at least once."

"My family background made that..." I searched for the word. "Complicated," I finally concluded.

"Ah."

He had to have noticed the anti-vampire wards on my father's house. If that wasn't a sign of "complicated" attitudes towards vampires, I didn't know what was.

I put my father and his new family out of my mind to focus on the present. "We may have another problem."

When he heard about the text from Trix, Simon sent a message to Che. "Let's make sure she didn't get stopped leaving the apartment," he said to me as he typed. That possibility hadn't even occurred to me, but before I could work up an appropriate level of panic, Che replied, saying he and Trix were already at Trinity College.

Since my apartment was possibly being watched, Simon convinced me to stay in one of the guest rooms at the club. "I'd let you stay at my apartment, but that might be worse." That I would be sleeping in a vampire club in the Butcher District wasn't even in the top five weird or traumatic things of the day.

Then we settled in with pens and legal pads to document everything we knew, which turned out to be... not a whole lot. We had a bunch of spelled bracelets from Mo's apartment that had been tampered with in the evidence lockup, another bracelet at Joshua's apartment that had caused one vampire to starve to death and another to be sent into the dangerous hunger. Someone had tried to destroy that evidence as well, and would have succeeded if I hadn't walked off with it. Plus, we had someone from the FBME at Joshua's apartment *before* we found the bodies, maybe others watching my apartment, and two possible attempts to kill Simon.

Given the paucity of information, we brought up the task force summaries from Seattle, hoping to find some links that would point us in the right direction, but they didn't have much either.

Over the last two months, fifteen vampires had suddenly starved despite draining the life force of nearby humans. As far as anyone could tell, there was nothing to tie the vampire victims together — they belonged to different clubs, lived in different areas, and hadn't interacted within the past month. There was nothing in the notes about any sort of jewelry found at the scenes.

At the end of the evening, our plan of action included tracing the source of the jewelry by talking to Mo (Simon), studying the blood magic books at the library to figure out what the jewelry was *supposed* to do (me), and keeping an eye out for anyone who might be following us (technically both of us, but Simon was the only one with training). Implicit in the plan was staying alive. We would document everything, and as soon as we found someone we were sure wasn't working against us, we'd read them in.

That last part would be difficult, but I wanted nothing more than to dump this mess on someone else's lap and let them deal with everything.

"Are you going to be able to go to the jail to talk to Mo tomorrow?" I'd finally looked at the wards around Simon's room and confirmed they were set up to keep him confined here. Not that he'd acted trapped. If anything, he seemed reluctant to leave.

He nodded. "The doctor will come by in the morning and clear me. He told me I could have left this evening, but there's a twelve-hour rule after the..." He trailed off.

"'The dangerous hunger," I supplied.

"Amanda told you about that? Yes. They wanted to make sure I'd remain stable. The syndrome can be tricky that way." A haunted look returned to his eyes.

"Knock it off," I said. "You didn't kill anyone, and you can't hold yourself responsible for something that happened when you were spelled." I covered a yawn. "It's been a really long day. I'm going to bed."

Before she'd gone off shift, Amanda had set me up with spare clothes and toiletries, and sent my work clothes off to be cleaned. They even had a bike locker in the back of the building; when I went outside to bring my bicycle in, the Butcher District was in full Friday night swing, with crowds of students, tourists, and other partiers clogging up the streets and sidewalks. But inside Silver Edge, none of that was audible. I could have been in a country house or some mountain retreat. The effect was disorienting.

The guest bedrooms were on the top floor. Mine had an expensive entertainment system, an incredible view of the ocean, and an enormous tub with whirlpool jets. On another evening, I might have taken advantage of all that, but I just wanted the day to be over. So I took a shower, shampooed my hair twice and scrubbed my skin until it was red, and then crawled between expensive sheets and hoped I wouldn't dream.

SEVENTEEN

Sleep had a funny habit of reviewing and re-prioritizing everything. When I woke in the morning, the idea that I'd nearly died twice seemed absurd, and if I hadn't exactly forgiven my father for having a secret family, I was more curious about this sister I'd never met. Unless the spells had been done by a friend, the bicycle in the yard said she was a magic user.

Why had I been the only child unable to do any magic at all?

That rankled, but life wasn't fair. Besides, I'd spent enough time complaining about it during my mad-at-the-world phase back when Julie and I had been pre-teens.

The memorial was Sunday, and I couldn't deal with more family drama until that was over, but at some point I'd have to decide if I wanted to have any sort of relationship with my new sister. And that would depend on whether she knew about me and, if not, whether it was fair to tell her.

Not until after Sunday, I told myself firmly. Get through the memorial first.

Today was Saturday and I had to go to the library. But first, I was going to get a cup of that insanely good coffee.

Armed with a bag of croissants and a thermos of coffee with the Silver Edge logo discreetly stamped on the rim — the man working in the restaurant had filled it and handed it to me when I'd asked if they had any to-go cups — I rode across the city, the chilly wind making my nose run. Through the Butcher District, across the river, and then through the streets to the university. It would have been faster to take the path on the other side of the river, but I didn't want to get too near The Vault.

The arcane library, officially known as the Coby Welch Memorial Collection, was housed in the south wing of the Floodmouth University Central Library and was world famous for its historical Western magecraft books and scrolls. Whoever had designed the interior had ignored the brutalist architecture of the building and filled the space with dark wood partitions and a gold and red palette. Because of that, walking from the main library into the arcane wing felt like being transported to a different century, when scholars were admired and the unwashed rabble wasn't allowed through the front doors.

To gain access to the collection, one had to be a student in the magical department at the university or qualify as a visiting scholar. I'd made sure to re-apply when I began working for the FBME. Even if I hadn't needed the information stored here, it was one of the safest places in the city, because the books could be catastrophic in the wrong hands. The vampire council and the mage concord both kept a close eye on who studied what, and the building was imbued with spells to keep the collection from harm.

At the main desk, a stooped white woman with too many wrinkles to count glared at me. When I'd first started

visiting the arcane library as an undergraduate, Mrs. Montcrief had intimidated me so much, I'd nearly changed my
major to accounting. In the decade since, she hadn't
changed at all, but I'd learned not to take her scowls personally — the dragon guarded the hoard.

She grabbed the chain holding her half-glasses. "Area?"

"Blood magic."

That earned me a long look before she flipped the pages
in her binder. "Subsection?"

This was where things got difficult. "Europe or North
America, in the last two hundred years. Either in English or
with an existing translation."

Indexing magical tomes was an art, not least because
many defied digitization. If I'd been looking for a particular
book, Mrs. Montcrief could have retrieved it in less than a
minute. But I was trying to trace the origin of an existing
spell, which meant I'd have to make an educated guess as to
where the mage had learned it. Blood magic was a relatively
small subset of the data in the arcane library, but it would
still take me months if I didn't narrow it down somehow.

The person who had created this spell hadn't been well
versed in theory. That much was obvious from the flaws in
the design. So I probably *wasn't* looking for a pre-Renais-
sance book, where everything was carefully coded in
ciphers to hide its true purpose. Also, until the late 18th
century, most European spell books were written in Latin or
French — again, tough books to wade through without a
classical education.

But just before 1900, there had been a movement
among practitioners to make knowledge more accessible to
the everyman. And yes, they'd meant men in particular,
because mages in the universities hadn't been particularly
enlightened then. We knew from other documents that

women had their own spells, but most had never been written down in books. As far as I knew, very little of the oral tradition concerned blood magic.

So... a recent book, in English, probably in the Western tradition. It was a reasonable place to start. Of course, it might turn out that I needed to look at the spells from a specific group of people in West Africa, but I'd cross that bridge if I got there.

One thing I hadn't needed to specify was a null room. The arcane library had five of them, and after an incident in 1981 caused by two scholars working at opposite ends of a table in the main — untreated — room, any potentially hazardous item could only be handled in a null room. If you looked up when you came through the entrance, you could still see the charred outlines on the ceiling. They kept painting over them, but the enamel reacted strangely with magic residues, and replacing the beams would require too much in the way of stabilization.

Mrs. Montcrief sniffed, perched her glasses on the end of her nose, and pointed to the right without looking up from her binder. "Room three. No food or drink is allowed in the room."

That last bit had nothing to do with my thermos of coffee, which was safely stowed away in my backpack with the mahogany cube; she'd repeated those words to me every time I'd used the library. I thanked her as I always did and moved into room three. On my way there, I stopped to pat the spine of my bound dissertation, untouched on the shelf with all the other magic department dissertations. Maybe nobody would ever use my attempt to advance the field, but just having it bound and available for any scholar was deeply satisfying.

Stepping over the threshold, I was rewarded with a

deep sense of calm. That was the effect of the null wards. In a city as full of magic as Floodmouth, a background buzz became the normal, in the same way that the constant stream of people at a cafe blended into its own soundscape. But a null room blocked everything that didn't originate inside the room. Some people found it disquieting, but I'd always loved the feeling, at least in short doses.

I wondered what Simon would make of it.

Scents of wood polish, dust, and the sweetness of decaying paper made me feel at home, in a way the apartments and townhouses of my childhood never had. Maybe that was why it had taken far longer than it should have for me to accept my career in academia would never work out. Too many people vying for too few positions, and the only people who could afford to work as a lecturer while applying for professorships were those who had enough generational wealth that they didn't need the salary. The rest of us went further and further into debt until we finally gave up and found jobs in industry. Or at the Bureau, in my case.

I didn't miss the low pay and financial stress, but I missed the library.

Mrs. Montcrief broke into my musings by entering with a cart stacked with seven wood containment boxes, each the size to hold a large hardback book or two. There would be more than seven on the list she'd compiled — seven was the maximum number of items that could be retrieved at one time. "When you're finished with them, return the ones you no longer need to the cart, and I'll bring in the next set." It was a speech I'd heard her give thousands of times.

"Thank you." That was my contribution to the play, which then led to her final lines.

"Wait until the door is closed before opening any containments."

And then I was alone.

Pulling the top box off the cart, I opened the lid to find *Forbidden Charms and Their Uses*, first published in 1913. The author was listed as Magister S, an obvious pseudonym, probably because the penalty for using blood magic before the Accords were signed — when vampires and magic became known to all — had been death.

Magister S might have been taking his life into his hands by publishing such a thing, but he was also prone to long-winded screeds about sinful deeds, including sex, gluttony, and, weirdly, swimming. He must have been a blast at faculty parties. I paged past another diatribe about the submersion of limbs being dangerous and reached a spell for curing *the French disease* that was all right angles and spirals. By the end of 700 pages, I knew two things: anyone who'd been stuck next to Magister S at a dinner party wouldn't have been fooled by the pseudonym, and the style of his spells was entirely different from what I'd seen on the bracelets.

I returned *Forbidden Charms* to its box and moved to the next book.

Four hours later, I'd waded through fifteen books and a scroll, and seen nothing close enough to what I was looking for to even need to open the evidence bag to check.

Most of the books listed the standard illumination spells and wards against vampires, stronger versions of charms that didn't require blood. A few claimed to summon demons, though they, too, had illumination spells in different colors and patterns, demon-summoning being the profession for charlatans with magic in the 19th century.

One of the demon-summoning books had a fire spell

that I was 90% certain would incinerate any caster unlucky enough to confuse left from right at a crucial juncture. That was the thing with blood magic — it provided more raw power, but that power had to go somewhere. I'd heard it described as the magical equivalent of a cheap space heater — it might be useful, but there was a decent chance it would burn down the house.

Those demon summonings must have been pretty memorable, though.

Mrs. Montcrief had clocked out for her one hour lunch break, leaving me in the hands of one of the underlings who changed so often they'd all gained the name Fred or Frederica, depending on perceived gender. The Fred/Frederica convention had started sometime prior to the current millennium, and the assistants wore the name with a sense of pride.

In this case, it was Frederica, though the woman looked vaguely familiar, which was a first. If Mrs. Montcrief had finally found an assistant whom she trusted and who hadn't been lured away by the employers who regularly poached the trained underlings, Frederica might one day become the new Mrs. Montcrief. Possibly, she would even be called Mrs. Montcrief as well. The arcane library had its quirks, and nobody bothered fighting them any longer.

While I waited for Frederica to bring the next seven books, I dug my phone out of my backpack. Simon had texted earlier in the morning, saying he was "going now", which I took to mean he was going to the prison to talk to Mo. Since our phones were FBME property, we'd agreed not to put any details in our texts.

Now I had another text from him, sent five minutes ago. *Stay there. On my way.*

We were *supposed* to be meeting at Silver Edge in the

evening, during which time I would allow myself to be talked into eating what would likely be the best meal of my life, if the coffee and croissants were anything to go by. Something must have happened to make Simon change the plan.

Text when you get here, I sent back. He wouldn't be able to get into the arcane library unless he flashed his badge, and maybe not even then. Since we were trying not to draw the kind of attention that would get reported back to The Vault, it would be better if I met him in the main library.

Frederica arrived with the next set of books. "Wait until the door is closed before opening any containments," she warned.

As soon as the null wards had snapped into place again, I opened the top box. *Amulets to Cast Out Demons* read the title in ornate gold script. The typed description on the outside of the box claimed the book had been published in 1842. From the title, I assumed the pseudonymous Mr. Thomas X had filled the niche opened by all the demon summoners, which showed a certain level of marketing savvy. Because, after all, if demons weren't actually summoned, how could anyone prove that the spells in his book didn't work as advertised?

When I paged through the introduction, though, I found I'd erred in my assumptions. The demons Mr. X had been trying to cast out were of the metaphorical variety — alcoholism, depression, and what I assumed a more modern person would describe as manic episodes. I was pretty sure psychiatric medicine gave up blaming mental illness on demonic possession long before the middle of the 19th century, but this author hadn't gotten the memo. Or maybe he knew and ignored it — if a spell to keep a person away from alcohol worked, it didn't matter if the person casting it thought they were altering brain chemicals or sending angels into battle. But I was glad I hadn't been around for Mr. X to experiment on.

These days, nearly a century after the Accords had been signed, everyone stuck with pharmaceuticals to address matters of the mind. Magic could induce feelings of euphoria or sadness, but it was short-lived, lasting anywhere from one to ten seconds. Plus, it was a little like using a sledgehammer to swat a fly — sometimes the rest of the brain took a hit, which might mean anything from memory loss to cerebral hemorrhage.

Mr. X had "solved" the problem of the spells not lasting long by introducing blood magic, which... Sure, that would change things, but I would have bet there had been a pile of bodies buried in the man's cellar. Or, more likely, the university or research institute where he'd worked had known how to quietly dispose of the subjects who didn't survive.

This was the kind of thing that made modern universities adopt institutional review boards to scrutinize the ethics of experiments before they were approved.

Nobody in their right mind would mess with psychiatric spells these days, but I kept paging through the book because it fit my criteria. Being stubborn had helped me far more often than being clever.

And I found what I'd been looking for.

EIGHTEEN

There it was — whorls and knots in a pattern matching what I'd seen on the bracelet next to Joshua. With a quick check to make sure the door to the null room was still closed, I opened the evidence bag and removed the containment box. With the bracelet next to the book, I compared them. Nearly identical. This was the blood magic spell that had been infused into the bracelet.

As soon as I was sure, I closed the containment box. Just because it affected vampires didn't mean it *only* affected vampires — Joshua must have been wearing it for some reason, after all — and I didn't want to find that out the hard way. Then I flipped a few pages back and actually read what Mr. X had said about this spell.

It was a spell to "restore good humours" and had a woodcut of a woman, head in hands, elbows resting on a table piled high with dirty crockery. An infant howled in a cradle at her knee. Reading between the lines, it was intended to cure depression.

My cynical side thought maybe giving the poor woman a chance to rest someplace quiet for a few days might have been more helpful than blood magic messing with her brain, but I was a century too late to point that out.

Later illustrations showed a spotless house and the woman standing with one arm holding a contented baby and her free hand curled possessively around an amulet hanging from her neck. It was an odd choice of images; despite clear evidence the recipient's coping skills had improved, the woman's body language was defensive, as if more protective of the amulet than the baby. Maybe that was supposed to indicate she approved of mother's little magical helper, but her look was nearly feral. Sure enough, the text claimed the woman refused to remove it, even when bathing. I wondered if that was a conscious choice or an addiction caused by the spell.

Just to be thorough, I flipped through the rest of the book, encountering entries on what appeared to be calming manic states, promoting pleasant behavior in children, and — horrifyingly — inspiring conjugal behavior in one's wife. This book was an abuser's treasure trove.

Closing it back in its null box, I set it aside from the others. If we knew who had accessed this book within the last year, that might be helpful. But Mrs. Montcrief wouldn't give us that information without a warrant. And it might not be that helpful anyhow. These spells may have been replicated in every arcane psychiatric text printed in the last hundred and fifty years.

But knowing what that portion of the spell did made the rest of the bracelet even more perplexing. Treating depression didn't require a power collector cell and a Moebius power circle. If anything, there should have been elements to dampen the powerful effects of the blood magic. Presumably, the wearer would want a low-key, pleasant buzz that didn't make them too tired to do anything. Dumping more power into the spell would leave the wearer lying on the ground. They might even forget to eat and drink. And maybe some people were looking for that sort of thing, but I thought if that had been the desired end point, it would have been packaged in something that would appeal to the party crowd.

The rest of the spell, the parts I hadn't yet figured out, had to somehow modify the effects created by the blood magic. But to do what?

My phone buzzed with a text from Simon. *I'm here.*

Be right out. After packing all my things, I loaded all the null boxes back onto the book cart and left the room, only stopping at the front desk long enough to tell Mrs. Montcrief that I had finished for the day.

"Always happy to help a scholar."

That she still referred to me as a scholar and not... whatever I was now, warmed my heart, and I smiled as I left the arcane wing and returned to the noise and bustle of the central library.

———

SIMON WAITED by the tables just outside the arcane doors. From his face, I could tell something had gone wrong, though there was an outside chance he was just really uncomfortable about the undergrad sending him come-hither glances as she leaned toward him, elbows on her calculus textbook.

He looked up in relief as I came forward. I tilted my head toward the main doors. "Let's go get lunch so I can tell you about what I found." And then halfway to the door, it occurred to me that with his attitude to being a vampire and his dietary abstinence, it might bother him to be around people eating. "Do you mind? I can always grab something after we talk if it bothers you."

"What? No, it's fine." He was first through the door and held it open for me. "I don't remember women staring at me like that the last time I was in a library."

I tried not to smile, but it was a losing battle. "Is this your version of fishing for compliments?" Saturdays near the campus weren't as busy, but I could smell the taco truck and I turned to follow the scent of fried fish.

"No."

He still looked confused, so I took pity on him. "The last time you were in the main library, you were probably one of a thousand undergrads who could be easily confused for each other in a line-up, right?"

Simon snorted, but didn't disagree.

"Now, you're older, but not actually *old*. You're not terrible looking. You dress well. And you move with the confidence of someone who carries a gun for work, which adds that hint of danger. Plus, you're a vampire. All that adds up to an attractive package for a twenty-year-old." We reached the truck, and I got in line. "Don't worry. Give her another few years and she'll have worked out that kindness is much sexier than danger."

He stood next to me, hands in the pockets of his slacks. "That puts me squarely in my place."

"My point is that her looking at you had nothing to do with you as a person and everything to do with her not being mature enough to *see* you as a person."

"Right." But he had the faintest trace of a smile.

He was silent until I'd been given my food, the fish taco platter with refried beans and tortilla chips. After I grabbed a handful of napkins, we lingered near a sculpture of Katie Tucker's horse, Shadow, which currently sported a pink top hat and a frilly garter above one knee. The horse had been a replacement for the statue of Atticus Leary, the founder of the university, which had been knocked down and thrown into the river in 1978. The students had been angry because they felt Leary had betrayed humans by not speaking out against vampires in the days before the Accords.

Anti-vampire sentiment had cooled since the riots, but plans for a replacement statue were scuttled when Leary's letters with a pro-slavery bent were uncovered. The university had quietly worked to remove his name from everything except the plaque on the central square giving the date the university was founded. Shadow, being a horse, was deemed highly unlikely to create a future scandal and was therefore chosen to fill the space.

Squeezing lime on my tacos, I said, "I found out what the blood magic part of the spell does." While he waited, I grabbed the soft corn tortilla with fried fish, cabbage, cilantro, and some kind of white sauce, and ate a quarter in one bite. It was amazing. After I'd swallowed, I said, "It's a spell to help with depression."

"Depression? Really?" He was paying attention, but his eyes were on my plate. "I thought the history of using magic in psychiatric cases was... not good."

Of course. As a doctor, Simon knew how magic had been used in medicine. "Exactly. Nobody does that now. And they certainly don't use blood magic." I scooped up refried beans with a tortilla chip. "But that's only about a quarter of the spell that's on that bracelet. I still need to figure out what the rest of it does. You want some of this?"

"No, thanks." But he continued to look at the plate as I started on the second taco.

"Okay. So I still need to think about what this thing is really doing. Did you find out anything from Mo?"

He sighed and looked at me. "Mo's dead. Killed by another prisoner in the cell before the guards could intervene."

I stopped chewing and stared at him. "Shit."

We'd been counting on information from Mo to trace the bracelets back to whoever had made them. Now, that was a dead end. Literally. And we still had no idea if someone from the FBME was involved.

I continued eating because stress makes me hungry, and it wasn't like *not* eating was going to solve anything, at which point Simon went back to staring at my plate.

"We may still have some leads," Simon said. "The police had been building a case against him for smuggling non-magical items. If we assume he had a regular route..."

"Then we might figure out where he got the bracelets," I finished. "Are the cops willing to share?"

"I have hardcopy of everything they have so far. I'm going back to the club to go through it all."

His club, because going to his home wasn't safe. My apartment probably wasn't safe, either, but I needed to go by to grab more clothes. "Can you take my stuff with you? I need to go by my apartment and I don't want to take the evidence or my notes with me, just in case."

"No." He abandoned my plate and met my gaze.

"You won't take my stuff with —?"

"No, you can't go back to your apartment. Don't be an idiot. I just told you someone *died*."

"Look, I have a family thing tomorrow that I really need to attend."

"Your sister's memorial," he interjected.

"Yes. And I can't go in this." With a wave of my hand, I

indicated the t-shirt and shorts I was wearing. "I just need to drop by my apartment to pick up my black dress and shoes. Two minutes, tops. Then I'll go somewhere safer." We needed to wrap this up before Trix came back from Dublin.

"They won't need two minutes. If they're watching your apartment, they could run you down the second they see you." When I opened my mouth to argue, he added, "Are you really going to make your parents mourn two children in one weekend?"

I glared at him. "That's a low blow."

"I'm right and you know it. Come back to the club with me. We'll continue going over the case and someone can bring you clothes."

"This sucks." Then I shoved the plate with the last taco at him. "Would you just eat this thing and stop staring at it like it's the forbidden love you can't allow yourself to think about?"

"I don't need —"

"I *know* you don't need to eat. But that's not the only reason to eat something and right now you are seriously pissing me off with this whole vampire hair shirt thing." Mostly, I was angry that I couldn't go home, but he was a convenient target.

Without another word, he took the plate from me, picked up the last taco, and slowly ate it. His eyes unfocused as he chewed. When he swallowed the last bite, he took a napkin and cleaned his fingers. "Happy?"

"Ecstatic."

NINETEEN

We spent the rest of the day in a private room on the third floor at Silver Edge, reading the police case file on the late Mohammed Murphy. Six months before, I would have been shocked by the amount of paperwork his case had generated, but I'd seen what an FBME investigation could engender, so the file seemed light in comparison.

Every so often, a Silver Edge employee would show up with more coffee or snacks or a "light dinner," which was far better than any meal I'd eaten in a year. It would have been a nice vacation if it hadn't been for the urgency of finding out who was behind it all. It was also a little too comfortable — I found myself wanting to know Simon better, on a personal level, and that was a disaster signposted in neon. Dating coworkers was at the top of my list of things to avoid. We needed to finish this before I did something stupid.

"What am I going to do when Trix gets back tomorrow?" I set down a report on the surveillance that had led the police to identify Mo as a person of interest. "I can't let her walk back into the apartment, but we're no closer to figuring this out than we were two days ago."

Simon regarded me across the narrow wooden table for a long moment. "Tell me again what the spell was supposed to do."

"It doesn't make any sense," I said, but when he waited patiently, I took a deep breath. "By itself, the blood magic portion treats depression. But that's only a small part of the whole spell."

"Explain the other parts to me. Dumb it down — I don't know anything beyond basic magic theory."

On the back of a witness statement, I drew the band. "There's a power loop going around the cuff and through the chain."

He nodded. "Which draws energy in from the person wearing it to power the rest of the spell."

"Yes." Then I stopped and frowned. "No." I stared at the line between the wall and the ceiling as I thought about it. "Huh." Then I remembered he was waiting and sat up. "That's the whole point of blood magic. The mage imbues the spell with all the power it needs when the caster adds their blood. So there's no need for a power loop."

"Okay, keep going."

In the center of the cuff, I drew a rectangle. "The power loop is connected to this collector cell, which is analogous to a battery."

He stared at my drawing. "If the power loop is always running, why would you ever need a collector cell?"

"Because you can't harvest much energy through the skin." Vampires solved this limitation by making an incision, which allowed them to drain energy faster. "Anyhow, for a spell that needs more power for a short period of time, you add a collector cell. It's what they use for short-term cosmetic glamour tied to something like a tiara — the user wears it for a few hours before the event, and then the spell draws on that stored power while the user walks the red carpet."

"But not for anything to do with psychiatric medicine," he said.

"What would be the point? Being happy for three minutes out of every hour would be worse than being miserable all the time." I shook my head. "And we have drugs for that. They're not perfect, but they mostly work."

"Unless you're a vampire," he said offhandedly.

He was right. The magic that maintained a vampire would make pharmaceuticals ineffective for more than a few minutes. I'd never thought about that. "So, how *do* they treat depressed vampires?"

"Therapy. That's why the council carefully reviews applications for people with any sort of psychiatric history. They do blood tests on candidates multiple times over six months, because if someone is using mood stabilizers, they may not be able to cope after the change."

"That would suck." Just another reason to stay human, though I wasn't crass enough to say that aloud.

"Agreed." He leaned back in his chair and rubbed his thumb along his lower lip. "Could the spell be intended for a *vampire?*"

It made sense, except for one thing. "Impossible. Blood magic only works on humans."

"Ah. They skipped that in my basic magic literacy course."

"It might have worked back in the twelfth century, though." When his brows raised, I waved a hand. "Sorry. My doctoral dissertation included an alternate theory for the second vampire plague."

"Yeah?" He leaned back in his chair, ready to take a

break from thinking about the case. "What was your theory?"

"*My* theory was that mages who were also vampires were casting spells to allow them to feed on other vampires in a quest to achieve immortality." At his look of disbelief, I continued. "It makes some sense, I swear. The limit on how long any vampire can live has always been the rate at which they can absorb energy from a human. At some point, the amount of energy needed to support an aging body is greater than the amount that can be taken in. But a *vampire* can store quite a lot of energy in concentrated form. That's why some can go days between meals. Theoretically, if you could take the concentrated energy from multiple vampires, that intake limit would increase quite a bit."

He raised a brow. "What does that have to do with the vampire plague?"

"Oh, that's the part where I sort of waved my hands and tried to make sense of the historical documents and the spells we know were in use at the time. If the plague was magical instead of biological, that would explain the weird geographic patterns, where some communities were wiped out but others were unaffected, even though we know they would have been in physical contact with each other." I drew a crude outline of the European continent and shaded in the clusters of known vampire settlements. "There were massive die-offs here and here, but this area was fine, even though there was a major trade route running right through it. But if you analyze the spell variants being used in each area, you can see there was a different magical tradition separating them."

I tapped the page. "Most scholars think that a virus mutated and wiped out the majority of vampires in Europe and Northern Africa. But the practice at the time was to burn vampire bodies after death, so we've never been able to find physical evidence to back that up. It also doesn't explain how the plague disappeared so completely. As far as magic users becoming vampires, multiple sources say that it drove them mad. That would be reason enough not to transform anyone who could work magic. But *I* think a plague spell was created by vampire mages and *that* is why the councils slaughtered every vampire who could perform magic. Changing a magic user has been prohibited since 1204, which is right around the time the second vampire plague ended, and there hasn't been a plague since."

For most of the thirteenth century, the vampires had waged war on *all* mages. At least now they just had a set of non-lethal tests to weed them out before they progressed in the application process.

When I looked up, I caught the amused look on his face and winced. "Sorry. I wrote 350 pages about it and I can get a little carried away."

"Don't apologize. It's always good to find out what people are excited about." He stared at the paper, where my map of vampire settlements bumped into the diagram of the bracelet. "So what you're saying is that before they were all wiped out in 1200 —"

"1204," I corrected. I couldn't help myself.

"Before they were all wiped out in 1204, a vampire mage could have used this blood magic spell to treat depression in vampires."

"Yes. Except the spell didn't exist yet." Blood magic wasn't my area of expertise, but I recognized at least three constructions in the spell first seen during the short-lived Blood Magic Renaissance of 1722. "And these bracelets are definitely not that old." I shrugged. "So we're back to where we started when I said that this spell makes no sense."

He reached over to fill my coffee mug from the carafe at the side of the table. "You haven't finished talking me through the bracelet yet."

With the amount of caffeine I'd ingested, it was a wonder my heart wasn't skipping beats, but it was *so* good. Maybe I *would* change careers and work for Silver Edge if that gave me access to this every day. "Okay. We have the anti-depression part, the power circle, and the collector, which, by the way, is the largest one I've ever seen. And then there's a puzzle lock." Because I really wanted to open the mahogany box and look at the bracelet to remind myself of the details, I grabbed my pen and added a little squiggle in the appropriate place on the cuff near the edge of the collector. I'd studied the bracelet enough at the library to remember the whole thing.

"And a puzzle lock is...?"

Right. Bowers hadn't studied magic theory. "A puzzle lock is basically like a physical lock, except it keeps the spell from triggering until the puzzle key is nearby. The most common use is in security applications, where wards drop when someone with the corresponding key is near. Sometimes you see them used by matchmaking companies — users suddenly appear more attractive if a prospective match is nearby. But mostly security. And I have no idea how that works with a spell to treat depression."

I held up a finger before Simon could speak. "But I *do* know the puzzle lock was damaged on Joshua's bracelet. So my guess is that some part of the spell was supposed to be intermittent, maybe when he went somewhere? But the aluminum bent and left the lock in the 'on' position." Flipping my pen in the air, I slumped in the chair. I'd figured out the failure state, but not the normal use. "The whole thing is a jumble of unrelated parts. I can't figure out what it's supposed to *do*."

I sighed and turned the paper over to re-read the witness statement. "Assuming Mo was the only person selling those bracelets, Joshua must have gotten it from him. Have you found anything connecting them?" While I'd been reading the file, Simon had been using his laptop to get the basics on the two men we'd found in the apartment the day before.

"They're both dead."

That *was* a connection of sorts, but it didn't really provide anything useful. "Other than that."

"Not yet. Joshua worked at The Speakeasy on Book-sellers Row. It's a literary bar."

"Don't remind me." I shuddered.

"Bad memories of Hemingway in twentieth century lit?"

"Brief relationship with a poet who expected me to be his cheering section. I drank a few Turn of the Screwdrivers to get through his seven turns on open mic night and I have never been so ill in my entire life." I blew out a breath as I shook my head. "Trust me, that thing I said about that girl in the library needing a few years to mature was based on personal experience."

He glanced up. "You're full of surprises."

"More than you'll ever know," I agreed, skimming through more surveillance logs.

"I had a pretty good inkling when I heard you arguing about whether a paddleboat could be considered a commuter vehicle."

Putting my finger on the page to keep my place, I looked up. That was something I'd said to Amanda when I'd been waiting for the team from Silver Edge to arrive. "You were *listening* to that?" That was a little embarrassing because I'd been talking without paying attention to what I was saying. I hadn't thought Simon had been in any shape to take it in. "And I still say it's a perfectly reasonable choice, as long as you don't have too far to go."

"I'll keep that in mind."

"Great. But back to the subject — the whole reason we went to Joshua's apartment was to serve a search warrant. That wasn't linked to Mo?"

"Doesn't look like it. A pawnbroker identified Joshua as the person who brought in a bunch of stolen charms. He was pilfering things from clients at the bar, but that seems to be it."

"Could he have stolen the bracelet?"

"If he did, nobody reported it missing. I checked."

By nine o'clock, I had fifteen pages of color-coded notes indexing all the material. And a headache. As tempting as it was to take some aspirin and power through, the next day was going to be hard enough, even with a good night's sleep. "I don't think we're going to figure this out tonight."

"No," he agreed. "What time is the memorial service?"

"At ten." Clothes had magically appeared in the guest room where I was staying, far nicer than anything I owned and also far better fitting. There were two outfits suitable for wearing to the memorial — one in black and shades of gray, and the other in blue and green tones. There were drawers of workout clothes, underwear, and casual shirts and jeans. Somebody had prepared for me to stay for a month, which was a little scary. But everything fit, even the shoes. When all this was over, I was going to track down whoever had been responsible for buying me clothes and learn their secrets.

"It's at Fairview Park, right? I'll have a car pick us up at 9:30." He caught my look of surprise and said, "If someone is trying to kill you, it's an obvious place to attack. The time and location have been publicized. You aren't armed and you can't cast spells. If I go along, they might think twice."

It was a sound argument for inviting him, but bringing a vampire to my sister's memorial would lead to a whole different set of issues. And while I didn't think anyone would say anything to Simon, he had to know what he was letting himself in for. "Before you... Do you know who Raiden Martin was?"

He gazed at me across the table. "The serial killer? Was he a suspect in her disappearance?"

"Maybe not officially. I don't know. I've never seen the case file." At the time, I'd been sixteen years old. As a magical technician, I couldn't request old cases, though it had occurred to me a few times since I'd started at the FBME that I could find someone else to show it to me. "But Julie was... I guess *obsessed* might be the right word for it. With vampires. She read everything she could find, watched any movie with a vampire character, wrote stories online about vampires. She even had a fake ID so she could get into the nightclubs that refund the cover charge if you feed a vampire at the end of the night." Most of those places catered to tourists and ranged from embarrassing to just plain sleazy.

Simon cocked his head. "You said she worked magic."

"Yeah. She knew she could never be a vampire. And that was probably a big part of it. You could always get Julie to do something by telling her she wasn't allowed to." I took a deep breath to calm my heart rate, which had spiked as it always did when I talked about my sister's death. "When we still hadn't heard from her after a few months, everyone kept saying there was still hope, but... Then Raiden Martin was arrested with all those bodies in the basement."

Simon nodded.

I continued. "Julie wasn't there. But the police always suspected he had more dump sites. And when they showed him her picture, he laughed." Pulling my hair away from my face, I said, "There was never any evidence that he did it, and he lied about other victims, so it's entirely possible he had nothing to do with her death. But my mother believes Julie was one of the victims that were never found." She still went to the prison every few months to ask him where Julie's body was.

"So you're saying my presence would be a problem."

"No. My mother will be delighted to meet someone I work with. But at some point, someone will make some bigoted remark about vampires."

"Ah." He nodded. "I'll try my best not to fall to the ground and wail in anguish."

I rolled my eyes. Tapping the papers in front of me, I changed the subject. "Can we leave these here, or should we store them elsewhere?"

"Leave them. I'll put everything in the safe when I'm done. Goodnight."

I left him staring at the papers in front of him and went to bed.

TWENTY

Patches of fog lingered in the hollows of Fairview Park, not yet burned off by the morning sun as Simon and I walked past the tour group forming at the north entrance. We cut west, toward the river. Most of the historical sites were in the east half of the park: the great oak where the Vampire Accords of 1925 were signed, a replica of a vampire safe house from 1902, and the Fountain of Fortune, where you could toss in a coin for good luck in the coming year.

"Fairview Park seems like an odd choice," Simon noted as we passed another brass marker set into the bricks of the path, this one commemorating the death of the vampire Manuela Armany, stabbed through the heart in 1924 after giving her famous speech on tolerance. He was wearing a dark gray suit that — like all of his suits — had probably cost more than my monthly salary.

"Because of all the ties to vampires?" When he nodded, I shrugged. "It was Julie's favorite place to go when we were kids. She could recite every plaque in the park by the time she was in first grade." I'd chosen the blue and green ensemble, with brown ankle boots, and was trying not to be mad that they weren't hurting my feet even though I hadn't had a chance to break them in. Rich people really did live life on easy mode.

"And your favorite place?"

"Floodmouth Public Library, the main branch on Cross Street. Well, any library, really, but that one had the best selection." At his low laugh, I added, "I know, I know. I haven't really changed much since then."

We walked past a plaque claiming to mark the location where Katie Tucker stole the governor's horse, an event that scholars agreed was apocryphal. Up ahead, I could see a white pavilion tent with paper streamers hanging limply. "That must be it, over there." I slowed my steps. "It's bigger than I was expecting." I'd thought there'd be maybe a few balloons and a big picture of Julie, with ten people, max. This was... more elaborate. Most of the people milling around were my parents' age. They'd never known Julie. "What was your favorite place as a kid?"

"Out on the water. My dad took us all sailing nearly every weekend unless the weather was bad." He took in the banner. "You didn't help your mom plan this?"

"At the ten-year memorial, I suggested she should spend more energy living her life. Which went over about as well as you'd expect." We hadn't spoken for nearly a year, and even now, our relationship was fragile enough that I was careful about everything I said or did. "So this time she did it all with her grief support group. My contribution was to track down my father to invite him. You saw how well that went."

Inside the tent, I spied my mother, in a black dress and hat with a veil, standing among a group of women I recognized from her support group. "That's my mom. I'll just go let her know I'm here."

To my surprise, Simon stayed at my side. We passed hundreds of photos of my sister, both alone and with my family, and I couldn't begin to explain how wrong it felt to have complete strangers staring at all my memories. At the back of the tent was a large poster with a fundraiser ther-mometer, titled "Bring Julie Home!" I sighed, wishing I'd taken something for the headache that had been building all morning.

"Jenny!" My mother hugged me, then held me at arm's length. "I love what you're wearing!"

"Hi, mom." I pulled away enough to leave room for Simon in the circle. "This is my co-worker, Simon Bowers. Simon, this is my mother, Gwen Perkins."

They shook hands, my mother sending me a quizzical glance afterward. But she didn't ask questions, just intro-duced us to the six other women, also dressed head to toe in black. "She looks just like Julie would, doesn't she?" one said. "I'm certain Julie's soul stayed to be with her sister."

That, in a nutshell, was what I *hated* about this group. They were so focused on the dead, they didn't care how they might hurt the living. But I couldn't say that, so I ignored the woman who'd spoken and turned to my mother. "I stopped by Dad's place yesterday and left a message, but I don't think he's coming."

There. That skirted the truth, but wasn't actually a lie. If I ever did tell my mother about his new family, it wouldn't be in front of the ghouls. At least one of them believed in reincarnation, and the last thing my half-sister needed was someone suggesting she was only born so my older sister could have a second chance at life.

My mother squeezed my arm. "I appreciate you trying."

Trix waved from the other side of the tent, and my relief was immense, because if I stayed any longer, someone would insist on telling me why they were raising funds, and I didn't think I could listen to that without screaming. "Oh, look, Trix is here. I'll be back in a bit."

"Of course." My mother smiled. "It was nice to meet you, Simon."

"The pleasure was all mine," he replied.

Trix, dressed in her usual riot of colors, stood out like a carnation in a bed of dead twigs. Having access to a private teleporter was a dream — two hours ago, she'd still been in Dublin, excitedly texting pictures of manuscripts. Throwing her arms around me, she whispered, "You can make it through the next hour." Then she must have seen the fundraising meter. "Oh, fuck. Not again." She pulled away and eyed the vampire standing next to me. "Hello, Simon. I assume you're part of the clusterfuck that led to the feds staking out our apartment?"

"It's not his fault," I said. "How was the trip?"

"Amazing and stop trying to change the subject."

After years of living with Trix, I knew she wouldn't drop it until I at least partially explained. "It's the case we're working on. Someone's determined to keep us from solving it."

"Ah. Well, fuck them, then." She looked between me and Simon. "Carry on. I'll crash at Amar's place until it's safe to come home."

"Amazing" suggested Che was indeed single and interested, but before I could ask, there was a squeal of feedback, and then a woman's voice came over two portable speakers on opposite sides of the tent. "Good morning, everyone, and welcome to the celebration of life for Julie Perkins on the fifteenth anniversary of her death. My name is Sonya Drennan. Some of you may know me from the Floodmouth Loss of a Child Support Group. We're going to start this morning with some memories of Julie, and then talk about our new attempt to bring her remains home to her family."

Sonya handed the microphone to my mother, who dabbed at her eyes and faced the other members of the support group. "Thank you all for coming today to help keep Julie's memory alive. Julie was the best daughter any mother could hope for. Kind, sweet, ..."

The week before Julie had disappeared, she'd set my favorite stuffed animal on fire using a spell I'd unearthed in a library book. It was payback because I'd used her computer to log into an arcane site my parents had blocked on mine. Due to the teddy bear immolation, she'd been grounded for a month, which was why she'd gone out the window without telling anyone on the night she'd disappeared.

But over the last fifteen years, the real Julie — smart, stubborn, lazy, and more than a bit vindictive — had been replaced by this anodyne version with a winning smile who never did anything wrong. This version had never stolen a bottle of whiskey from the corner store, or ditched school for two days to wait outside the hotel her favorite band was staying at, or cut my hair while I was sleeping because I'd laughed at her. And that was just the stuff my mother *knew* about.

"Saint Julie rides again," Trix muttered as my mother continued speaking about the perfect child who had never existed. Simon glanced at Trix with one raised eyebrow.

"Whatever makes her happy," I whispered back.

"Right." Sarcasm dripped from her voice.

Julie's disappearance had destroyed our family, in every possible way, and my mother had gone through a series of therapists who had tried a slew of different drugs to keep her from lying in bed all day, every day. That lasted until she found the current support group, which gave her life purpose again. That the purpose was finding Julie's remains seemed unhealthy to me, but I didn't get a vote. Maybe it didn't matter, as long as she was able to get up in the morning.

It made me wonder how vampires handled that sort of grief. Yes, the vampire council could screen applicants to filter out those who needed pharmaceuticals to help their brain chemistry, but they couldn't keep every vampire safe from trauma. Bad things happened.

My mother's stories about perfect Julie continued. In the beginning, I'd been hurt because none of her gilded memories ever included me, but I'd eventually realized it was because the minute she added me, with all my flaws and foibles, it made her idealized version of Julie feel hollow. My mother couldn't deal with that, so she kept her memories of us separate. And because the real Julie had been around during most of my childhood, the memories of me had gradually been erased.

Trix thought I should be more angry about that. But I understood. Julie's death had broken all of us in different ways.

My mother wound down and handed the microphone back to Sonya, who raised it to her lips. "As many of you know, we have a new tip on the location of Julie's remains." She paused for a round of applause. "Raiden Martin himself gave us this information."

Sonya emphasized the vampire's name, as if he was some kind of celebrity. Which, in a messed up way, he *was* for this crowd. Most of the people at this event would have described my mother as "the woman whose daughter was killed by Raiden Martin, the vampire serial killer." It was probably how my mother would have described herself.

Personally, I wasn't convinced Raiden Martin had been involved in Julie's death. He had recalled things about Julie he couldn't have known unless they had crossed paths, but every interview with him had shown how good he was at cold reading people. Dredging up new details was just his way to keep torturing my mother. The minute Julie's remains were recovered, she would stop visiting him and Raiden Martin would lose one of his few sources of entertainment.

"But it's going to take a lot of resources," Sonya continued. "So while we invite everyone to remember Julie as the angel she was, we also ask that you consider donating so we can bring her back home to her family. We're having a silent auction of these generously donated items, and for a small contribution, I'll be signing copies of my book about my journey toward acceptance after my son was murdered. So while you're walking around looking at the pictures of our angel, Julie, don't forget to get those bids in so we can bring her back home to her family."

The commercialism was too much for me. "Let's go." I'd done my duty.

The three of us ducked out into the bright sun and I felt a weight lifting off my shoulders. I'd survived the memorial, and I had five years to come up with an excuse to avoid the next one.

Trix paused on the path, one hand on my shoulder for balance, to switch from her purple heels to the red sneakers she wore when walking around town. "What is that, the fifth time?"

"Something like that," I said. It was actually the sixth, but it didn't matter. "Number of times the support group has gone searching for Julie's remains," I explained to Simon.

"My mom believes Raiden Martin will tell her the truth if she just keeps asking."

He kept his face still. "That seems unlikely."

Trix snorted as she shoved her heels into her bag, and we resumed walking. "I bet a forensic accountant would find something if they went over that support group's books."

It was possible, but I thought the group fed on its own trauma, not monetary reward. "Thanks for being here."

"Any time." She hitched her bag higher on her shoulder. "I'm off to tell Amar he has a roommate for a while. You promise to let me know if there's anything I can do, right?"

"Of course."

She waved away Simon's offer of a ride, hugged me fiercely, and finally frowned at Simon. "Che says you're a good guy, so I'm trusting you. Don't blow it." Then she struck off to the northeast across the grass toward the river while Simon and I continued along the path to reach the waiting car.

WHEN WE RETURNED to Silver Edge, I saw that Simon had printed out more paperwork after I'd gone to bed the night before. "Everything about the investigation into Joshua's death so far." At my questioning look, he shrugged. "It's not my case, but I still have access."

For the first time, I read the name of the vampire who'd died in agony after slicing up his neighbor. Evan Maguire. He was forty-two, owned a souvenir shop on Booksellers Row, and had been a vampire for fifteen years.

Maguire. That name had come up before. I paged

through my notes until I found it. "Evan Maguire was one of Mo's buyers for the legal goods."

"What? How did that get missed?"

I dug through the stack of paperwork until I found the statement. Whoever had written it up had spelled his name "MacGuire" and they hadn't noted that he was a vampire, but it had to be the same person. "Right here. Three cases of Bloodmouth U sweatshirts, a gross of novelty pens, and one case of Katie Tucker salt and pepper shakers. If that doesn't say crap for tourists, I don't know what would."

The investigators had contacted Evan and questioned him about his association with the smuggler, but everything about him had appeared aboveboard and he'd become one of a thousand other footnotes in the investigation.

"We've been looking for the wrong connection," Simon said. "Instead of Mo selling the bracelet to Joshua, it must have gone from Mo to Evan to Joshua."

Something about that felt wrong. "But... Joshua had an anti-vampire ward on his front door. I can't see him hanging out with Evan."

"Right." Simon sat back in his chair and regarded me. "We assumed the bracelet belonged to Joshua. What if we were wrong?"

TWENTY-ONE

"But..." Then I stopped and closed my mouth as I shifted connections around in my head. The bracelet had been near Joshua's arm, but Evan's attack had been frenzied as he'd tried to open enough skin to keep from starving to death. The only thing that definitely tied the bracelet to Joshua was the blood magic. "Blood magic doesn't work on vampires."

"Ignore that for the moment. If we assume it was Evan wearing the bracelet, things make more sense. We have the tie from him to Mo. And that would explain why we can't find any way to connect Joshua to Evan — because they had nothing to do with each other... until the spell went wrong and Evan broke through the wall."

I nodded slowly. "That would fit with the neighbor saying Evan was pounding on *her* wall and yelling. Because he wasn't being affected by something Joshua had been wearing, but by his own bracelet."

Suddenly, the damage to the bracelet made sense. "The broken collector. There was nothing to limit the power draw." I pictured the layout in my head and marveled at the terrible design. Excess power and zero experience had combined to create a disaster.

After two seconds of silence, Simon said, "I'm going to need a hint or two."

Flipping back through my notebook, I found the page with the map of trade routes in Europe and the basic diagram of the spell on the bracelet. "The power loop feeds energy into the collector, right?" I still didn't understand what that was used for or where the blood magic came into play, but that didn't matter for this.

"Right."

"Here's the thing. I have a PhD in magical theory, so I would approach this in a completely different way. But I'm pretty sure the person who created this spell doesn't have any formal training. The bracelet's made out of aluminum, for starters, and aluminum is prone to bending and warping, which any entry-level class would emphasize. Plus, there's this collector cell, which is so big that it's bound to fail at some point."

When I looked up to see if he was following my explanation, he nodded. "Keep going."

"Okay, so Evan is wearing this bracelet for whatever reason." Not for fashion — that bracelet wasn't something most forty-two-year-olds would wear, and it hadn't fit his style. "And he bangs his arm against something, bending the aluminum. The collector is damaged, so it's leaking energy, and the power loop starts pulling more from Evan to refill it."

"And he starves to death," Simon said slowly.

"And he starves to death," I confirmed. "An experienced mage would have rate limited the power draw, but there's nothing like that here. And it wouldn't be a problem for a human, because our skin limits how fast energy can be extracted. But vampires? I don't think that's the case." Vampires were literally coated with magic. That was why the anti-vampire spells worked, and that was why I could tell Simon was a vampire just by looking at him.

Simon's brow furrowed, and I waited for him to ask the question he was trying to form. After a few seconds, he said, "I understand why Evan lost so much energy he went into the dangerous hunger. But I didn't put the bracelet on. Why did it affect me?"

Tapping the cuff on the drawing, I said, "Because of the Moebius loop. It only has one side, so it's taking in energy from the wearer and anyone nearby. The vast majority is going to come from the wearer just from skin contact. You sometimes see it used for spells when people are going to be in crowds. In this case, you were the only living vampire within range, so it pulled energy from you. Evan might have realized at the end what was happening and taken it off, but he didn't get far enough away, so it still killed him."

We fell silent then as we both stared at the drawing.

"What I *don't* understand," I said finally, "is why someone in the FBME is so worried about this being discovered that they're soaking evidence in saltwater and torching a CSI van. I mean, this is obviously a lawsuit waiting to happen, and maybe criminal charges, but people have died. Why are they protecting whoever's creating these things?"

Simon ran a hand through his hair, which was getting increasingly rumpled. "It has to be related to whatever the rest of the spell does, doesn't it?" He stood and paced along the length of the table. "If blood magic doesn't affect vampires, but a vampire is powering the spell, doesn't it follow that the blood magic part of the spell must be affecting humans in some way?"

I considered that while Simon continued to pace. "So

he's what... making the humans around him feel better?" Then I remembered the strength of the blood magic spells. "Knocking them out through bliss?"

I could think of ways this could be used as a weapon, but nothing in the information we had about Evan suggested he was that sort of person. And I certainly hadn't felt any effects, even when I'd handled it, though it *had* already been damaged by then.

"I don't see the point of it," Simon admitted.

"There's another possibility," I said. "Maybe it wasn't intended to be worn by vampires, but Evan just..." My thought fell apart. "No. I can't see it. Nothing else Evan was wearing fit with this bracelet."

"It had to be doing something for him, even when he was alone in his apartment, or he would have taken it off."

I remembered the woodcut of the depressed woman with the amulet. "The blood magic spell may be addicting," I said slowly.

"Which means..."

I nodded. "Everything points to Evan being the target of that spell. It's *possible* that someone figured out a new way to make blood magic affect vampires. There's a group in Guelph that was trying, but last I heard, all they'd done was melt a lot of silver." I shrugged. "I'll check with some people I know — maybe they had a breakthrough."

"We need more information about Evan," Simon said. "Maybe he talked about it to someone."

"We need to figure out who we can trust in the FBME," I countered. "I can't stay here forever. And we won't have any FBME resources to help with research if we don't go in to work tomorrow."

"We could take away the incentive for getting rid of us."

I leaned back in my chair. "How?"

"Document everything we know and make sure there's no way to bury it." He sat in his chair and leaned forward. "You turn the bracelet in to the evidence lockup tomorrow morning." He held up a hand when I drew breath to protest. "It's the only way to get this info out there. As soon as it's in the system, you attach your report to it. And when that happens, I copy the report to everyone on the task force, both here and in Seattle. They can't *all* be involved in a coverup."

And if things started disappearing in the system, we'd be able to trace who was doing it.

"Tomorrow's going to be a shit show," I warned.

"There was always going to be a price to pay for not logging that bracelet into evidence on Friday."

He was right. I drew in a large breath and slowly released it. "Okay." It wasn't what I wanted to do, but I didn't have a better idea. "Then I guess I should get that evidence report written."

TWENTY-TWO

Though I had multiple replies to my queries overnight, nobody was aware of any breakthroughs involving blood magic and vampires. The negatives all came with requests for more information if I found someone who *had* figured it out, and I was fairly certain the entire grapevine was humming. My questions had been chum in the water for the sharks of academia.

Simon and I got to The Vault at seven, and our first stop was the evidence counter, where I logged in the bracelet, still in its mahogany containment box, and Simon counter-signed. We waited as the officer on duty entered everything into the system and attached it to the correct case.

"You two are in early," he said as he printed out the receipt with the transaction number. It was just the usual small talk that happened when everyone was waiting for the computer to finish, but paranoia made it seem more sinister.

"Getting a head start on the week," Simon said.

"You can always tell the new employees," the other man said with a laugh. But he handed over the receipt and turned back to his paper and coffee.

My phone buzzed with yet another notification, the fourth since we'd entered the building. At Simon's raised brow, I shook my head. "News about the fundraising."

Somehow, I'd ended up on the group chat for the *Bring Julie Home!* committee, which was mostly people from the grief support group, including my mother. The silent auction and other donations at the memorial had brought in nearly half the amount they needed to drag ground penetrating radar into a national forest, or whatever it was they planned to do. Monetary updates would have been bad enough, but each bit of news was followed by a flurry of responses — hearts, affirmations, and celebrity reaction gifs. Each one caused a new notification and another round of comments. I'd been hoping the activity would die down, but it was only getting worse. "Give me a minute?"

While Simon pretended to read something on his phone, I removed myself from the group chat. My mother would see that change, which was why I hadn't done so when the first texts showed up at four in the morning, but it couldn't be helped. Shoving my phone back in my bag, I looked up. "Thanks."

From there, we went down to the basement where the magical evidence technicians worked. Nobody was there, which wasn't a surprise at seven-thirty on a Monday morning.

While I booted my laptop, Simon looked around. "This is very..."

I waited, eyebrows raised, to see what he would come up with.

"Secure," he finished.

"A window or two would be nice," I said, "but I guess we can't all have offices with views of the city." When the login prompt came up, I inserted my ID card, typed in my name and password, and held my breath. The screen flashed to display the normal background, so I started the evidence reporting program, ignoring the messages waiting to be read.

The report I'd written the night before was a thing of beauty. Forty pages of diagrams, citations, and theories about both the bracelet as it was when we'd recovered it and as it had been before the damage. If this went to trial, no prosecutor would have difficulty understanding the summary, and no defense lawyer could complain.

Not that this would go to trial any time soon — so far, everyone involved was already dead.

The evidence number came up as valid, and it had the right information associated with it, so I copied my report into the program, saved it, and then brought it back up again just to make sure it was all there. Theoretically, it couldn't be deleted now without director-level authorization.

"I think we're good to go," I said.

Simon rolled another chair over and opened his laptop next to mine so I could see what he was doing. He'd written the email the night before, but now he downloaded the official evidence report and attached it to the email, which gave us one more copy in case it was deleted elsewhere. Then he hit send.

"I hope this works," I said.

"It'll work." He closed his laptop and slid it into the case before standing up. "Stay in public spaces today. They've tried to make everything look accidental up to now, so I think you should be safe enough in a group."

I looked around at the empty office. "We need to have a talk about your speeches of reassurance."

That got me one of his rare smiles. "I realized that right after I said it, but I was hoping you wouldn't notice. I'll stay here until there are more people around." Then he moved over a little to give me more room, and we worked in companionable silence for the next twenty minutes.

When my phone rang, I was expecting something work-related, so I answered before I checked the screen. "This is Perkins."

After a moment of silence, I heard my mom's voice. "Jenny?"

My whole body flinch made Simon look up sharply. "Hi, Mom." She would be calling about me removing myself from the group chat — not a conversation I wanted to have in front of anyone, much less the vampire sitting next to me. But we had already established that going off on my own would be a bad idea. "Sorry about taking myself off that list. It's just that I need to use my phone for work and —"

My mother cut me off. "Jenny, relax. It's okay. I didn't mean to have you on that list in the first place."

"Oh." Now I felt like an ass.

"I just wanted to thank you for coming to the memorial yesterday."

Somehow, that made it even worse. What was I supposed to say now? *You're welcome?* Julie had been my sister. Of *course* I'd go to her memorial service. "Looked like a good turnout." Right after I said it, I slapped my palm against my forehead. Our last huge fight had been when I'd suggested there was a performative element about the grief shown by some others in her group.

There was a long moment when I thought my mother would dig into that statement. Thankfully, she moved on. "We didn't really get a chance to talk with everything going on. What do you think about having dinner next week? Just you and me."

This was new. The last few times we'd met, at least one of her friends from the support group had come along.

"That would be really nice." *As long as nobody is trying to kill me,* I added silently. We agreed on a date and time.

Relief laced my mother's voice. "Well, I'll let you go. You probably have to get to work."

I stared at the phone after the call disconnected.

Simon looked over. "Everything okay?"

"What? Oh, yeah. It's just... My mom wants to have dinner. Just the two of us." Could she finally be ready to move forward with her life? With a shake of my head, I put my phone away. "I'm probably reading too much into it."

My email was a mix of the mundane — a reminder to everyone to clean up any spills in the break room, and a request to clear out any bikes no longer being used from the bike storage room — and the highly specific. There were seven forms I needed to fill out for the events of Thursday and Friday, and a complaint from the armory that I'd turned in damaged bracers covered in some sort of burned substance. That was followed immediately by a reply from a supervisor that said the bracers would be replaced and I didn't need to do anything. Reading between the lines, I *would* have been getting abuse from various low-level employees just because they could get away with it, except their supervisors recognized my name and shut them down. The Perkins Maneuver must have really impressed someone.

Hamilton and another technician, Trace, had just walked into the workspace when our laptops dinged with an incoming priority message. It was from Supervisory Agent Salt. *My office. Now.*

I looked up to see Simon watching me.

He tipped his head. "Here we go."

TWENTY-THREE

Salt's office had a view of the river and half of Floodmouth. Paneling with sound muffling spells had been installed on the interior walls in front of the glass. Hers was the only office on the floor that was truly private once the door was closed. Diplomas, awards, and photos of her shaking hands with people even I recognized were scattered over the paneling. She had a masters in criminology, I noted. I wondered what the subject of her thesis had been. If I still had a job at the end of the week, I'd look it up.

When we entered, she was seated behind her desk reviewing a stack of papers. The carefully tailored red suit jacket almost hid the broadness of her shoulders. "Close the door," she said. Her voice was pleasant, but she didn't look up and she didn't invite us to sit. "So. That was an interesting memo you two sent out this morning." Venom dripped from every word.

Silence seemed the best way to get through this, so I kept my mouth shut. Simon had obviously reached the same conclusion.

On the bright side, if I didn't get fired, this would definitely get me sent back down to my safe and boring job in
the basement as a magical evidence technician.

Finally looking up, Salt growled, "Would you like to tell
me why vital evidence in the case wasn't logged last Friday
when it was recovered?"

No yelling yet. Maybe we'd get through this all with
polite conversation.

Simon opened his mouth, but Salt cut him off. "Bowers,
you had to be carted away before you hurt someone, so I
can't imagine this was your call."

In the silence as Salt stared at me, I could hear the
ticking of the building's air conditioning. Someone had once
told me that giving some sort of explanation, even one that
made no sense at all, gave managers a face-saving path for
any problem. Maybe that would work here.

I reworded my sentence three times before I opened my
mouth. "I was concerned about the saltwater flooding in the
evidence room, and I needed to compare the spell on the
bracelet with some reference texts at the university's library,
so I kept it in my possession during the weekend."

"Saltwater flooding," she repeated slowly.

"Like what happened to the evidence we collected the
day before," I explained.

She held my gaze for three long breaths while I tried my
best to look innocent. Then she shook her head in disbelief.
"Pull that stunt again, and I'll have you up on obstruction
charges, understand?" Before I could respond, she kept
speaking. "One way or another, the two of you have opened
up the investigation. What's your next line of inquiry?"

It was like bracing for a category five hurricane only to
see it veer off at the last moment. My brain glitched, but

luckily, Simon had an answer. "We'd like to concentrate on Evan Maguire, to confirm he really was the owner of the bracelet and determine its intended purpose."

Salt regarded him for a full three seconds, and then nodded once. "Fine. I'll have your assignments reflect that. The task force morning briefing is in..." She checked the time. "Fifteen minutes. Don't be late. Now get out of my office."

I didn't need to be told twice. We were almost out the door when she yelled, "And if you pull that crap again, I'll have you collecting evidence in the sewers for the next two years!" She hadn't yelled her threats until everyone else could hear. That was interesting.

"Better watch out, Bowers," said a blond vampire man leaning against another agent's open door frame. "At this rate, you won't get invited to the mayor's Accords Day party."

Simon didn't slow. "Already got my invitation in the mail, Lampinen. But if you're free that evening, I heard they were looking to hire extra security for the door."

The woman inside the office laughed. Red spots showed on Agent Lampinen's cheeks, but he merely turned and resumed his conversation.

When we were back in Simon's office with the door closed, I craned my head so I could see down the hallway. "I don't think Agent Lampinen likes you very much."

"He had a couple cases go south recently, and I broke his top closer streak last quarter. He'll get over it, eventually." Simon looked at his pristine desk as if searching for something. "Well. Now we're on the task force. I'll admit, I didn't see *that* coming."

"She was supposed to realize I'm not meant to be

anywhere but the basement." I flopped into the extra chair. "It *can't* be her, can it? If she's the one trying to screw up the investigation, she would want us as far away from this as possible."

"Unless she wants to keep an eye on us."

Simon's completely reasonable response made me want to growl at him. What he was *really* saying was that the targets wouldn't be off our backs until this case was over.

If that wasn't an incentive to find out what was going on, I didn't know what was.

THE TASK FORCE briefing was mercifully short, which was good, considering nearly everyone who worked in The Vault was crammed into the conference room. The wall screen showing the video link to Seattle showed a similarly crowded room — this was the most important FBME case on the west coast and they were throwing every resource at it.

Salt took her seat five seconds before the meeting was scheduled to begin. "Is the audio working? Let's get started. We have some new info." Despite the crush of people, she glanced directly at the corner where Simon and I stood before looking down at her tablet again.

She went through the highlights of what Simon and I had found, though I didn't think anyone needed the summary. They'd either been copied on the email or had been told to go read it by their direct supervisors.

Nothing was said about evidence disappearing or being damaged.

Salt stuck to her agenda, which I appreciated after

many years of rambling departmental meetings. When assignments were handed out, the humans on the Seattle team were charged with going back through their case files with a specific eye for any jewelry or other spelled items that might have been taken into evidence by the police. "Even if that doesn't get us any closer to an answer, we need to get those things out of circulation — or the next vampire to set foot in the police evidence lockup might be affected." In the meantime, the vampires would go back and talk to friends and relatives of the vampire victims, looking for the source of the spelled jewelry.

The Floodmouth agents were allocated in roughly the same fashion. "Lampinen, Kim, Mann, and Wong, talk to everyone Mohammed Murphy knew. Find out where he was getting those things. Bowers, you and Perkins follow up on Evan Maguire to confirm the bracelet really was his and he got it from Mohammed Murphy."

I tried not to squirm as everyone in the room turned to see who "Perkins" was. Luckily, Salt plowed forward and the moment passed.

"Everyone else, I need you looking over the case notes. This is a big break, but what else got missed? Split up the files; make sure there's overlap. I want summaries and a list of people we need to interview or re-interview before the end of the day. Any questions?" She waited exactly three seconds before nodding. "Thank you." And then the meeting was over and everyone scattered to their tasks.

Since Simon and I didn't have gear to carry, we walked the twelve blocks to Booksellers Row to talk to people who'd known our vampire victim, Evan. But first, Simon insisted on taking a detour three blocks north to a gun range. "If, for no other reason," he said drily, "than to keep you, an employee of the FBME, from asking a random civilian how to unload a gun in the future." The range was a dark, low-ceilinged hall with three lanes and a very bored proprietor who relaxed and went back to watching a movie after Simon showed his badge.

"I could have just tossed it in my duffle bag and hoped for the best," I said as I picked out ear protection. "And she was hardly a random civilian."

"Nevertheless." He checked out a bag of dummy rounds with orange tips and spent ten minutes walking me through basic gun safety and how to unload and load his Glock. Then he had me load the gun with live ammunition and I got to shoot at a paper target with the outline of a man. Even with the ear protection, the bang as I pulled the trigger made me flinch.

When I'd fired all seventeen rounds, Simon had me eject the magazine and latch the slide back before stepping away. Then he brought the target forward so we could examine it. Though I'd been aiming at center mass, I'd missed the paper completely with fifteen rounds, hit the target's hairdo once, and tagged the very edge of the shoulder with my last shot.

Simon cleared his throat. "It's probably good that I didn't know what a terrible shot you were when I gave you my weapon on Friday."

"Didn't need a gun to take out that pterodactyl, though, did I?"

"Were your eyes actually open during any part of this?"

"Maybe your gun is just broken. Did you ever think about that?"

He shook his head, clipped on another target, and loaded his gun. His shots rang out at steady intervals, and when he was done, only one hadn't hit the center ring. He reloaded his gun, secured it in his holster, and then held up my target. "We'll work on it. Do you want to keep this as a souvenir?"

"Can't the next person just reuse it? They might as well save the paper."

Simon wiped a hand over his face. "Promise me you won't tell anyone I taught you to shoot. I don't think my reputation can take the hit."

I rattled the target. "You really think I'm going to brag about this?"

"I've given up trying to predict what you'll do." But he said it in a way that sounded amused and not irritated, so I decided it was a good thing on the whole.

After we picked up the casings and returned the dummy bullets, we went back outside to fresh air that smelled of river water and stale popcorn instead of gunpowder and oil.

Dodging around a toddler who had plopped down in the middle of the crowded sidewalk to remove her shoes, I said, "Maybe we should show that target to Salt. She can assign you a partner who can have your back while I stay in the basement."

"We'll be fine." Simon sidestepped to avoid a tiny sneaker hurled by the child. "Let's have a quick look at Evan's shop and then talk to the employees nearby. Someone must have spoken to him regularly."

That clearly hadn't been the neighbors on either side of his apartment, since they had warded — or tried to ward — their rooms against him. Thinking of that reminded me of something. "You know who I want to talk to? The woman who lived next to him in number four."

"The one who told you a female vampire from the FBME visited Evan on Friday morning?"

"Yeah. I never asked her to describe the woman. Salt's

pretty distinctive." If we could get a description that proved it *wasn't* Salt, we could tell her all our suspicions.

Simon nodded. "Okay, we'll start at Evan's apartment, talk to the neighbors, and then go to his shop afterward."

I smiled. "I can't wait for Evan's neighbor to see *you*."

TWENTY-FOUR

Apartments two and three were both still sealed, but Simon cut the tape on unit three — Evan's apartment — and we let ourselves inside. The layout was the reverse of the unit next door, with the kitchenette to the right of the door and the bedroom sharing a wall with the neighbor in number four, the woman who'd spent money on an anti-vampire ward that covered her entire apartment.

It had the air of a place someone rented when they were planning on staying just a month or two. If Trix and I had lived here, the scuffed and dented beige walls would have been buried under posters, shawls, and strings of lights. Evan had left them completely bare, which made the ragged hole that led to the apartment next door really stand out.

There was a queen mattress with no frame in the bedroom, and a sofa that had seen better days in the living room, but other than that, the place was empty.

I stood in the middle of the living room and turned in a circle. "From the look of this place, I'm assuming Evan broke up with someone recently."

"And they got all the furniture," Simon agreed.

"Probably all the friends, too." This didn't look like a place that had seen many visitors.

As we went through the apartment, everything we found strengthened that view. He had a copy of the rental agreement, signed four months ago, in the empty silverware drawer. The refrigerator sat unused, disconnected from power. "I don't get it," I said, as I looked inside the vegetable drawers just to be thorough. "Maybe it's not *required*, but don't you sometimes just want to enjoy the taste and texture? I think I would still eat even if it wasn't necessary."

Behind me, Simon looked through the other cupboards, which would have held pots and pans if there had been any. "I don't get hungry, so I forget." He stood. "Nothing. I'm going to look in the bedroom."

Half an hour later, we were finished, and the only useful personal possession we'd found was a photograph of a smiling girl, maybe ten years old, on the floor next to his mattress. She had windblown brown hair and was wearing some sort of school uniform, with a dark blue sweater, a white collared shirt, and a pleated blue skirt. From the license plate of the car she was leaning against, the picture had been taken somewhere in Great Britain. The silver frame had the words "#1 Dad" embossed at the top.

Simon handed it to me. "His daughter?"

There was no obvious similarity with the withered vampire we'd found lying on the floor, but when I compared the girl to the photos we had of Evan when he'd been alive, I could see the resemblance around the eyes and mouth. "I think so. It's sad."

"Why?" Simon took a photo with his phone, then took the back off the frame to check if there was any inscription on the other side. It was blank.

"Because that's what you send for Father's Day when

you have no other connection with them." A study of parenting skills would show a strong correlation between complete physical or emotional absence and a high number of items in the house labeled "#1 Dad" or "World's Best Father."

Assuming that was his biological daughter, Evan had become a vampire within the last ten years — the magic that kept vampires alive played havoc with fertility. Prospective vampires didn't need to be rich, but they did need to have the resources necessary to take care of themselves. Nobody wanted an impoverished vampire snagging humans off the street for a quick meal. But even more than financial stability, applicants needed to prove they would be a credit to vampires. The application process was like interviewing for a really important job. This didn't look like the apartment of someone who had their life together. What had happened to Evan in the last ten years?

The bathroom wasn't particularly spotless, but since Evan had only been there a few months, it wasn't too gross. With no humans living there, the cabinet was free of painkillers, prescription drugs, and other medical junk that might have accumulated there.

"I hope he spent his free time elsewhere," I said when I'd finished looking. "Otherwise, I feel sorry for him."

"His online accounts might be more interesting," Simon said. He looked around. "Are you done? Let's talk to the neighbors."

Unit one was occupied by the owner of the tattoo parlor downstairs, who also owned the building and rented out the remaining apartments. He was a thin white man in his fifties with sandy hair and a vast quantity of facial piercings. I stopped counting at fifteen. Wearing a loose t-shirt and sweatpants, he had the rumpled look of someone who'd just climbed out of bed. Tattoos covered all the skin I could see on his arms and neck.

He was also angry at the FBME, or maybe just law enforcement in general. "Do you know how much it's going to cost me to get the apartment cleaned? And the wall needs to be repaired and repainted. But I can't even schedule the work because you guys still have everything closed up. Every day I don't have those apartments rented is another day I'm losing money. And this guy's parents are talking about suing me for not providing better security, so now I need a lawyer I can't afford."

Simon stayed impassive. "Sir, the sooner you talk to us, the sooner we'll finish our investigation."

The man's nostrils flared and his lips tightened, as if he had bitten back an obscenity. "Fine. What do you want to know?"

"Joshua and Evan. What kind of tenants were they?"

The man crossed his arms over his chest. "The guy in number three just moved in. Quiet. Paid his rent on time. I would have called him the ideal tenant if this hadn't happened."

"Anybody visit him?"

"Not that I ever saw."

"And Joshua, the man in two?"

Since we were pretty sure Evan was the link we wanted, I assumed Simon was asking just to be complete. But then again, making assumptions had led me to think the bracelet belonged to the wrong person for most of the weekend.

"The guy in two was like every other guy living in the Row in his twenties. Liked to play his music a little loud, but not so loud that everyone complained. He's been late on the rent a couple times in the last six months, but always got it to me before the next week." He shrugged. "There were a few girls, but none that stuck around long, and I wouldn't recognize any of them."

"Did they ever have any problems with each other?"

"As far as *I* know, they never even talked to each other. Mary, number four, found out number three was a vampire when he moved in and got everyone else all wound up about getting anti-vampire wards, as if that was necessary. She and number two spent three days arguing about where to get them."

He stopped for a second, possibly realizing for the first time that a decent ward might have saved Joshua's life, then shook it off. "Whatever. Mary's always complaining about something. When number two moved in, she was convinced he was a drug dealer and wanted me to install another dead-bolt on her door. She's a pain in my ass. Though," he added, as if forcing himself to be fair, "she's better than any alarm system. Nobody breaks into these apartments. She's constantly calling the cops about something or other."

Simon looked over at me. "You have any other questions?"

I tried my best to look like I knew what I was doing. "Not right now."

Nodding once, Simon turned back. "Thanks for your help."

"Yeah, yeah." The door was halfway closed when the man suddenly yanked it open again. "Hey, when can I fix those units so I can rent them?"

"Should be someday soon," Simon said as we walked away. "I'll have someone get in touch."

The door slammed.

Mary, the woman in unit four whom I'd talked to on Friday, didn't answer her door. Since she was the kind of person who would never miss a chance to insert herself into any drama, I assumed she wasn't home.

Simon tucked his card in the door with a note asking her to call. "We can come back later," he told me.

The woman in unit five had an infant in her arms. She'd never met Evan or Joshua, didn't know a vampire had moved in — she'd avoided Mary since the other woman called CPS because her baby was crying — and hadn't heard anything at all on Friday. Given the bags under her eyes and the dried baby food on her sweatshirt, I was inclined to believe her.

As we went down the stairs, I apologized to Simon. "We should have gone to the shop first. This was a waste of time."

"I have a better sense of Evan now," he said, brushing my apology away. "That's important. Let's go see what he did during the day."

TWENTY-FIVE

Two blocks away, we found Evan Maguire's souvenir shop. It was on a busy corner and we had to fight our way through a herd of tourists to get to the front door.

"Nice location," I commented, using my body to keep pedestrians from running into Simon as he picked the lock with a snap gun. We hadn't seen the keys to the shop at Evan's apartment, which meant they had probably been checked into evidence in The Vault along with everything else the vampire had been wearing.

Simon grunted acknowledgement and opened the door, locking it behind us. Inside, the narrow aisles were stuffed with every possible souvenir, from "Bloodmouth U" clothing, to greeting cards, hats, plastic blood stains, and candy fangs. A plastic sign near the register offered a selfie with a vampire for twenty dollars.

I tried to imagine spending every day surrounded by the clutter. "Is it more or less tacky that this was all being sold by an actual vampire?"

While I'd been taking it all in, Simon had opened the pass-through so he could get behind the counter. "Ah, this ought to get us somewhere." He lifted a stack of receipts and invoices. "Maybe now we can find out what he did with his days."

Apparently, what Evan did with his days was sell junk to tourists, replace the holes on the shelf with new junk, and watch cooking and baking competitions. We learned that last one when we found the Hot Bakery Prize calendar with personalized signatures by all the contestants.

"You agree that's weird, right?" I asked as I flipped through the pages, reading what he had written in the daily squares. "Being obsessed with baking competitions when you don't even eat?"

Until four months before, weekends had noted sports tournaments, birthday parties, and museum visits, while weekdays had been nearly empty aside from the occasional dance recital.

Simon paged through a stack of invoices. "I used to watch those shows to relax, and I've never baked anything in my life."

He had a point. I pushed the calendar closer to him. "Until recently, it looks like the typical divorced dad weekend schedule. Then , everything stopped. I think his ex moved to Great Britain with their daughter. He no longer needed extra space, so he moved to a smaller apartment. But I don't see any sign he ever met up with anyone outside of work."

Removing two smaller pieces of paper from the pile, Simon passed them over. "Restaurant receipts. Three times in the last two weeks, but nothing before that. Maybe he met someone?"

"Fingers crossed it was someone who asked why he was wearing such an ugly bracelet." The calendar slipped easily back onto the nail where I'd found it.

Simon ushered me toward the door. "Let's go see if anyone remembers who he was eating with."

"NOBODY," the Korean-American woman working the hostess desk at Katie Tucker's Slippery Fish Sushi Restaurant said when we showed her Evan Maguire's picture. She wiped plastic-coated menus with a towel as she talked. "He came in alone, ordered the calamari tempura and sashimi, ate his food, and left without talking to anyone other than the staff. Good tipper. Did something happen to him?"

Simon and I looked at each other. I said, "You're sure it was this man?"

"Positive. He's the vampire that runs the souvenir shop around the corner, right? Owen or Ian or something. My dad orders our t-shirts through him." She used her chin to indicate a red t-shirt tacked to the wall. It had the restaurant's logo emblazoned on the front and had a price sheet next to it. "I thought it was kind of weird that he started eating here after all this time, but vampires *can* eat, right?"

"They can," I agreed. "Do you remember the first time he came in?"

"Three weeks ago Monday," she answered promptly. "Is he in trouble?"

"He died last week," I said, and I felt Simon sigh next to me. Oops.

She scrunched her face, in the way people do when they need to look appropriately solemn, but the death doesn't directly affect them. "That's sad. He seemed like a nice enough guy."

"Did you know anything about his personal life?"

"What personal life? He worked seven days a week."

Her hands stilled as she looked into the distance. "He said something about a daughter, once. But she didn't live in Floodmouth." Setting down the stack of menus, she said, "Is that it? I need to get things set up for the lunch rush."

"Thanks." We had turned to leave when another thought struck me. "One last thing. Did you ever see him wearing a silver bracelet?" I mimed a cuff around my left wrist.

She snorted. "That thing with the cheap glass on the top? Yeah, it kind of stuck out. I think his daughter must have made it or something. I asked him about it the first time he came in, and he said he wore it because it made him happy." She shrugged and smiled. "That's the best reason to wear anything, isn't it? So what if it looks like something only a tourist would buy? If it makes you happy, enjoy it while you can."

A sharp voice called from the kitchen, and she waved a hand. "I've got to get back to work."

I followed Simon out to the street, where we stood blinking in the suddenly bright sunlight. "At least we have confirmation that he was the one wearing the bracelet. Someone, somewhere, figured out how to get blood magic working on vampires."

"Agreed."

"Other shops next?"

"Yes. Find out who his friends were. I'll take this side; you take that one."

Booksellers Row catered to tourists and, so almost every shop involved one or the other. The staff in the magic supplies shop next to Evan's store knew him to talk to, but hadn't talked much about his personal life. Two confirmed that he'd mentioned a daughter who lived elsewhere and the third maybe saw the bracelet, but none of them remembered seeing him with anyone who wasn't a customer.

At the doorway of a bookstore, I paused to look at the anti-vampire ward. While they were legal for private residences and clubs, blocking vampires from a public business was illegal and could lead to fines. The woman in charge saw me looking. "It's an advertisement for our services. If any vampire wants to come in, they just need to ring the bell and we take down the ward."

She was a willowy white woman with platinum blond hair, wearing a black robe with stars and planets embroidered in red thread, so I wasn't surprised to find entry-level books and kits meant to be given to children as holiday gifts. None of the spells would cause much damage — if they did anything at all. Certainly nobody who could cast that anti-vampire ward would rely on anything found here.

While I doubted Evan had ever rung the bell to have the ward taken down, I still had to ask my questions. Holding up my phone so she could see Evan's picture, I said, "Have you ever seen this man? His name is Evan Maguire."

"Well, obviously I haven't seen him in *here*," she said, with a theatrical wave of her hand to indicate the store.

She couldn't have known Evan was a vampire from looking at a photo. "But you've seen him elsewhere."

"He owns the souvenir shop on the corner. Used to run it with his wife, but they split up a couple years ago. He sometimes has his daughter in the shop with him on weekends. Though I haven't seen her in a while. I think he said she and her mother had moved away."

I found it weird that she knew Evan well enough to talk about his personal life, but still kept anti-vampire wards on her business. "Did you ever see him with anyone else? Maybe a friend?"

"Sorry, no." Then she held up a finger. "Though I think he took his meals to go, if you know what I mean." At my blank stare, she elaborated. "Two people from In Vein showed up at his shop every day. It's a feeding service for vampires. Their bags have a distinctive logo once you recognize it."

I jotted down the name of the service. "Thanks for the info."

"No problem." She glided off to help a group of people wearing "Welcome to Floodmouth" hats with fake blood dripping from the letters and didn't look back.

SIMON and I met up at the caramel pretzel cart to compare notes while I ate a pretzel and he surreptitiously observed me. I offered him a piece, but he shook his head quickly. "I've never been into sweets."

"Your loss," I said and shoved another piece of bread into my mouth before the caramel sauce could drip to the ground. "Everyone I talked to said Evan didn't have friends, at least not any that came to see him here."

"Same. And whatever else the bracelet did, I don't think it affected the people around him."

I thought about the woman in the bookstore and agreed. She'd have been suspicious purely because he was a vampire — a spell would have to be extra subtle to get past her. "I concur."

Simon typed a note into his phone. "Did you get anything else useful?"

"No. Oh wait, yes. Have you ever heard of In Vein? It's

some sort of mobile vampire club service. Apparently, they came by every day."

Simon raised his brows. "That's interesting." He grabbed another handful of paper napkins for me. "It's in the Butcher District. Let's drop by before we head back to the office."

First, though, we went by to see if Mary in unit four was home. Nobody answered the door, but Simon's card was gone. Simon slipped another card under the door. "We may need to come back and camp on her doorstep."

As we went down the stairs, he called back to The Vault to let them know our new destination. According to Simon, it was only sporting to give your fellow agents a starting point if you disappeared. He'd meant it as a joke, but it didn't make me any more excited to leave my job in the nice, safe basement.

In the subway, we had half the car to ourselves, and I sat sideways on the bench so I could raise my aching feet. "You upstairs people walk a lot more than we do down in the basement."

"It's good for you."

"Yeah, yeah. Hey, why is it interesting that Evan had his meals come to him? Workaholics live on delivery food."

From the way his shoulders stiffened, I'd hit some sort of nerve.

I held up a hand. "If that was an inappropriate question for some reason, I'm sorry. Forget it."

"No. It's fine. I'm trying to figure out how to explain. Vampire clubs aren't just..." Simon trailed off and started again. "When I was first transformed, I tried to pretend nothing had changed."

His powers of imagination were impressive if he could manage that. Simon had gone from being a surgeon to not being allowed through the front doors of the hospital. Change didn't get much more significant than that.

Simon's mouth quirked up, as if he'd read my mind. "Yes, that plan was doomed from the start." He rolled his shoulders to loosen them. "A vampire club isn't just a restaurant that serves the right food. It's also a place to relax, where you don't have to laugh at some jerk's vampire jokes. Or have a stranger fixating on you because they're fascinated by vampires."

"It's a place you can be around people who are like you," I suggested. "A community."

"Yes." He shrugged. "It felt like I shouldn't need that, but I did. I think everyone does. A quick meal at work or home every once in a while is one thing, but every day?"

Silver Edge had replaced the social circle Simon had left behind when his medical career had come to an abrupt halt. But I thought I understood where he was going with this. "So, given Evan's lack of social contact, it would make sense if he spent time at some club. But as far as we can tell, he didn't belong to one."

Simon shrugged again. "Maybe he was just one of those people who was fine being around humans all the time. Or having In Vein come to him could have been his substitute. Maybe the employees were his community. Let's hope he talked to one of them."

TWENTY-SIX

In Vein had its offices at the very edge of the Butcher District, on the second floor of a modern eight-story building that seemed to mostly house insurance companies and law firms. When I saw their shingle with the name, I realized I *had* seen the logo before. The light blue "I" superimposed over a slightly darker blue "V" didn't suggest vampires or blood, which I supposed was why they had chosen it. In Vein seemed to value discretion above all else.

"How did you even know where this was?" I asked, slightly breathless from climbing the stairs. Simon preferred stairs, and I was pretending I wasn't lazy enough to take the elevator one floor when my legs worked just fine.

"My mother's law firm has the top two floors." He held open the stairwell door. "You okay? Or should I see if I can find an oxygen tank?"

I glared at him. "I'm fine. Is your mom upstairs right now?"

"Probably." He lengthened his stride, leaving me staring at his back as I tried to catch up. "I'll drop by and say hello after this."

We were definitely going upstairs together — on the elevator — before we left.

In Vein didn't have a large office, which made sense if they did most of their business away from the premises. The outer door led to a reception desk and a tiny waiting area, with two doors beyond, both of which had card readers. Nothing about it hinted at what type of business it was. It could just as easily have been a dentist's office or a spray-tan salon.

Behind the reception desk sat a Latina in her fifties who exuded a capable air. Given what Amanda had told me about her training at Silver Edge, I was guessing being able to stay calm during a crisis was a requirement for employment. The receptionist looked up as we entered, gave me a high-wattage smile, and then relaxed when she saw Simon, shifting her body to the left. "How can I help you, sir?"

In Vein might be a relaxed, public business, without all the visible security of a club like Silver Edge, but they were prepared for anti-vampire attacks. I would bet money there was a panic button under the desk and she'd had her hand on it before she'd noticed the vampire next to me.

Simon showed his badge. "We need to talk to people who knew Evan Maguire."

"Just a moment." She picked up the phone, spoke briefly with someone, then smiled at us again. "This way, please."

Door number two led to what was clearly an employee lounge, with lockers along one wall, a refrigerator and microwave, two sofas, and a television. Two men and a woman — all human, all probably undergrads — lounged on the couches with laptops and textbooks, and a male vampire sat at the table. He was an Asian man in his fifties, just going gray around the temples, wearing khaki slacks and a polo shirt with a tiny In Vein logo on the sleeve. When he saw us, he closed his laptop and stood. "Darwin Chu. Belinda said you had some questions about one of our clients?"

Simon introduced us and informed Chu of Evan's death. "We're trying to find people who knew him." The three humans stopped pretending to study, and everyone showed real signs of sorrow.

Chu recovered first. "I'm sorry to hear that. Of course, we'll help in any way we can. I saw Evan nearly every day, and most of our employees were there at least once a week. He was In Vein's most steady customer."

That matched with what Simon had said about most vampires only occasionally using that sort of service. Leaving Simon to talk to the other vampire, I looked at the humans. The woman had Taylor's *Basics of Magic Theory* in her stack of books, making me smile. "You taking Intro to Magic Theory with Kessler?"

She was tall and rangy, like a distance runner, and had dark brown skin and long black hair in ringlets. With a heavy groan, she said, "My friends convinced me to take it for one of my humanities electives, but they didn't say anything about needing to do math." She lifted her stack of books and balanced them on the arm of the couch. "Have a seat. You look like your feet hurt."

FBME agent training probably emphasized physical safety when talking to witnesses, but I wasn't really an agent and my feet *did* hurt. I sank down with a grateful sigh. "Thanks. What's it like, working here?"

"Better than working in the dorm cafeteria," she responded promptly. "Actually, it's a decent job if you aren't squeamish and don't mind feeling exhausted the day after. We get paid for a four-hour shift with a bonus if we have a client, they give us a comfortable place to study, and the handlers are always careful about our safety."

I glanced at the vampire seated at the table. "Darwin is a handler?"

"Yeah. They always have two scheduled. James is out on a call with Trina right now. There are always a couple clients that just drop in — we have a room over there." She tilted her head toward the wall, to a room where the other door led.

"How long have you been doing this?"

"A couple years, but I take time off during spring when we compete. Rowing," she answered before I could ask. "I still train during the off-season, but I can't do this and stay in peak condition." She shifted on the couch. "Evan's really dead?"

I nodded. "You knew him?"

"Not well, but we talked a bit. He seemed like a nice guy. That sucks. He was just starting to get his life back together."

"In what way?"

"His marriage imploded, and that really knocked him back. They say that something like eighty percent of marriages fall apart when one partner becomes a vampire, but he truly thought he was going to beat the odds. And then his ex moved to England a few months ago, and it was rough only seeing his daughter on video calls. He was pretty cut up about it. Understandably, I guess, but he was having a hard time just getting through the day. Had to pay the after-hours fee a couple times because he forgot to schedule an appointment earlier."

"But that had changed recently?"

"Yeah. A few weeks ago, he suddenly had all these plans for how he was going to get his daughter to stay with him when she wasn't in school, and he was talking about expanding the business, hiring more people, that sort of thing. It was like he suddenly had inherited money. He always tipped, but he started tipping us *really* well."

That was interesting. Maybe it would be worth checking Evan's bank statements when we got back to the office. Had someone been paying him to wear the bracelet? Maybe he'd been a test subject? It all went back to figuring out what the stupid bracelet had done before it was damaged.

The other two students, Jesse and Constantine, confirmed the recent increase in tips, though they were more vague about Evan's personal situation. "We always just talked hockey," Jesse explained.

Similarly, Evan and Constantine limited their discussions to music. "He had some good classic jazz recommendations. I did get him to try out some new stuff last week. He said he enjoyed it."

Simon looked at me, eyebrows raised. I thanked the students and we left, going to the atrium of the building to talk.

Gesturing at In Vein, I said, "Everything we've learned points to Evan being depressed. Then he started wearing the bracelet and suddenly he was getting out more and making plans for the future. Someone figured out how to get blood magic to work on vampires. But nobody has said anything that gives us any idea what the rest of the spells were doing."

Simon said, "If we could find an intact bracelet, I could test it easily enough."

I grimaced, thinking about the second woodcut in *Amulets to Cast Out Demons*. The artist had chosen the woman's pose carefully, showing her protecting the amulet.

And Evan had kept the bracelet on almost until the last minute. He had to have guessed what caused his madness if it came on as soon as he damaged the metal. "That's not a great idea. We don't know if the addiction would disappear when the bracelet is gone."

Simon frowned in thought. "That might explain why nobody who's been wearing one has come forward yet."

" Until we understand exactly what the spells do, you should keep your distance."

"Understood." He looked over his notes. "I'm going to make a quick detour upstairs and then check in to see what everyone else has found out. You want to get a coffee and meet me outside in fifteen minutes?"

I narrowed my eyes at him in a mock glare. "You've met all of *my* family."

"You won't thank me when you realize later that you signed up to help with five letter-writing campaigns. My mother works on civil rights lawsuits and she recruits heavily." When I didn't back off, he shook his head with a smile. "Just remember that I warned you."

On our way to the elevators, we sidestepped around two vampires coming out of the stairwell on their way to In Vein. After waiting until we were out of earshot, I asked, "I get why someone would use the service, but why come to their offices?"

Simon ushered me into the elevator. "Avoiding someone at their club, maybe? Some places have a lot of drama."

Reality television had missed a huge opportunity. "So, do people switch clubs or join a second one?"

"I have no idea."

The doors closed and the cab moved up for twenty seconds before the elevator ground to a halt. The doors remained shut and a distant bell rang.

I leaned my back against the wall, prepared for a long wait. "Normally, I'd be upset about being stuck in an elevator, but at least while we're in here, nobody can try to kill us again."

"Something's wrong," Simon said.

"Yeah, the elevator's broken." I looked over at him. He'd gone pale. "Are you claustrophobic or something?"

He backed into the corner opposite me. "No, there's something wrong. It feels like it did on Friday. You didn't check that thing out of evidence, did you?"

"No."

He was pushing himself against the wall, as if trying to go through it to get away from me. "There's something on you."

"We haven't even been back to The Vault since this morning. How would..." I gave up on that sentence and knelt on the floor, upending my bag. My wallet and keys were followed by a shower of change, tissues, cough drops, and all the other detritus that ended up in the bottom of my purse. I shook the bag to make sure everything was out.

The aluminum bracelet with a glass sun on the band — the same one I'd checked into evidence that morning — fell to the floor. "Fuck!"

Someone had dropped it into my bag, probably right before we'd gotten on the elevator. Then they'd disabled the elevator, leaving me and Simon trapped in here together.

"Can you get the doors open at all?" If we could shove the thing through a gap, it would drop multiple stories, which might get it far enough away that it wouldn't affect Simon much. Not an ideal solution, sure, given the other vampires in the building, but we could evacuate until I could get down there with a containment box.

Simon swallowed. "I'll try." He waited until I'd moved

the bracelet to the back of the cab, then tried to get his fingers between the doors.

If I'd been able to work magic, I could have broken the spell, burned out the power circle and kept it from pulling energy from Simon. But I couldn't. Years of study and research and I couldn't even do the most basic wards. I was useless, helpless to disable the spell that would kill us both.

Unless I could *fix* it.

"Give me your gun," I ordered.

Simon stopped trying to pry the doors open, pulled his gun from his holster, and held it out. "If you need to use it, aim for my chest and don't stop shooting until I'm dead." His hand was shaking as he passed me the weapon.

"Swear to god, you are *such* a drama queen." I hit the button to release the magazine and let it clatter to the floor, then racked the slide to eject the round in the chamber. The bullet flew off to the side, pinging against the metal wall of the cab.

"What are you doing?"

"Keep trying to get those doors open." Taking a deep breath, I examined the collector. I'd been staring at this thing for three days now, and I knew every part of it, even if I didn't understand its full purpose. It had been damaged when Evan bent the cuff. If I could bend it into the right configuration, the collector should fill again and stop pulling energy from the power circle.

Holding the aluminum cuff against the handrail, I hit it sharply with the butt of the gun. It deformed, but not enough, so I hit it again, harder this time. The collector went back into a more stable configuration. Even better, I'd scratched the power loop and the whole thing was heating up in my hand. I let it drop to the floor.

A wisp of smoke curled up from the carpet, and then the whole spell failed.

"Ha!" I said. "Problem solved." That thing would no longer pull energy from any vampire.

Then I looked up and saw Simon fixated on me, his face tense.

Holding up one finger, I slowly leaned over to pick up my phone, wishing I had the ill-fitting bracers. "You turn around and stand in the corner. I'm going to call Silver Edge."

TWENTY-SEVEN

At Simon's insistence, I reloaded the gun before I called Amanda and told her we needed help again. She had a team on the way before I finished explaining. "And we'll need someone to fix the elevator," I added. Just as I said it, the cab jolted and slid upward. "Never mind. It's moving again." One less worry. "We're going up.

"Do you think you can safely get the elevator to the ground floor?" Amanda asked.

"Yes?" I drew the word out to three syllables.

"Just a few more minutes."

I repeated that to Simon's back. He didn't move. The elevator slowed as we approached the top floor.

Amanda spoke. "The team is almost at the building. They'll be waiting for you in the lobby."

They must have sprinted down the street. "Remind me to schedule all my emergencies nearby."

The doors opened to a crowd of people in business suits waiting to enter. Simon turned around to look at them, his features nearly feral.

"FBME emergency," I said, careful not to raise my voice. "Stay back."

The suited crowd took a gratifying collective step backward, though that was probably because I was holding a gun.

After ten long seconds, the doors closed again and we descended. Sweat trickled down my spine. "We're going back down," I told Amanda.

"You're doing great," she said warmly

Naturally, the elevator stopped at every floor on the way down. I had a bad moment on the fifth floor when a man intent on his phone conversation stepped forward the second the doors opened. Then he saw my gun and screamed. Simon's head jerked around, his nostrils flaring.

"Come *on*," I muttered. Oblivious Guy stopped screaming and froze, staring at Simon. I moved between the two, gun pointed at Simon, and shoved the stranger sideways, hearing him stumble and fall behind me. "Bowers," I said in a low voice as I backed into my corner so I could stab the door close button, "I need you to turn around and look at the wall. We're almost there."

On the phone, Amanda said, "The team is set up and waiting."

I repeated that to Simon and blew out a breath as the doors closed. He turned and rested his head against the wall of the cab, and I clamped the gun under my elbow so I could wipe my sweaty palms on my trousers.

By the time we made it to the lobby, Simon was shaking. The second the doors opened, I inched backward and felt a hand grab my shirt to guide me to the side. It was the same female vampire who'd pulled me from Joshua's apartment. She took the gun from me as she pushed me behind her. I couldn't blame her.

Thirty seconds later, the other two vampires led Simon to a car idling by the front doors, and I blew out a shaky breath. People edged back into the lobby, unsure if it was safe.

I went back into the elevator to collect everything I'd dumped out of my bag. I even found the bullet that had originally been chambered. The last thing I picked up was the mangled bracelet, all traces of magic permanently erased. "It wasn't his fault," I told the vampire waiting for me. "Someone slipped this into my bag. When it was still spelled," I added.

"Someone wants the two of you dead," she commented while unloading the Glock. "Does anyone in the building need medical assistance?"

"Not because of us."

"Good." She handed me Simon's gun, the slide locked back to show it was empty, and then the magazine. "You should probably take care of whoever's trying to kill you before someone gets hurt."

"That's the plan." Except I didn't know how to investigate this sort of thing. I didn't even have a badge to convince people to talk to me. The only thing I had going for me was that I was human — if I'd been a vampire, Simon and I might have slaughtered every single human on the eighth floor before anyone could stop us. One of those people was Simon's mother. "Thanks for the help. Again."

She raised her first two fingers to her temple in a casual salute, and then left, leaving a lobby full of people staring at me. The elevator doors closed, and I heard the cab hissing its way to the upper floors.

I moved to a quiet spot near the wall so I could figure out what to do next. Calling Supervisory Agent Salt was high on the list, but whether she was involved in the coverup or not, the minute I told her the bracelet had been removed from evidence and dropped in my bag, someone at the FBME would start covering their tracks.

No. Wait. The person who had done this would have covered their tracks the minute they'd retrieved the bracelet from evidence. Even if I teleported back to The Vault this instant, I wouldn't be there in time. But someone had dropped that thing into my bag, and I was pretty sure I knew when.

If this building had security cameras in the interior corridors, I could put a face to our attackers.

"Jen? Jen Perkins?" A woman's voice broke into my thoughts. I looked up to find a white human woman in her fifties, her salt and pepper hair styled in a pixie cut. Though her suit hid her figure, she looked like the type of high-energy person who lived on coffee and exercise. And I recognized her features. This had to be Simon's mother. She thrust out a hand. "You *are* Jennifer Perkins, aren't you? I'm Claire Bowers."

"Nice to meet you." I meant it, but I hesitated. "I'd really love to talk, but I need to check in at work and let them know what happened." And get a copy of the security recordings before anyone could make them disappear — if I could get whoever was in charge to hand them over. Then it struck me that Claire might be able to help with that. "Do you know who to talk to about getting copies of the security videos? Someone just tried to kill your son, and this may be our break."

CLAIRE not only knew the security supervisor by name, she introduced me to him and stood there while I asked for a copy of the recordings. Without her, I think I would have needed a warrant. But after one glance at Claire, he copied everything onto a USB drive and handed it over without another word.

When I suggested he forget we'd ever been there, he blinked. "Who are you?" Then he smiled and wished us a good day.

"Simon's probably not going to be happy that I got you involved with this," I warned her as we went back to the lobby.

"Too bad." She gestured toward the cafe next door. "Do you have time for a cup of coffee or tea?"

"Give me just a minute."

My call to update Salt felt like a weird echo of Friday, though at least this time I hadn't just found two bodies. Plus, I already had her number stored in my phone now. She told me to get back to The Vault as soon as possible and to go straight to her office. I decided she'd never know if I spent fifteen minutes having a cup of coffee with Simon's mother — public transportation could be notoriously unreliable.

The cafe sold tiny cheesecakes, and I ordered one with my coffee. I'd been right about Claire — they didn't bother asking for her order, just handed her the largest mug filled with black coffee.

"Che thinks you're a good influence on Simon," she said as we sat down.

On a normal day, her leap past small talk to a more personal subject might have thrown me off, but nothing was normal anymore. "I've known Simon less than a week." The coffee at the cafe wasn't as good as Silver Edge, but it was still miles ahead of the break room swill at The Vault. "Do you talk to Che a lot?"

She smiled, as if I'd just confirmed something. "I've been worried about my son since he changed. Oh, not because he became a vampire, in itself," she said, waving away that thought. "But because so much of his sense of self was tied up with being a surgeon. He's wanted to be a doctor since he was five years old. It was a big adjustment."

I thought about the way Simon stared at food but didn't eat. "He needs time to work some things out."

"And we've been giving him space," she agreed, "but you're the first person from the FBME that he's introduced to anyone outside of work."

"Yeah." I stretched out the syllable as I remembered why I'd met Che. "I'm not sure that was a deliberate move. The visit to Che was professional after I got chewed on by a... never mind."

Her knowing smile didn't waver. "Trust me. If my son hadn't wanted you to meet his closest friend, he would have found a reason to take you to a different hospital." She leaned forward. "All I'm asking is that if you see him struggling... Well, a phone call to me, or to Che, if you think that would be more appropriate. I just want to make sure he gets back on his feet."

She was worried Simon was going to hurt himself, I realized. There was some irony to her asking *me* to watch over him — I'd held a gun on him twice in the last week. "This thing today, it's going to be another setback, even though he couldn't have done anything to avoid it."

"See? You understand." Claire finished the last of her coffee. "If I could have convinced him to do something else, I would have. But if he had to join the Bureau, I'm glad he has people like you working with him."

"I'm an evidence technician," I protested. "Normally, I

never leave the basement at The Vault. I'm not the best person to be keeping Simon safe."

With a smile, she touched my hand. "Simon doesn't need someone to keep him safe," she said. "He needs someone to keep him whole."

TWENTY-EIGHT

When I got to The Vault, I went downstairs to grab my work laptop. The USB drive with the security video was burning a hole in my pocket, but I didn't dare view it here. With all the evidence technicians back from Seattle, the basement had its normal level of activity, everyone settling in after a week away and picking up where they'd left off. My boss, Mimi Bambury, watched me walk across the room from her corner office, but didn't say a word. That didn't mean anything, though — she would wait until my next review to go through a list of things I'd done wrong.

Predictably, Hamilton was the one to comment. "Welcome back, Special Agent Dr. Perkins! We're honored to be graced with your presence."

Flashing the expected middle finger at him, I said, "Want to trade, Hamilton? I have to go see Salt next." My laptop clanked against Simon's gun when I dropped it into my bag.

"Hard pass. But don't forget us little people when you have your own office on the sixth floor."

"I'm more likely to hit you up for a loan while I'm

standing in line for unemployment benefits, but sure." With a bright smile and a beauty pageant wave to my fellow magical evidence technicians, I walked out.

Supervisory Agent Salt was waiting for me by the elevator on the sixth floor. "Enjoy your coffee and cake?"

She couldn't *possibly* have known about my detour with Simon's mother, but I still had to work not to flinch.

Luckily for me, she didn't give me a chance to stammer out an excuse. "My office."

She walked off, and I had to lengthen my stride to keep her in sight. When we went into her office, she said, "Close the door." After I had, she added, "Sit."

It felt more like a command she would give to a dog rather than an invitation, but I was too tired to quibble. I sat.

Salt leaned forward and rested her forearms on her desk. "Now tell me exactly what happened."

"We were looking for people who knew Evan Maguire," I started, unsure about where she wanted me to start. When she moved one hand in a circle for me to hurry it up, I skipped forward. "We finished talking to some people he'd known at In Vein." I paused and she gave a sharp nod, showing her knowledge of the business. "Bowers wanted to say hello to his mother while we were there, since she works in the building. The elevator stopped between floors and then he said he felt the same thing he'd felt on Friday at Joshua's apartment. That was when I found the bracelet in my bag."

"You hadn't checked it out of evidence earlier?"

"No. And I don't think it could have been in my bag long, or it would have affected the other vampire at In Vein." My stomach lurched. "It *didn't* affect the vampire at In Vein, did it?" It hadn't even occurred to me to check. Darwin Chu had seemed fine when we'd left, but there had been three college students in there with him.

"Everyone there was unaffected," Salt said, not as if she particularly cared, but as if she knew I wouldn't continue until I was reassured I hadn't left a massacre in our wake. "What happened next?"

"Simon tried to get the elevator doors open so we could drop the bracelet down the elevator shaft. While he was doing that, I tried to fix the spell so it wouldn't keep drawing energy from him."

Salt frowned. "Your file says you aren't a mage."

It was unnerving to have her know so much about me, but maybe also a little flattering. "I'm not. But the spell was malfunctioning because the aluminum bent, so I thought if I could get it back to the right shape, it would go back to normal."

A calculating look crossed her face, and she leaned back in her chair. "Interesting approach. And that worked?"

"No. Maybe. I mean, it *might* have worked, but I scratched the power circle while I was trying to bend the metal back, and the whole thing burned out. The entire spell is gone." And that was fine, as far as I was concerned. Hopefully, Salt wouldn't be upset that the evidence had become worthless.

"I see. Where is it now?"

Grateful to have an excuse to look away, I dug around in my bag until I found it. "Here." The aluminum clanked as I set it down on the glass of her desktop.

Without a word, she opened a drawer in her desk to retrieve a mahogany containment box, used a pen to drop the bracelet inside, then closed the box and sealed it in an evidence bag. Both of us knew the bracelet was no longer spelled, but there were rules. Once that was done, Salt set it on the side of her desk and looked at me for a long moment.

Even without any magic behind it, Salt's stare made me want to run and hide. If I'd had anything to confess, I would have spilled my guts right then. Instead, I ignored the trickle of sweat running down my spine and really, really hoped she wasn't involved in the coverup.

Finally, she drew a deep breath and let it out. "Why do you think someone targeted you and Bowers?"

"I don't know." More than anything, I wanted to tell her everything that Simon and I had talked about. But the neighbor in unit four had seen a woman from the FBME, and it could have been Salt. "We hoped that if it was work-related then making the report public this morning would have stopped it."

That wasn't giving anything away. Salt was smart enough to have figured out the reason, even if she didn't know the specifics of why we were concerned.

She looked at me a moment longer, then nodded. "I need you to write up an incident report."

"Can I do that from the club? I'd like to check on Bowers."

"He uses Silver Edge, doesn't he? That's fine. Just make sure you keep your mobile switched on in case I need to reach you."

"Of course."

I stood, and when she didn't say anything else, managed not to run while leaving the room, but just barely.

From behind me, I heard her yell, "And make sure your report explains why an evidence technician was waving a gun around in public."

TWENTY-NINE

Since Simon and I had come in by a hired car that morning, my bicycle was still at the vampire club. So I took the water bus downriver to the Butcher District and walked the eight blocks to Silver Edge. I'd considered going to Booksellers Row first, to talk to the neighbor in unit four, but that was in the opposite direction and I really needed to sit in a secure space and look at the security video on the USB drive.

It was possible the neighbor had tried to get in touch, but she would have called Simon's number and he would have been in no shape to answer. As I dodged a tourist on a rented scooter, I remembered the landlord in unit one. *His* contact details were in my notes. When I called, he sounded as if I'd woken him up again. Two minutes later, I had Mary's phone number. She didn't answer. I left a message asking her to call as soon as possible.

By now, the afternoon staff members at Silver Edge felt like old friends. Since Amanda was busy with a client, I took a seat in the lobby to wait. I wanted to take out my laptop, but I needed to be sure I was the only one watching.

Amanda finished calling a car, saw the client off, and then came to me. "Jen, you really are an angel."

"How's he doing?"

"Not quite ready for visitors, I think. What can I get for you in the meantime?"

"Can I borrow the office Simon and I were using yesterday? Or any room, really. I need to write up an incident report."

"Of course! Come with me." Amanda led the way to the elevator. As we waited for the cab to come to ground level, she said, "How are you doing after everything that's happened today?"

I went with the truth. "Someone tried to kill us. Half of me is hiding under the bed and the other half is relieved to have proof I wasn't imagining things."

Her eyebrows rose, but before she could say anything, the elevator doors opened. Two vampires came out, and I recognized Delia Tarragona. She was wearing a long burgundy sequined dress that shimmered with every movement. With her was a middle-aged white man in a tuxedo. He looked familiar, but I didn't think I'd ever met him.

Delia saw me and smiled. "Jen! How lovely to see you!" She turned to the man she was with. "Perhaps you can have Amanda show you the best place to see the fireworks. We'll just be a moment." Then she took my arm and drew me to the side. "I was just about to message you. A few minutes ago, I got a call from a friend who's in charge of the Ferugia Project. Are you familiar with it?"

"Of course. Deep water exploration and research." By combining magic and technology, the multinational research group had successfully sent robotic probes into areas of the ocean never previously seen. Everyone wanted to work there. I didn't even bother applying, because there was no way I could compete with people who were on my level at theory *and* could cast spells.

"Well, they have a rather urgent need for a theoretician and Jane asked me if I knew anyone who might fit the bill. And of course I told her I had just the right candidate."

Me? Work on the Ferugia Project? "I... There must be a hundred people better suited..."

She tilted her head in a disappointed but fond way. "Nonsense. You would be *perfect* for this position. And since you work for the FBME, you already have the necessary clearances." She smiled. "Can I tell them you're interested?"

"Oh my god, yes!" Working on the Ferugia Project had been something I'd never even let myself dream about. I'd have to move, of course — they had multiple satellite offices, but none were in Floodmouth. I'd have to find someone to take over my half of the lease, but Trix would understand. Me! The Ferugia Project!

"Wonderful. The only drawback is the timeline. As I said, it's an urgent need. They have fifty people waiting for a spell glitch to be resolved and they're in danger of losing funding. You'll need to be in Hawaii as soon as possible."

"The end of the month?" It would be tight, but I could put in a two-week notice. By then, Simon and I would have at least figured out who we could trust in the FBME, so I wouldn't be leaving him in the lurch.

Delia shook her head. "They would want you on a plane tomorrow," she said gently. "I *might* be able to push it back to Thursday, but even that might be difficult."

My emotional high crashed. "That's too soon. There's a case at work..."

"Jen. Listen to me." Putting her hands on my shoulders, Delia looked me in the eyes. "When you're making career decisions, you need to think about yourself. Don't worry about what's going on at work. Nobody is irreplaceable. If the FBME decided tomorrow to cut the staff in half, they wouldn't worry about how it would affect *you*. You *cannot* be more loyal to a job than they are to you."

She was right, and there was a good chance I *would* be out of a job when Salt found out we'd been holding things back. But right now I was literally the only person in the FBME that Simon could trust. I couldn't leave. Not now.

Taking a small step back until Delia's hands dropped from my shoulders, I said, "I can't. I really appreciate you thinking of me, and if this had come up a week ago, I would have jumped at the chance. But I can't. Not right now."

For a moment, she merely looked at me, and the disappointment in her gaze tore at my heart. Then she sighed and offered a gentle smile. "As much as I think you're making a mistake, I respect your refusal to compromise your principles. Don't worry. Something will come along again in the future."

"Thank you for considering me," I said helplessly.

"Of course, my dear." She straightened and turned her attention back to the man she'd come off the elevator with. "Jonathan, are you ready?" The vampires swept away to their evening entertainment and Amanda rejoined me.

"You look disappointed," she remarked, as the elevator whisked us upward.

"Delia offered me a job," I admitted. "It would have been perfect for me."

"But?"

"But they needed me to start now. And I can't abandon Simon in the middle of this mess."

Amanda nodded decisively. "I knew I liked you." When the doors opened, she ushered me into the corridor. "My nan used to say that anything that happened once can happen again, so if you aren't ready, you shouldn't jump just because an opportunity appears." She laughed. "She was talking about marriage, which tells you something about my nan, but the idea is the same."

Then she opened the door to the office Simon and I had been using the day before. "I'll have coffee sent up. If you need anything else, I'm just a phone call away."

"Thank you."

I had my laptop out before her footsteps faded. The format of the files on the USB drive stumped me for a few minutes, but eventually I figured out the naming scheme and found the files for the second floor cameras. Then it was just a matter of moving forward until I found the correct time.

Starting with the camera that covered the hallway in front of In Vein, I sped forward until I saw Simon and me, walking away from the camera, enter the business. There were a few other people in the corridor, but nobody got close enough to drop anything in my bag. That was expected, though, because the vampire at In Vein hadn't been affected, so I was fairly certain I hadn't been carrying the spelled bracelet at that point.

I scrolled forward until we emerged. This time, we were facing the camera and I had to stop critiquing how I walked and concentrate on everyone around me. We passed under the camera and disappeared with nobody getting near us.

The view of the camera above the elevator entrance overlapped the first camera slightly, so I skipped forward to that time and watched us walking. The stairwell door opened, and a Black man and a white woman in business casual came out. Simon and I moved to the side to accommodate them, and...

Backing up the video five seconds, I went through frame by frame. The woman's heel caught on something and she staggered, nearly running into me, but caught herself at the last second, throwing her arms up to keep her balance. One hand came near my bag. The metal of the bracelet never made an appearance, but there had been something dark in her other hand, impossible to see clearly in the grainy video.

It was the shape and size of a containment box.

In the next clear image, she had her hand in her pocket, and a second later, her hands were empty.

From the security video, it was impossible to tell if they were vampires or humans, but I had a vague memory of swerving around two vampires in that spot. The woman had pulled the bracelet from a containment box, dropped it in my bag, and they'd walked away before it could affect them.

Those were our enemies.

Three cups of coffee later, I'd reviewed the rest of the video, searching for clearer pictures and looking at what else they had done in the building. Though the two vampires had done a good job of avoiding the cameras, I caught clear images of their faces in two spots.

A minute after Simon and I had entered the building, they had followed. Then they checked the building's directory, and went into the stairwell where they had waited, looking like two colleagues casually taking a break, until they'd seen us through the window in the door. They'd *known* where we were. That fit with a mole in the FBME — Simon had updated our log to say where we were going next. Multiple people could access those logs; taken alone, it didn't condemn or clear Salt.

But now I knew there was a female vampire who *wasn't*

Salt working on the coverup, so the evidence of the neighbor in unit four wasn't so damning.

As if she could tell I was thinking about her, Salt sent a text. *Need that incident report ASAP*.

Working on it right now, I texted back. Then I quickly typed up everything I'd told Salt earlier. Would it look worse or better for both of us if I said Simon had given me his gun so I could shoot him? But clearly someone had complained, probably the guy who had blundered between us on the fifth floor, so I added a section saying Simon had given me his weapon to use as a last resort to keep bystanders safe and that the gun had not been aimed at any members of the public. With any luck, the security videos would back me up.

After I filed the report in the system and texted Salt to let her know it was done, I closed the laptop. I had images of the people who had tried to kill us, but I didn't know who they were or what to do next.

Picking up the house phone, I pressed the button to be connected to the lobby. "Amanda, do you know if Simon is ready for a visitor yet?"

"Let me check." There was a brief pause, and then she was back. "He is, though apparently he's in a bit of a mood, so be prepared."

Thinking about what Simon's mother had said earlier, I thought about inviting her or Che for a visit. Then another idea occurred to me, and I texted a question to Claire. She replied with gratifying speed, and a few minutes later, I rode the elevator down to the medical floor.

The room was the same one Simon had been in on Friday. As I'd been warned, he was in no mood for polite words of encouragement. "Don't say anything," he growled from the couch when I came into the room. "I don't want to hear about how well I'm doing."

"Wouldn't dream of it," I said, and sat down uninvited on the other side of the couch. "I have two things that will cheer you up."

The first was his gun. Both of us were relieved when it was back in his possession. He slid the magazine in place, racked the slide, and set it on the end table next to him. "What's the second thing?"

"Information." I pulled my laptop out of my bag and showed him the stills I'd saved of the two vampires who had been waiting in the stairwell. "Do you know these two? They're the ones who dumped the bracelet in my bag."

He looked at me — really looked at me — for the first time since I'd entered the room. "You found out who tried to kill us."

"What, did you think I was going to spend my time picking out the perfect get-well card for you? I found them on the security video, but I have no idea how to figure out who they are. So if you want to stop moping around and help, it would be nice."

He took the laptop without comment, but there was a hint of a smile on his face. Then he narrowed his eyes as he looked at the images. "Hang on. I've seen them before. And so have you."

THIRTY

It took Simon five minutes to find the information he was looking for, during which time a staff member knocked on the door and wheeled in a cart with dishes covered in a silver cloche. When Simon raised an eyebrow, I waved him back to his search. "I haven't eaten a real meal since breakfast."

But I left the cart untouched while he worked.

Finally, he handed my laptop back to me, with a web page that had a publicity photo of a group of people in FBME jackets behind a table laden with daggers and swords. "Spelled weapons bust in Seattle last year," he said, then pointed at the two people on the edge of the group. "That's them."

From the photo's caption, I got their names. "Haley McMair and Dion Sharpe."

"They were in the task force meeting this morning," Simon said. "In Seattle."

Even depending on a public teleportation site, it would have taken them less than an hour to get to Floodmouth. "Is it a good sign they had to use agents from Seattle? Maybe nobody here is involved."

"Or maybe," Simon countered, "they thought we might recognize any local agents and ask what they were doing there." He glanced at me. "You really want to dump this all on Salt and be done with it."

"Yes." The more people we could trust, the faster this whole thing could get cleared up. Trix could move back to our apartment, Simon and I would stop being targets, and I would be free to accept the perfect job that Delia had found for me. "But you're right. This doesn't actually clear anyone." I set down the laptop between us and pushed up to my feet.

Under the cloche, I found two grilled cheese sandwiches cut into one-inch strips and a tureen of tomato soup with a side of sour cream. The kitchen had included two small bowls that fit on the plates, so I ladled soup into both bowls, then moved back to the couch with one plate in each hand.

Simon stared at me when I handed him his plate. "Why do you have such a hard time understanding that I don't need to eat?"

"Why do *you* have such a hard time understanding that acquiring calories is only one of the many purposes of food?" Curling up at the other end of the couch, I inhaled the fragrant steam, smelling basil and garlic, before taking a bite. How the kitchen had produced tomato soup on demand was a mystery — this hadn't come from a can. Whether it would be the same as what Claire had served was a different question, but I'd passed along her instructions and the kitchen hadn't disappointed. Whatever cheese they'd used in the sandwich was going to ruin my appreciation for the cheap stuff.

"I take it you met my mother today?" He picked up a strip of grilled cheese and sniffed it.

"We had coffee and cheesecake. Well, I had cheese-cake." Ignoring his prodding and sniffing of the food, I continued eating. "I like her. The meeting would have been much more awkward if I'd had to shoot you."

"I'm sure you would have muddled through anyhow."

"Naturally." In reality, if I'd had to shoot her son to save my life, she might have understood, but she never would have forgiven me — or herself. She'd already been worried something bad would happen, even without knowing the mess Simon and I had stepped in. Back when he'd been human, she would have pushed him to see a psychiatrist for some short-term pharmaceutical help until he got through this transition, but the minute he'd become a vampire, that was off the table.

It proved there really was a need for the bracelet Evan had worn, preferably without the addictive nature and sudden, messy death. If I had a time machine to go back nine hundred years, I could have worked with an insane vampire mage to create a better version without the drawbacks.

The mass of murky information swirling in the back of my brain suddenly clarified and my hand froze with the grilled cheese halfway to my mouth. "Holy shit. That's it. It doesn't make any sense, but that has to be it."

I had an answer that seemed obvious to me, but was it a case of everything looking like a nail because I'd spent years building a really big hammer?

Simon took a bite of his sandwich and waited for me to continue.

"I'm an idiot. They didn't create a new technique for getting blood magic to work on vampires. It was obvious from the start that whoever put that spell together didn't have any training. The whole thing uses power to hide a lack of finesse."

"Okay, but —"

Excited about my theory, I cut him off. "Someone figured out a way to treat depression in vampires and *they didn't make it public*. What does that say?"

He considered that, taking another bite as I nearly vibrated in my seat. Finally, he said, "It tells us they were doing something shady."

"Exactly. If it had been done in a university, there would be fifteen papers published by now. And if it was being done commercially, you'd see ads for a Vampire's Little Helper Amulet plastered all over the city. But instead, we have absolute silence."

"Okay..."

I leaned forward. "I couldn't figure out what the second part of the spell did. But if I'm right, it all fits together. Because they didn't create anything new, they used something *old*. Somehow they transformed mages. Vampires are making a play for immortality."

THIRTY-ONE

Simon's eyes narrowed. "Immortality? Like your theory about the second vampire plague?"

"It makes sense. We're not looking for a place with a spell that matches the puzzle lock. We're looking for a person. Another vampire." Transferring energy from one vampire to another would also require a blood magic spell. At least, it did in humans, and I saw no reason why vampires would be different. We didn't have any evidence of this second blood magic spell. Yet.

Simon didn't say anything, so I kept talking.

"Eight hundred years ago, European vampires had a strict hierarchy, with newer members beholden to the group that transformed them. So setting up a spell that siphoned energy from younger vampires could be done without the younger vampires questioning it. That wouldn't work today — you'd just walk away. But if someone developed a mind-altering product, a spell which some vampires *needed*, it could be coupled with a spell that secretly siphoned energy." The addictive part would keep them from stopping, even if the victims figured out what was happening.

Simon set his empty plate down. "Except this all requires a vampire mage."

"At least one." The process of creating a vampire was kept secret, but Simon would have gone through it recently. "Is that likely?"

He exhaled slowly. "If you'd asked me yesterday, I would have said no. Now?" A head tilt indicated his uncertainty. "That would mean some *very* high-ranking vampires are involved. How much do you know about the transformation process?"

Everything I knew about modern vampire culture was stuff Julie had told me, because she'd been *obsessed*. But her sources hadn't been reliable. "Not much."

"The selection process is akin to a background check. But the transformation itself requires a *magna decem* — ten senior vampires working together over four days."

I had no idea what made a vampire powerful enough to be part of that, but it didn't matter. "How many vampires are there that could be part of the process?"

"Worldwide? Maybe a hundred. They transfer to different cities, because nobody wants one nation to have that power. The idea is that if you have ten vampires, but they're all from different places, the group as a whole will follow the rules."

It was a good plan... if nationalism was the only worry. But there were other things that could corrupt: ideology and money were the two obvious choices. "I think somebody suborned a group, at least temporarily."

Simon looked at me. "I have no idea how we would track them down." Then he nodded. "But it explains why they wanted *you* out of the way."

"It does?"

"Of course. You're the one person most likely to put all the pieces together."

"But would *they* know that? You're overestimating how many people read my dissertation." While every other department at the university made their dissertations available online for anyone to read, the magic department kept one bound copy in the arcane library. As far as I knew, the tome had remained unopened from the day I'd turned it in until now. But Simon was right. I was one of the few experts on the vampire plagues, and certainly the only one working at the FBME. "Now I feel kind of stupid for not realizing what was going on earlier."

"It's only been five days."

It felt like it had been months. "So... What do we do now?"

"We have hard evidence that two FBME agents were involved in an attack on us."

I nodded. "And we aren't sure who else is involved." After I set my empty plate on the floor, I curled my legs under me. "I guess we could do the same thing we did this morning: send the information out to everyone, so there's no point in coming after us."

"Which worked so well," Simon said, his tone dry.

"Good point." I sighed. "I think we may just have to trust Salt."

He hummed a partial agreement. "Let's see if we can get that neighbor to confirm that it wasn't Salt she saw on Friday morning first."

"I'm starting to think that woman is avoiding us." Lifting my phone, I said, "I left her a message earlier, and she hasn't gotten back to me."

"We can go by on our way to work tomorrow and show her a photo array that includes Salt and the Seattle agent."

"Haley McMair." The name of the person who'd nearly killed me today was burned into my brain.

"Right. We'll show her a photo array that includes Salt and McMair. Assuming the neighbor doesn't pick the wrong one, we dump this all on Salt."

I nodded. "And if Mary does pick Salt?"

He shook his head. "Then things get complicated."

THIRTY-TWO

When we met in the lobby early the next morning, Simon looked like his usual self, well rested and capable. I'd found more clothes in "my" closet the evening before, better than anything else I owned, and the casual luxury was starting to really make me feel weird. I didn't belong here, and surely even the bricks of the building knew that.

But though I didn't belong in the rarified air of Silver Edge, the soft sheets and comfortable mattress — to say nothing of the feeling of safety — had given me a great night's sleep and my brain had churned out something new. "I had an idea while I was sleeping," I said.

"Good morning to you, too," Simon said, holding open the door for me. We walked out into a dense fog. "I didn't bother ordering a car. Subway's going to be the fastest this morning."

"It usually is," I said under my breath, but he was already five steps away, almost invisible in the mist. By the time I caught up to him, we were already descending the stairs to the Joy Street station. "We might be able to find out who's siphoning the energy since we know the shape of the puzzle key."

He looked over without slowing. "How does that help?"

Our train was just pulling in at the platform, and we ran down the last few stairs and onto the nearest car. It was still early enough that there were seats available among the other drowsy commuters, but we moved to the back and stood, holding onto the pole so we could continue talking.

"If my assumptions are correct," I said, "the energy generated by the power loop built up in the collector. I *think* whenever Evan got near someone with the corresponding puzzle key, the energy from the collector would transfer."

Simon leaned in as we went around a curve. "You don't think he would have noticed?"

"Maybe not. Even if he *did* notice, he might have thought it a small price to pay."

Simon didn't respond to that.

"But my idea was that we could create our own spell to alert us when someone with the matching puzzle key is nearby." I paused, waiting for him to get as excited about the idea as I was.

Instead, he cocked his head. "*We* are going to create a spell? Neither of us can cast."

"Stop trying to rain on my parade. I'll design the spell and then we can have someone else cast it."

We stopped at a station and a new group of people entered, taking the last of the seats and partially filling the aisles.

Simon stepped closer so nobody would get between us, giving me a whiff of some woodsy aftershave. "Who?"

I opened my mouth to say any of the people in the basement of The Vault could do it for us — I was literally the *only* magical evidence technician who couldn't cast spells — and then I saw what he was driving at. Until we knew the extent of the conspiracy, we couldn't assume *anyone* was safe. But I had a solution for that. "We'll use one of my contacts at the university." There had to be at least a few people who would do a favor for me, despite my defection from academia.

"It wouldn't need to be done with a vampire mage?"

"No. That part of the spell could be done by anyone." Anyone other than me, of course. My life would have been so much easier if I'd inherited that one little trait.

"How long will it take you to design something?"

I shrugged. "A few hours? I'll just be reusing bits and pieces from other spells."

He shifted closer to let people go by. "I think we should bring it up with Salt."

The unspoken "if we can trust her" hung in the air as the train doors opened to admit the next group of commuters.

ABOVE THE TATTOO shop in Booksellers Row, the crime scene tape had been removed from units two and three, and smooth jazz floated out from the open door of unit two, along with the sound of someone sanding.

"I'm surprised they released the apartments so quickly," I said as we turned toward unit four.

"I doubt they did," Simon replied.

Maybe if I'd been a more dedicated FBME employee, I'd have cared, but I didn't think we would get any more information from the apartments and I had no desire to start enforcing laws. If I couldn't spend my time teaching and researching magic theory, then at least I could confine my work to documenting and containing magical artifacts that would hurt people.

"Pretty sure there's nobody in there," Simon said, but he knocked on the door for unit four anyhow. We both listened for any response. Nothing. While Simon crouched to peek through a gap in the curtains covering the window, I called out, "Mary? It's Jen Perkins. We talked the other day."

Nobody responded, so I knocked again. Booksellers Row followed tourist hours and was much more active in the late evening, so she might have just been sleeping heavily. Or she knew who it was and didn't want to talk to us.

"There's food on a plate that's got mold on it," Simon said. He stood. "I'll call in a welfare check."

"Hang on a sec." A welfare check would involve the regular police, so we'd be stuck waiting for hours. But the landlord seemed to keep track of what was going on around the place — he might be able to tell us if she'd gone to the hospital or left for the week. Maybe she was just terrible at housekeeping.

I backtracked to Joshua's apartment, where the door was open and music played. "Hello?"

The sanding stopped, and the man I'd talked to in unit one appeared, t-shirt and shorts covered with white grit. His first expression when he saw me was guilt. That rapidly evolved into grievance. Since I didn't want to listen to him complain about how he needed the apartment rented out immediately, I ignored the pleasantries. "Have you seen Mary recently? We've been trying to get in touch with her and she's not responding. And it looks like there's some food that's been out for a while."

It was the last bit that galvanized him into action. He grabbed the key ring clipped to a belt loop and walked past me. "Dammit, I tell my tenants all the anti-vermin spells in the world won't help if they leave food out."

I gave Simon a smug smile over the landlord's shoulder as I followed him to unit four. "This will be faster," I whispered as we stood back and waited for the man to unlock Mary's door.

The scent of old pasta and sandalwood incense wafted from the open doorway. Simon's business card was on the floor, apparently untouched. I followed the landlord inside, leaving Simon stuck on the landing due to the anti-vampire ward.

Mary's apartment had a modern eccentric feel, with colorful shawls draped over lamps, mismatched but clean furniture, and an array of weak charms dangling from the key hooks mounted next to the door. Sorting through the charms, I found a few that made the wearer look younger, one for aching joints, and a final one that gave the wearer an aura of mystery.

The kitchen had the disordered look of a post-cooking, pre-cleaning meal, with a pot of spaghetti sauce on the stove, an empty pot in the sink next to a plastic colander, and a wedge of parmesan cheese on a cutting board. A half-eaten plate of pasta waited on the tiny formica table.

"Look at this," the landlord said in disgust. "It's a wonder we don't have ants and cockroaches running all over the place."

Before he touched anything, I took pictures. Then I left him scraping things into the sink and checked the bedroom — no Mary, just an unmade bed and a counter full of glass perfume bottles. In the bathroom, cosmetics were scattered over the counter and the cabinet held two prescriptions, both to be taken every day.

Sometime between Friday and Monday, Mary had left in the middle of her dinner and hadn't come back. That didn't sound good.

Legally, we didn't have an excuse to be in the apartment, and I couldn't destroy the anti-vampire ward to let Simon in. The landlord might be able to make a case for entering to deal with a hazard, but even that was iffy. If I'd been trained in anything other than the legalities of entering an apartment with a search warrant and destroying the anti-vampire ward, I might know what we could and couldn't do, but I didn't. And it was looking like the apartment might be a crime scene.

Going back to the kitchen, I stopped the landlord from taking the kitchen trash out. "We need to leave everything as it was, as much as possible."

"This is already starting to smell," he protested.

As a compromise, he knotted the top closed and put another bag around it. Then he agreed to leave the apartment and lock it behind us.

Out on the landing, I shook my head when Simon looked at me. He gestured toward the roof overhang. "No security cameras?"

The landlord made a face. "No. If you get the cheap ones, they're useless. And I can't afford the good ones." He tilted his head toward Mary's door. "Besides, everyone walking up the stairs sees her staring at them through the window."

Nosy neighbors provided the second best security, right behind owning a dog, but Mary might have paid the price for that. "On Friday morning, Mary said she saw an FBME agent go into Evan's apartment. A vampire." At his blank look, I added, "Number three."

"Oh, right." He turned toward Simon, confused, as if trying to work out why we would want to trick him. "That was you, though."

I shook my head. "No. We didn't get here until after lunch. There was another person here earlier that day. Did you see them?"

"Nah, I didn't see anyone enter number three."

I sighed. It had been worth a try since his kitchen window looked straight down the walkway in front of the apartments. "Thanks for your time." I turned away to follow Simon down the stairs.

"Wait, you're not talking about the *lady* vampire who was at Mary's door, are you?"

Simon and I stopped and turned. I said, "Lady vampire?"

"Yeah. There was a vampire who was a woman talking to Mary for a while that morning. Seemed kind of odd because Mary's pretty anti-vamp, if you know what I mean. I guess she could have been an agent."

He'd assumed I was talking about a man. I'd have to learn to be more careful with my questions. "Did you get a good look at her?"

He shrugged, but Simon was already pulling up the photo array he'd put together on his phone. He held the screen toward the landlord and slowly paged through the six images.

"That's her."

From where I was standing, I couldn't see which photo he'd chosen.

Simon's voice stayed level. "Let me show you the rest of

them." He finished scrolling, then went in the reverse direction.

"That's her, I'm telling you."

"Thanks." Simon turned the phone so I could see the screen.

It was Haley McMair, the Seattle FBME agent who'd dropped the spelled bracelet into my bag.

THIRTY-THREE

We made it back to The Vault thirty minutes before the daily task force briefing, and I followed Simon to Salt's office, not even detouring to the basement to set my things down. Hamilton would give me a hard time about "being too good for all of them now" if he found out, but there was no help for it.

Supervisory Agent Salt was on the phone when we arrived, but she waved us inside. While she finished her conversation, I looked at the commendations on the wall. She'd been part of every major operation I could name over the past twenty years. If she was dirty, she would have the experience to hide it.

"I look forward to seeing that. Let me know if you need help." Salt hung up the phone. "And no, I *won't* do your work for you," she added under her breath. I was pretty sure we weren't meant to hear that. She typed something on her computer, then dropped her hands from the keyboard and looked up. "Someone has it out for the two of you."

Seated side by side, Simon and I looked at each other. If we made this decision, there was no going back. I nodded.

He set his laptop down on Salt's desk. "Yes." Angling his screen so she could see it, Simon started the security video showing our encounter with the two Seattle agents before getting on the elevator.

Frowning, Salt said, "What's this?" She pulled the laptop closer and restarted the clip.

"That," Simon said, enunciating carefully, "is Agents McMair and Sharpe trying to kill us yesterday."

There was twenty seconds of silence as Salt watched the clip again. "I was told," she said slowly, watching it yet again, "that there had been a hardware glitch that had erased the recordings."

"The FBME has a problem," Simon said. "And we finally have proof."

"You didn't bring this to me earlier." Salt leaned back in her chair and narrowed her eyes at us. "Is there some particular reason I ended up on the suspect list?"

Her voice hadn't changed, but suddenly I would have given anything to be anywhere but that office. If I'd accepted Delia's job offer, I could have been downstairs packing up my personal belongings.

Before Simon could respond, I blurted out, "There was an FBME agent in Evan Maguire's apartment *before* we found him. A woman. Vampire."

Her gaze pinned me in place. "And you assumed that was me."

I was still frozen, so Simon took over. "It was a possibility. But we just talked to a second witness who identified Haley McMair."

"And the first witness?"

"Missing."

Salt's face took on a calculating look as she stared at us, though I couldn't tell if she was thinking about the case or merely whether she could fire me without going through the hassle of a personal improvement plan. Finally, she sat up. "Okay. I'll start quietly looking into who in the FBME is involved. You two need to stay far away from *that* investigation. This stays with us for the moment."

From her top drawer, she took out a pen and notepad and then jotted something down. When she was done, she looked up. "Everything up to yesterday can be explained by you two being in the wrong place at the wrong time, but yesterday, you were targeted. Why?"

Simon looked at me to see if I had recovered my wits yet. I swallowed and said, "My PhD dissertation was on an alternate theory for the cause of the second vampire plague. Not many people study that field, so anyone doing research would have come across my name. I think what's happening with the vampires now is related." Having already gone through this with Simon, my two-minute summary of why I thought mages had been transformed to vampires was reasonably coherent.

By the time I was finished, she was staring out the window, her gaze unfocused. She sighed and looked back at us. "You know, if I'd taken the transfer to Bangor last year, this could have been somebody else's problem." Then she shrugged. "But then I'd have to deal with snow." She sighed again and straightened her shoulders. "Okay. We have a theory and no evidence. But if the two of you repeat your performance from yesterday morning..."

Her lips twitched, the first sign I'd seen of any sense of humor. "The part where you ignored communication protocol and sent your report to everyone, not the nearly dying part." She sobered again. "Write up your theory and send it out to the same group. Hopefully that will make you less of a target, though I'd stay away from elevators. And for pity's sake, get a bag that zips closed," she added, looking directly at me. "You're a pickpocket's dream." She glanced at her phone. "Is that it? I have to prepare for the briefing."

Simon didn't budge. "Perkins has an idea to track down who's involved. A spell that would alert on anything that has the other half of the..." He stopped and looked at me.

"Puzzle lock," I said. And for once, I didn't have a problem keeping myself from explaining everything about the concept.

Salt snorted in disbelief. "The two of you are *determined* to get yourselves killed." She held up a hand before Simon could speak. "No, no, it's a good idea. But we'll need to be very fucking careful about how it gets implemented." She blinked and rolled her shoulders. Then she pointed her pen at Simon. "You write that report. Work on it after the briefing and get it out as soon as possible." The pen moved in my direction. "And *you* design that spell. If anyone asks, you're working on a ward to deploy against those damned pterodactyl spells."

Setting down her pen, she said, "Nothing about other agents being involved gets written down *anywhere*. Do you understand?" When we nodded, she waved a hand. "Good. Now get out of my office so I can prepare for this briefing."

AFTER THE TASK force morning briefing — an uncomfortable affair during which I tried not to stare at McMair and Sharpe sitting among the rest of the agents in Seattle — I went down to my desk in the basement to work on the spell. Simon offered space in his office, but all my reference books were downstairs and I doubted anyone would try to kill me within the FBME building.

Someone had left a plastic dinosaur on my desk. I held it up so everyone in the room could see it. "Very funny."

Hamilton laughed. "Shouldn't you be out kicking down doors or something?"

"Nah. I might break a nail." I scanned the books on my shelf. "Have you seen my Sung & Franklin?"

He waved a hand toward the far side of the room. "Cottell was asking if anyone had a copy yesterday. Check his desk."

Cottell was in the break room loudly arguing sports with Stenberg. The book in question, *1001 Spell Combinations for the Modern Mage*, sat on his bookshelf, despite my name printed in black ink on the spine. For a law enforcement organization, it was shocking how many people regarded all books as communal property. Back at my desk, I sat down and flipped to a new page in my work notebook.

To head off complaints from my boss, I brought up one of the reports in my work queue and typed random characters every minute or so. Bambury monitored the program to see who was logged in and active, but she couldn't see what we were typing. As long as I hit at least one key every minute, it looked like I was working. Hamilton had taught me that trick in my first week after the third time Bambury had stomped over to complain that she wasn't paying me to scroll on my phone, only to find me concentrating on my task.

During my time in academia, I'd created spells regularly, some to explore concepts in classes and others for projects I'd been involved with. But since coming to work for the FBME, I'd only worked on documenting existing spells and safely disabling the dangerous ones. So it was kind of fun to work out what I would need in order to alert someone they were near the other piece of a puzzle lock.

Sung & Franklin gave me a few ideas, but I glanced through a stack of other texts.

The lockbox Hamilton had been working on last Thursday was slowly making its way around the room, accompanied by shocks and muffled swearing. When a particularly loud yelp echoed around the room, I looked over at Hamilton. "You warned everyone, right?" The FBME had recruited some fairly powerful mages, and if the lockbox reflected their full strength back at them, someone might lose an eye.

"Yeah, yeah, yeah." He raised his brows at the books I had spread out on the desk. "What do they have you working on now?"

I picked up the plastic dinosaur and waved it at him. "Live through *one* pterodactyl attack, and suddenly you're the expert." There. It wasn't a lie, exactly. "How about you?"

He nudged a box filled with evidence bags. "We're redoing the forensics on all the Seattle victims' personal possessions."

"Sounds fascinating."

"I'll save you some if you want."

The ringing of my desk phone cut off our conversation. The display said it was the guard at the front desk, and I wondered what my coworkers had ordered that required me to go up front — a singing telegram by people in dinosaur costumes, maybe? Hopefully not a male stripper. I didn't want to have to deal with HR on top of attempts on my life. Lifting the handset, I said, "This is Perkins."

A bored man on the other end of the line said, "There's a Maya Perkins here to see you. Says she's a relative."

I frowned at the phone. "Who?" I didn't know anyone named Maya. My mom had a second cousin named Maria who had visited once about twenty years ago, but she wouldn't know where I worked. Plus, her surname wasn't Perkins.

Then I realized who it had to be. I hadn't even known her name. "I'll be up in a minute." After disconnecting the phone, I closed my eyes.

An unexpected wave of anger hit me. How dare she come to my *work*? I shouldn't have to deal with this while trying to maintain a professional face.

But even as I thought that, I knew why she had come here. How *else* would she get in touch with me? My father didn't have my current address, and I wasn't in any city-wide directory. In fact, it was pretty impressive she'd tracked me down just from seeing the FBME logo on our gear.

And she was just a kid. No matter what had happened, none of it was her fault. I opened my eyes and stood up.

Hamilton was looking at me with concern. "You okay?"

Plastering a smile on my face, I said, "Yeah. Family thing. Don't let Cottell steal my books while I'm gone."

"What's it worth to you?" he asked, but I was already at the door and didn't bother with a reply.

THIRTY-FOUR

On the way up the stairs to the main lobby, I tried to work out a plan. Be calm. Find out why she was here and then put her off for a week or two when I would hopefully have more space to deal with this.

Maya — my sister, I reminded myself, even though she was a total stranger — stood in the lobby, leaning one shoulder against the wall with her arms crossed.

She hadn't seen me yet, and I paused before walking forward. Now that I knew who she was, I could see more differences between her and Julie. Maya's face was thinner, her hair a little curly where Julie's had always been straight, and there was a nervous energy coming off her I'd never seen in my older sister.

Then she turned her head, saw me, and pushed away from the wall. Caught out, I walked forward. She didn't return my polite smile. "Does he have two families?"

My dysfunctional family was not something I wanted to discuss in the lobby of The Vault with all my coworkers within earshot. "Let's get some hot chocolate." And then I walked past her, out of the building.

She caught up with me halfway to the sidewalk and grabbed my arm, pulling me to a halt. "I don't want anything from you. I just want to know if he's had two families all this time."

Twisting from her grip, I said, "Depends. How old are you?"

Her scowl was electric. "Almost thirteen."

"Then no. He and my mom split up fourteen years ago. So he may be a shitty person, but he's not a bigamist."

We stared at each other. She hadn't had her final growth spurt yet, so I had the advantage of height, but a rage I'd never felt simmered in her eyes. Sorrow versus anger. As sisters, we were broken in different ways.

"So why didn't he even tell me you existed?"

"Ask *him*." Opening up old wounds to satisfy her curiosity wasn't my job.

"I did. He says I'm imagining things, and you were just someone selling magazines. What did you do? Kill someone or something?"

After years of being ignored, I'd thought my father no longer had the power to hurt me. His denial still took my breath away. And all he'd accomplished was widening the gap between himself and both of his daughters. Maya would find out the truth one way or another. "Come on. Let's grab a seat and I'll tell you."

The benches along the Flood River were half filled by tourists eating and watching the boats go by, but we snagged a seat. Maya swung her backpack around and hugged it to her chest.

Waiting until the water bus had gone by, I said, "I — we — had an older sister, Julie." I took out my phone and pulled up the photo album, then passed my phone to her.

Maya scrolled for a few seconds, then said in disbelief, "She looks just like me."

"Yeah. The Perkins genes are strong."

That made her snort, and she scrolled some more before saying, "What happened to her?"

"She disappeared. Fifteen years ago." Nearly to the day, but Maya didn't need to know that. "Her body was never found, but... Have you ever heard of Raiden Martin?"

Maya looked up from the phone. "The vampire serial killer?"

I nodded. "He claims she was one of his victims." Then I shrugged. "He might be lying — he's manipulative, and he has his own reasons for saying what he does — but even if he is, we're pretty sure she's been dead all this time. She never would have run away and stayed silent forever."

We both watched as two boats sculled down the river, the muscles on the rowers' arms and legs straining as they raced. Behind them, a bright red tour boat cruised slowly, the recorded spiel incomprehensible at this distance. The air tasted of popcorn and peppermint. Next to me, Maya hugged her backpack and jiggled one leg.

Circling back to the original question, I said, "Our dad didn't handle things well. Not that there's any *good* way, but he just sort of checked out. Then he and my mom split up and I didn't see him much. If I had to guess, I remind him of what happened to Julie, so he's just pretending I don't exist."

"That's a total asshole move."

Her words made me laugh, because of the raw truth and the incongruity of the swearing coming from a pre-teen. "Yeah. But I don't think it was intentional. It was just the only way he could cope."

"Even so."

The tour boat passed in front of us, and now I could catch phrases. "...on the left is another famous building known as The Vault..." Everyone seated on the deck turned to take pictures.

I twisted to look at Maya, curious about her as a person for the first time. "You make that ward on the bicycle in your front yard?"

She ducked her head and mumbled, "It's just a stupid thing I wanted to try. Not like what *you* do."

"Not me," I protested. "I focused on magic theory in school, but I can't do anything. That was Julie's thing."

"But you work at the FBME." She was frowning again.

"I do. Most of the time I sit in the basement and document evidence that's part of a case. I don't need to have any magic for that."

"But when you came to our place, you were working with a vampire."

"Yeah. It's been a weird week." My phone rang before I could say anything else. "Speak of the devil." I hit the button to connect the call. "Hey, Bowers."

"Where are you?"

"Outside, watching river traffic. With my sister."

"Oh."

In the ensuing silence between Simon and me, Maya said, "Tell him to come out here. I want to meet him."

"If you have time, Maya wants to meet you," I repeated into the phone. It felt a bit like I was bribing my sister so she would like me, but I wasn't above that. Besides, letting her meet a real live vampire was the only present I could afford.

"Be down in a minute." The call disconnected and I put my phone away.

At Maya's questioning look, I said, "He's coming outside." It finally occurred to me it was mid-day on Tuesday. "Shouldn't you be in school right now?"

Her lip curled. "Shouldn't *you* be working?"

And just like that, all the credit I'd gotten for inviting a vampire to meet her vanished like smoke. Maya's phone rang then, and she declined the call without looking at it. Maybe I was just a magical evidence technician, but even I could see the signs that there was more going on here than my sister just deciding to meet me on a whim.

"You're not going to get me in trouble for contributing to the delinquency of a minor, are you?" I'd meant it as a joke, but she rolled her eyes and went back to staring at the river.

Fine. We both had a lot to process.

I checked over my shoulder and was relieved to see Simon striding toward us. Though I tried not to look like I was fleeing the scene of a crime, Simon's left eyebrow went up at my speed as I walked toward him with Maya.

Once I'd performed the introductions, he said, "No school today?"

It was the exact same question I'd asked. But instead of giving Simon the cold shoulder, Maya shrugged. "I got suspended."

As I watched, bemused, she explained. "They *say* there's a rule about no spells at school, but it only applies to some people. Kerry and Isobel have been putting shockers on my chair in the middle of class all year, but the *one* time I do something back, I get suspended. And it was mostly an accident."

Simon's gaze met mine and the laugh lines at the corners of his eyes deepened, but his voice remained grave. "What happened?"

"I *meant* to make all of Kerry's books stick to her desk, but I sort of set everything on fire." She shrugged again. "It wasn't a big deal. Nobody got hurt. Kerry can live with short hair for a while."

"Ah."

Maya's shoulders hunched. "Mom says I can't come home until I apologize to Kerry, but screw that. She deserved it. I'll live somewhere else."

I couldn't help closing my eyes when I heard that. This hadn't just been a trip to meet a previously-unknown sister, or even a fact-finding mission to find out if our father was a bigamist. She was angling for a place to stay.

Maybe I was wrong. I'd wait until she asked before explaining that even *I* couldn't stay at my apartment.

Trix would find this all hilarious whenever I had a chance to tell her.

Simon took it all in stride. "How about I give you a tour of The Vault?" As Maya lit up, he said to me, "Meet us in my office in fifteen minutes? I need you to check over the report before I send it out."

As I followed Maya and Simon back to The Vault, I sent my father a text letting him know Maya was safe. No matter how we'd left things between us, I wouldn't leave him wondering about that.

Once inside, Simon and Maya went to the guard station to sign Maya in and get her a visitor's pass, while I went downstairs to grab my notes and a few books. My books had been moved, though they were still stacked on my notepad. When I checked, the Sung & Franklin text was still there.

Hamilton saw me looking. "I nearly got knifed in the kidney, but I protected your stash."

"Appreciate it." Piling up everything I needed to finish the design, I said, "I'll remove the temptation so you don't need to worry about your vital organs."

"Safe except for all the mind control drugs they pump into the city's water supply," he countered. "That's why there are so many dialysis centers."

"Except for that," I agreed. I still couldn't tell if he was serious when he said things like that.

He grabbed another bag out of the overflowing box and tossed it down on the workbench. Then he glanced up. "Hey, if you need someone to create that thing when you're done with the design, let me know. Any excuse to spend some time away from the death-by-a-thousand-pieces-of-evidence-that-have-already-been-looked-at."

"I may take you up on that." The plan was to have someone at the university create the spell, but I hadn't lined anyone up yet. And as a human, Hamilton was unlikely to be part of a conspiracy to allow vampires to cheat death. Besides, he was too focused on imaginary conspiracies to take part in a real one.

"Let me know. I'm cheap."

"And easy, from what I've heard."

"Who's been talking?" His bark of laughter followed me out the door.

THIRTY-FIVE

In Simon's office, I had a glorious ten minutes to myself, which gave me a chance to solidify my design. Without the original spell to look at, I had to rely on my memory of the puzzle lock, but I'd spent hours studying it at the library on Saturday, so I was fairly confident I had the details correct.

In the end, I went with a simple power loop which triggered an audible alarm when the matching puzzle key was nearby. Lenihan's *Tips and Tricks for Perfecting Your Spells* had a duck quack that could be mistaken for a cell phone notification, which seemed a safer route than having a rainbow suddenly appear in the air or the sudden smell of sulfur.

As I redrew my updated design on a clean sheet of paper, my father finally replied to my text. I'd expected an indication of how many minutes it would be before he arrived to collect Maya, and possibly even a thank you for letting him know. Instead, I got a one sentence response. *She's welcome to come home as soon as she apologizes to her classmate.*

Had he changed that much in fifteen years? He'd *never*

responded like that any of the times Julie had run away. My mom would never have let him. Maybe Maya's mother set the tone of his relationship with his youngest daughter.

Simon and Maya were coming into the office, so I flipped my phone over to hide the conversation. Simon rolled another chair in. "Have a seat for a few minutes. Jen and I need to get a little work done, then we can all get lunch."

Maya sat and began paging through *Tips and Tricks*, which gave me a panicked moment as I tried to remember if anything in there would get her into more trouble. Then again, fire was the accidental endpoint of most spell disasters and she'd already lit a girl's desk on fire. There wasn't much else to worry about in that book.

Sitting shoulder to shoulder with Simon, I exchanged my phone for his laptop. Maybe he could convince Maya to apologize. If I was the one who suggested it, my sister would probably go torch the girl's house. Simon read the exchange with my father and raised one eyebrow. "That's not good." He handed back my phone. "Let me work on it."

As I read through Simon's report, I only found two points that needed to be clarified. He'd done a better job than I had of explaining the basics to an audience that didn't know magic theory. Then I added references to five statements and heard him sigh. "It's important," I said. "You can't just say stuff like that without backing it up."

"Nobody is going to read them."

"That's their loss." I pushed the laptop back to him. "Looks good to me. Think it will work?"

"Fingers crossed."

Both of us wanted to get back to normal.

He saved the report and then attached it to the same email list he'd used the day before. When he clicked send, I pushed my chair back. "Now there's no reason to come after us."

Simon's lips thinned. "Yeah. We thought that last time, too."

THE STREETS near The Vault were home to every culinary experience possible, and if my budget had allowed for it, I would have eaten at a different restaurant every day. Simon offered to buy lunch, and I made a list of ten places within two blocks that I'd been meaning to try.

So it was a disappointment when Maya chose a chain restaurant with boneless, over-processed chicken tenders and reconstituted mashed potatoes. Part of me was convinced she'd chosen it purely because she knew how I'd react, but she probably just had a limited palate.

Simon didn't complain, but then again, Simon wasn't planning on eating anything. Plus, he was amused by Maya's strong preference for him over me. Short of me becoming a vampire, I didn't see that changing anytime soon.

As I worked my way through all the different dipping sauces, trying to find one that tasted of something other than high-fructose corn syrup, Simon drew Maya out, asking her questions about her hobbies. Those turned out to be entirely geared toward learning and practicing magic, of which her parents strongly disapproved. They signed her up for robotics camp and coding challenges, and she sent parts flying through the air and accidentally blew up six computers. In their professional lives, Maya's mother retrofitted buildings to withstand earthquakes, and our father contracted with tech firms to optimize their assembly lines.

I got the picture of two engineers shoving their daughter toward STEM activities, to the frustration of everyone involved.

It explained why she'd accidentally set her classmate's desk on fire. (If one believed it *had* been an accident — I had my doubts.) Maya had learned magic from a combination of library books, internet videos, and popular fiction. If her parents continued to deny reality, I hoped they had good property insurance, because — like Julie — Maya showed every sign of becoming a powerful mage. And untrained powerful mages were a danger to everyone around them.

I suppressed a sigh, not allowing myself to be jealous of this pre-teen. If I'd had even a tenth of her magic, my career would have been wildly different. I'd have probably had a tenure-track position, or maybe an industry job that would have paid off my loans the minute I graduated. The Ferugia Project might have come calling years ago.

Instead, I had a job where the first time I'd left the basement something had tried to kill me.

Once Maya and I had finished our meals — this time, I didn't push Simon to eat, because he would have taken it as punishment and rightly so — Simon rested his forearms on the table, carefully avoiding the sticky residue at the corner. "I happen to know someone who can advise you on crafting an excellent apology letter."

My sister had been leaning forward, but now she drew back and folded her arms. "I'm not apologizing to Kerry. She deserved it."

"No." Simon caught her gaze and held it. "At the very least, you frightened her, and that's not okay. Part of growing up is learning the importance of saying you're sorry when you do something that hurts another person, whether you think they deserved it or not."

To my surprise, Maya looked down at the table and stayed silent.

Simon took his victory and moved on. "Like I said, I know someone who can help you craft the perfect apology, and she's going to drop by The Vault to pick you up this afternoon. Assuming you agree to that, between now and then, Jen will tell you what you did wrong to make your spell light the desk on fire."

Raising my eyebrows, I said, "I will?"

"You know, don't you?"

"I have a good idea." The spell Maya had been trying to cast relied on a few advanced techniques. Knowing she was untrained made it easier to guess where she'd gone wrong in such a catastrophic manner.

Now Maya was looking at me, as if reevaluating my place in her world.

Simon held out a hand. "Do we have a deal?"

"Deal." Maya put her hand in his. "But I still think Kerry deserved it."

AS WE WAITED for Maya to return from the restroom, I loaded the trash onto our tray and dumped it in the garbage. "Who is this miracle worker?"

"My mother spent a decade doing criminal law. She's had to guide a lot of clients through writing decent apologies to use during allocution. I sent her a text to see if she had any ideas." He shrugged. "She's the only person I could think of who would know what to do. The other option was to call CPS."

Shoving my hands in my pockets, I said, "Even aside from the whole disaster at school, they *need* to get her into some sort of training. But it won't help if I get in the middle of things."

"My mom will know where to start."

"Thanks." And I could be grateful that he had a great relationship with his mother, while also feeling sad that I'd lost out on that with my own.

THIRTY-SIX

Back in Simon's office, I set Maya practicing a turn-loop spell, which had the advantage of both being tricky and not having fire as a failure state. Even though I wasn't a mage, I knew the curriculum the schools followed. Simon was reading through the mountain of reports generated by other agents, hoping to find anything that would give us a clue to which high-level vampires were involved.

I was working on the final iteration of the spell I'd created, in between trying to find someone unrelated to the FBME who could cast it for me. Of the four people I'd contacted, two no longer lived in Floodmouth, one was on vacation in Italy, and one was sitting by his dying grand-mother's bedside. Jun had offered to create the spell anyhow, if I could bring everything he needed to the hospice, but I told him not to worry about it. I'd find someone else.

Across the room, Maya ripped up another sheet of paper. The turn-loop spell was meant to be attached to something flat, like paper or stone, and the floor around her was littered with her attempts. "It keeps collapsing before I can finish it," she said, her voice perilously close to a whine.

"Because you're not bracing the first turn correctly," I replied. "And that's exactly what happened when you set the desk on fire." Leaning over to point at the textbook, I tapped my pen on the Mayhew lines near the start of the design. "Don't ignore these. They aren't just for decoration."

That was the problem with learning things from random videos instead of following a curriculum that built up from zero. Teaching spells often had unnecessary elements, but if you got in the habit of ignoring anything that looked difficult, bad things could — and did — happen. Mayhew lines seemed unnecessary and often were... until some later part of the spell added stress to the initial structure. Maya had gotten around her sloppy casting by using extra power. The results were predictable. And flammable.

Leaning back in the chair, I stared at my contact list. The four people I'd talked to were the ones I trusted to have my back, no matter what. If we'd had more time, I'd have waited until one of them was available. But this was something that needed to be done now.

Did I trust my dissertation advisor with something like this? All her decisions, from whom to hire in her lab to which gym to exercise in, came down to funding and publishing, though those were often the same thing — without constant publications, her grants would dry up. If someone offered her enough money to create spells for illicit vampire mages, she would sign the contract before the paper fully emerged from the printer.

That was the trouble with academia. It was nearly impossible to exist without compromising your ethics in *some* way.

Meanwhile, Hamilton had offered to help. He wasn't

particularly cozy with the vampires, *and* this was the type of conspiracy he'd be warning everyone about if he'd heard anything. So he was probably the safer choice. Plus, Hamilton wouldn't spend the entire conversation making snide remarks about all the time and effort he'd wasted on me, just to have me sell out in the end.

Decision made, I shoved all my scrap paper into a pile, then picked up the notebook holding my final design. "You okay if I go down to the basement for a bit?"

Simon looked up, exchanged a glance with Maya, and then nodded. "We'll try to keep from destroying the Bureau while you're gone."

Since he was the one who had signed my sister in to the building after lunch, she was his problem.

Downstairs, Hamilton was typing listlessly, but he perked up when he saw me. "Tell me you're here to take care of some of these," he said, backhanding the box still half-full of plastic evidence bags. "The boredom is killing me."

Swapping my open notebook for the box, I said, "I'll work on these if you can make two copies of that." One copy for Bowers and another for Salt, the only two vampires I was sure I could trust. I could have had him make a third for me, but I was only near vampires when Bowers was around, so there was no point.

Hamilton frowned as he examined my diagram. "You have anything I can use to test the final product?"

"Nope. You'll just have to get it right the first time."

"So demanding. Do I at least get some decent coffee out of this deal?"

"For you, Hamilton, anything. What do you want?"

After I'd taken his order, and then the orders of all our

coworkers who found out I was heading to the coffee cart, I left him to it.

Thirty minutes later, he was still working, so I set his coffee on a spot clear of the magic swirling around his bench and settled in to examine the evidence.

EXAMINED IS *a first edition mass market paperback titled* The Scandals of Kiley Rae *by Annabelle Christina. There are no additional markings or notes. A receipt for the purchase of the book dated January 15th was found between pages 152 and 153. Condition of the spine is consistent with the receipt being used as a bookmark. No magical residue detected. Minor damage to cover consistent with being carried in the purse where it was discovered.*

Blowing out a long breath, I shoved the book back into the evidence bag, sealed it, and scribbled my initials and the date on the log sheet. Then it went into the box containing the processed items. "Stop malingering over there, Hamilton. You just missed out on a chance to read some really filthy sex scenes."

His head shot up. "Really?"

I shrugged. "Now you'll never know, will you?" It had been almost an hour, and he was still working on the second copy. My spell wasn't *that* complicated — he was probably dragging it out so I'd get more of his work done. Still, it was hard to complain that he was taking too long to do this favor for me. "You want me to leave the second book for you?" I held up the bag with another dog-eared paperback showing a naked male torso on the front and a wolf's silhouette in front of a full moon. "*Pack Me In, Pack Me Out,*" I read from the cover. "Apparently it's a werewolf romance, not a guide to hiking."

He stood up and slapped two small squares of cardstock on my workbench, then grabbed the paperback. "Gimme that." As he walked back to his desk, he gave a delighted laugh. "I thought you were making the title up."

"As if I would ever lie to you." The box, with substantially fewer items remaining, went back onto his desk with a thud. "Thanks for this," I said, holding up the spells as I walked to the door.

Already flipping through the book, Hamilton just grunted an acknowledgement, and I grinned all the way to the elevator.

THOUGH I HADN'T EXPECTED the spell to trigger on anyone in The Vault — the vampires I normally came into contact with were unlikely to be high in a secret organization — it was a relief to get back to Simon's office without hearing the duck quack that would warn me about a power-eating vampire nearby.

The first thing I noticed was the lack of a teenager. "Where's Maya?" Surely Simon wouldn't be naïve enough to let my sister wander The Vault unsupervised.

Looking up from his computer, Simon said, "My mother took her back to her office."

"She has fire insurance, right?" Before he could answer, I slid one spell across the desk to him. "It should fit under your phone case."

He studied the card. "How close do I have to get?"

"About three feet." It had taken me a while to decide on the distance. Too limited and we risked nobody getting close enough. Too far and it would be impossible to tell which person it had alerted on. Plus, the larger the area it covered, the more power it would burn. Even at three feet, we would have to renew the spell in a week.

His left eyebrow quirked up. "And it *quacks*."

Lenihan's *Tips and Tricks for Perfecting Your Spells* had a cheap binding, so I placed it carefully on the desk in front of him. "Feel free to look through the chapter on common alerts and pick out something you like better for next time. Maybe a loud burp? Or you can explain why everything suddenly smells like skunk." After multiple semesters spent grading third-year projects, I was familiar with the common variants. We had rules in the lab classes, but there was always one student who tried to be funny.

He held up his hands in surrender. "I was just checking. Quacking is fine."

"Trust me, quacking really is the best option." Retrieving *Tips and Tricks*, I placed it on my stack of texts. "If it works at all," I added as an afterthought. "We don't have any way to test this thing."

He shrugged his unconcern. "It's a long shot, anyhow. We know there must be someone in Floodmouth who's siphoning energy, but the chances of Salt or me getting within three feet are pretty low. Even if we do, we would still need to build a case. We'll get there without it. It just might take a little longer."

And in the meantime... "At some point, it would be nice if I could go home again." If it took too much longer, Trix might move back to the apartment before it was safe. She'd already sent me a text asking if I knew dinosaurs had feathers, which was her subtle way of pointing out that staying at Amar's place was getting old. I'd owe her a case of margarita mix *and* a free pass on the chore wheel by the time this was over.

"At least wait until McMair and Sharpe are in custody." Simon picked up the second spell card and stood. "I'll give this to Salt and see when that might happen."

THIRTY-SEVEN

Spending the rest of the afternoon re-examining evidence made me feel a little less guilty about all the extra work dumped on my coworkers while I'd been doing other things. By the time Simon messaged to say he was going back to Silver Edge for the night, I'd made a respectable dent in the pile and learned almost nothing new.

There had been multiple items of jewelry processed, but only a few could have been used to hold a spell. None were cheesy ornaments glued to an aluminum band, but I did find a broken rhinestone necklace, the metal links torn apart. Though there was no hint of magic, salt sparkled in the hollow where the rhinestones had been inexpertly attached. Unless McMair and Sharpe had unfettered access to the evidence locker, they weren't the only problems in Seattle.

That was my cue to leave. If I stayed any longer, I'd give in and eat the pepperoni pizza cooling on Hamilton's work-bench. It always amazed me that he avoided the sports drinks provided during his ultramarathons because he was convinced they sensitized him to magical interference, but he would eat the cheapest pizza available in Floodmouth, which contained ingredients even *I* side-eyed. Unfortunately, after a few days with the amenities of Silver Edge, my standards had risen. Going back to my own cooking — or rather, heating cheap frozen meals — would be rough.

When he heard me collecting my things, Hamilton looked up. "Skating off early?"

"It's almost seven," I said defensively. "What are *you* doing here still?" Normally, he timed his departure so he'd put in eight hours, not a minute more or less. Hamilton didn't *do* overtime.

"Taking a half-day tomorrow, so I need to get my hours in now." He gave a languid wave. "Enjoy your beauty sleep."

"I will." I glanced in the box to see how much was left. "If you work hard enough, you can probably finish all those in an hour." Patting him on the shoulder, I added, "I believe in you." It was a phrase that had been repeated ad nauseam during our last team building workshop, so it had become a standard sarcastic comment. Our shared hatred of team building had brought the basement together.

Then I dodged the pen he threw at me and left.

SIMON and I had just reached the Silver Edge lobby when his phone buzzed with a text. He read it and gave a tiny smile. "My mother is taking Maya to dinner at the Magic Hatter as a reward for successfully navigating the apology."

"Your mother is a miracle worker." Granted, the Magic Hatter, a restaurant that combined food and magic and had reservations six months out, was a potent bribe, but I was still impressed. "Thank her for me. I owe her." Now I could stop wondering if it would be safer to take Maya to my apartment or trust her to find other accommodations. Silver Edge wasn't an option.

Delia Tarragona stood by the elevator, wearing a black velvet dress with a blue cape. "Jen! And Simon! How are my two favorite federal agents this evening?"

Simon dipped his head in greeting as I answered, "Well, thank you." Seeing her reminded me of the job offer I'd turned down because of this whole situation. My mood dipped. But surely another opportunity would come up in the future. Maybe not at the Ferugia Project, but there were other places to work. Pushing my regrets down, I smiled. "You look like you're off to an event."

"*La Bohème.* Hopefully, I'll get to enjoy the singing this time and not have to spend the entire first act in the foyer discussing changes the foundation needs before supporting a bill." The elevator opened, and we followed her on.

"Your last chance to see..." I paused, trying to remember the name she'd told me when we'd gone for coffee.

"Attilio Pagano, yes! How clever of you to remember." She pressed the button for the fourth floor and waited with her hand near the controls.

"Three," I said, and she pushed the button. "I love that cape."

As we glided upward, I almost managed to forget I was in an elevator with two vampires.

Delia smoothed the fabric. "It's very dashing, isn't it? It took me years to build up the confidence to dress the way I wanted, and now it feels like I wasted so much time." She shook one finger at me in mock seriousness. "Take my advice. Don't let anyone tell you who you are."

"I'll do my best."

The elevator door slid open. As Delia shifted so we could pass by, my bag erupted in a prolonged farting noise, so loud that it echoed from the metal roof of the elevator cab. No human anatomy could have produced that volume, but it still made me want to drop through the floor in embarrassment.

I knew that exact sound. College students found it as irresistible as twelve-year-olds, and *Tips and Tricks* helped them bring it to life.

Delia burst into delighted laughter as she turned to look at me. "You should see your face, my dear!" As the doors closed to take her to the next floor, I could still hear her laughing.

When I looked at Simon, he was doing his best to hide a smile. "You were supposed to be *watching* her," I said, pulling my bag to the front so I could dig through it to find whatever spell on a timer Maya had hidden inside.

"Sorry." He almost looked contrite, though his lips quivered.

"It's all fun and games until someone's jacket catches fire," I groused as I rummaged through my bag. Salt had a point about using a bag that zipped closed, though it wouldn't have helped in this case, since my sister clearly wasn't being monitored when Simon was there.

"You have to admit, it's a little funny." Simon's fingers were tapping on his phone.

"That better not be a message to your mother to tell her how hilarious it was." There. At the bottom of the bag was a slip of paper that I hadn't put there. I grabbed it and followed Simon into our temporary office.

But the more I thought about it, the more impressed I was. Timing spells were notoriously tricky to get right, the difference between one minute and one day a matter of arcs and energy. If Maya really had been trying to time it to go off this evening, she had more control than I'd thought.

Then I looked at the spell on the slip of paper and froze.

This wasn't a simple sound after a delay. Maya had cast *my* spell to find the vampire with the other half of the puzzle lock.

And Delia had triggered it.

THIRTY-EIGHT

I stared at the paper, still not believing the evidence in front of me. "Maya cast my finding spell. It's *Delia*."

Simon's eyes met mine for a long moment. Then he took his phone from his pocket, removed the case, and picked up the card I'd given him before we'd left The Vault. "This one didn't go off."

I took it from him and sat down at the table, my hands shaky from adrenaline. "Maybe Maya made a mistake."

That would be the simplest explanation. She was an amateur with no training. The chance she'd messed up a line and somehow made it sensitive to an altogether different trigger was high.

Simon nodded toward the slip of paper. "Be sure. We know where Delia will be tonight, so let's not jump the gun."

But as I traced each line of power on the scrap of paper, I couldn't find her error. The audible portion of the spell was completely different, of course — a high volume fart instead of the muted quack I'd chosen — but I could safely ignore that part.

Nothing. I spent nearly half an hour and couldn't find the error in Maya's work. As much as I needed Delia not to be involved, my sister's spell had activated. So why hadn't the one Simon carried?

It took another thirty minutes to find the fault with Hamilton's casting, a matter of two lines crossed that changed the entire puzzle lock. It would have been a perfectly plausible mistake for Maya to make, but Hamilton was a professional, with decades of experience. Hamilton would have found it himself if he'd checked over his spell, but he never put any more effort into his work than he had to. I'd been an idiot to entrust him with something this important.

I lifted my head. "Maya's is right. It's definitely Delia."

Simon and I looked at each other for a long moment.

"I'll call Salt," he said.

While he told Supervisory Agent Salt that Delia appeared to have the other half of the puzzle lock on her person, I stared at the two spells in front of me. Maya's was full of minor wobbles and energy fluctuations, though technically accurate; if I'd had her in my advanced spell construction class, I'd have sent her back a level for remedial work. In contrast, Hamilton's casting was all controlled lines and perfect angles, just as I expected from someone working in the field.

Even the paper reflected their expertise: Maya's was a scrap roughly torn from a larger piece — warping of the surface from pulling on it could cause the whole spell to fail. Hamilton had used a pre-cut rectangle guaranteed free of defects.

Simon held the phone to one side. "Who cast the spell?" he asked, pointing at the neat rectangle in front of me.

Hamilton had been doing me a favor. To repay him by

getting him in trouble with Salt for a simple mistake would be a truly asshole-level maneuver — *if* it had been a mistake. If it hadn't been, he was part of the conspiracy, with access to our computer systems and the entire evidence locker.

We couldn't take that chance.

"Hamilton." If I was wrong about this, no amount of expensive coffee from the cart across the square would repair our relationship.

Simon repeated the name into his phone, listened for a few seconds, then hung up. "She'll call back in a couple minutes. She's in the middle of something."

"Scooping up McMair and Sharpe?" Unable to sit still, I got up and walked over to the window overlooking the pavement. The usual evening chaos of the Butcher District had started, and crowds of people clogged the street. If I dropped Hamilton in the middle of everything and he'd made an honest mistake, I'd never live it down. But that would be better than the alternative, that the only person who'd welcomed me to The Vault had been involved with the group trying to kill me.

A weight lodged in my chest. How could *Delia* be involved?

"Let's hope," Simon said, referring to the Seattle agents. "Probably something related to that, anyhow." He eyed me speculatively. "When's the last time you ate something?"

"About an hour before you let the little felon stow a spell in my bag." I shook my head. "Promise me you'll never tell my sister her spell helped crack the case. She's already impossible to be around."

He smiled, then picked up the wall phone. "It might be a long night. I'll have them send up food. And coffee."

"Thanks." I forced myself to sit down, then gave up and resumed pacing. Even after I'd designed the spell today, I hadn't expected results so soon. My timeline had involved getting the spell redone in a week, and maybe again another week after that. Having it go off just hours later meant I hadn't envisioned the next steps.

Simon finished talking to the front desk, sat down, and opened his laptop while I paced.

Maybe having it go off so quickly made some sense. We knew the vampires gaining strength from the spell were powerful enough to have secretly created vampire mages. Silver Edge was the most exclusive vampire club in Floodmouth. This was the obvious place to look.

How many *other* vampires in the club would set off the spell? Were we safe?

I could drive myself crazy thinking about this while we waited to hear about the Seattle team's apprehension, so I switched tracks. "How can you afford Silver Edge on an FBME salary?"

He looked up and I could almost see his brain bookmarking what he'd been reading so he could switch gears. "I can't. My parents pay for it."

"Nice."

Though I hadn't meant it as a rebuke, he shrugged. "It isn't entirely for my sake, though I appreciate it. With Silver Edge, nothing scandalous is likely to happen, and if it did, there wouldn't be videos of it on the internet ten minutes later." My blank look must have clued him in. "You *do* know my father is a US senator, don't you?"

"Oh." How had we spent five days together without that coming up? "Really?"

He huffed a laugh. "I thought the entire building knew. It certainly gets brought up enough at work."

"The basement is its own little world," I said, after thinking about it for a second. "I don't think the upstairs gossip makes it to us." Not being clued in on the drama sounded better than admitting the technicians didn't care what the vampires did, though the latter was closer to the truth.

"Huh. That would explain it. I didn't even know there were people who *worked* in the basement until last week."

"That interdepartmental team building is really going great, isn't it?" I dropped into my chair. "So, is that how you became a vampire so quickly?" Right after I said the words, I realized what a rude question it was. No choice but to plow ahead. "It's just that Che mentioned that you only recently found out about the... illness." For the life of me, I couldn't remember the name Che had used. "And I know it usually takes about five years for the application to go through, so... But I guess having a father in the Senate explains things." Babbling was not helping my case at all. I shut my mouth with a snap.

He kept his gaze on me, as if trying to make up his mind about something as the silence stretched. Finally, he said, "That wasn't why."

Clearly, this was something he didn't normally talk about. I hadn't intended to force him into a confession. "Sorry. I didn't mean to pry. Forget I said anything."

"No, this is something that could potentially come up in the future, especially with this case." He took a deep breath and let it out. "My biological father is a vampire on the council. He and my mother broke up while she was pregnant with me. It wasn't until I became ill that she thought to track him down to find out about his family's medical history. Once he found out I was ill... well, let's just say my application was fast-tracked."

"Oh." It seemed like I needed to say something else since I'd brought it up. "Have you met him?"

"Once. I don't think we'll ever be close, but he *did* save my life, so I can't complain."

I'd finally caught up to what he'd said. "You don't think *he* has anything to do with this, do you?"

"No, because I'm fairly sure he has someone keeping track of what I do. If he wanted me off this case, he would have had me transferred, not killed."

Before I could respond to that, Simon's phone rang. "This is Bowers," he answered.

Work, then, not personal. Thank god. That meant we had an excuse to abandon this increasingly awkward conversation.

Simon tensed. "Okay, then we should..." He paused while waiting for the other person to speak. "The opera." He waited again. "Right. We'll meet you there."

I was already back on my feet. "What happened?"

"Seattle botched the pickup. McMair and Sharpe are in the wind. We have to assume everyone involved has been warned. Salt is heading over to pick up Tarragona before she disappears. Let's go."

THIRTY-NINE

Part sculpture, part mid-twentieth-century municipal boast, the Floodmouth Opera House took advantage of its waterfront location with a magnificent glass wall facing the ocean, connected to a long rectangle with its famous three waves in stainless steel plating on the top. In the daylight, the glare was blinding, but at night, the reflected city lights were beautiful.

We'd arrived after the start of the fourth act, forcing Salt to threaten an usher until the kid showed us to the box where Delia was sitting. Salt pushed the door open just enough to see that Delia was inside and that there wasn't another exit. Then we waited in the hallway for the performance to finish, listening through the nearly soundproofed doors as Mimi got on with dying in Italian.

"Your job," Salt told me in a low voice, "is to record everyone who looks like they might be thinking about coming over to talk to her as we leave. Discreetly," she added. "There's a chance we'll be able to connect some dots later."

Relieved to have a reason for being there, I nodded and

got my phone ready. Simon had insisted I come along, but it wasn't as if I could do anything useful during an arrest. Analyzing a spell and determining its likely country of origin wasn't exactly a high-stakes-moment skill.

We waited in the quiet hallway, the orchestra barely audible through the doors. Simon's phone buzzed with a new text. He angled the screen so I could see the message from his mother saying my sister had returned home.

The muscles in my neck relaxed. This might be only a temporary win — Maya's parents needed to get her training, and soon — but at least I knew she wasn't sleeping on the streets tonight. "Thank her for me, would you?"

Salt glanced up from her phone. "What's that?"

I waved a hand, hoping she wouldn't press for details. "Just some family drama. It's sorted out for the moment."

The supervisory agent held my gaze for an uncomfortable moment. "As long as it doesn't impact the Bureau, I don't care. But the minute it does, I need to know. Got it?"

I nodded. In truth, I wasn't sure where this particular problem landed as far as the Bureau was concerned, but I wasn't getting into it tonight.

"Good." A wave of applause sounded from the theater and she put her phone away. "It's time. Let's go."

The cheering hit me like a wall when Salt opened the door. Onstage, the cast held hands and bowed. Flowers rained down on the stage. Delia looked up as Salt stepped forward to stand by her side. The other three people in the box expressed a range of surprise and confusion, but only the silver-haired man seated next to Delia looked like he was objecting. I made sure to capture his face in my recording. Delia put a hand on his arm and spoke quietly. Whatever she'd said, he still wasn't happy, but he stopped protesting.

Delia stood, settled her cape around her shoulders, and walked toward the door with Salt on one side and Bowers on the other. When she saw me, a wrinkle formed between her brows, but it was quickly smoothed away. She stopped at the threshold where I waited. "It was that spell in the elevator, wasn't it? I should have known." She made a small sound. "But if I had, I would have missed a truly magnificent performance. On the whole, I think it was worth it." She turned her head to look at Salt. "I assume it was your decision to wait until the end? Thank you."

Then she swept by me, head held high, as if the two FBME agents were escorts meant to protect her.

AN HOUR LATER, Simon and I were in his office at The Vault, watching via a remote feed as Salt and Deputy Director Diego Bowdey questioned Delia. If I'd needed any confirmation that this case was important, Bowdey's presence in the building would have removed all doubt. In the six months I'd been working there, he'd been in The Vault twice, both times on scheduled visits during working hours for meetings and award presentations. But watching him and Salt together, it was obvious they knew each other well.

All of Delia's jewelry had been removed and placed in the safe in Salt's office — not the evidence vault. Hopefully tomorrow I'd have a chance to examine everything, but Salt wouldn't let anybody touch anything unless she was there in person.

Next to me, Simon was researching public records and looking through Hamilton's social media. Salt had already sent a team to watch his apartment, just to make sure he didn't disappear if he *was* involved in all this, but so far, the place was empty. He'd left The Vault two hours ago. Without going inside his rooms, the team couldn't tell if he'd fled, or he was just out late.

In the interview room, Delia was saying, "It's no good asking me for names." So far, she hadn't denied anything, though she also hadn't given any useful specifics. "They've put spells in place to prevent that. My heart would stop if I tried to tell you."

"She didn't ask for a lawyer," Simon said, frowning as he rubbed his thumbnail against his lower lip. "Something's not right."

I kicked off my shoes so I could sit cross-legged in the chair. Not dignified, but it was late. On the desk in front of me, I was tracing the lines of the spell Salt had been carrying. Like the copy I'd handed to Simon, it hadn't alerted when Delia was near, and I found the same modification. I yawned. "Same thing on this one." Dropping my hands, I pushed the card away. "But I can't swear it wasn't an honest mistake that he repeated." I really didn't want Hamilton to be involved with this.

On the monitor, Salt tapped her pen against the desk. "Where are the vampire mages?"

Weirdly, Delia looked *proud*, of all things. "Jennifer Perkins figured it out, didn't she? I *told* them we should hire her, but at the last minute, they got cold feet. What a wasted opportunity." She blew out a breath and gestured to her surroundings. "And look where it got us. By the time I convinced them I had been right all along, it was too late."

No lie — it was an ego boost to hear her say that. *The bad guys knew me by name!* Probably I needed to find another therapist.

"Where?" Salt repeated.

"Can't tell you," Delia said. "And truthfully, I don't

know where they are now. I visited once... No, I can't say more about that without triggering the spell. But they moved them after I visited anyhow, so it wouldn't do you any good."

Simon clicked through to another website. "Hamilton plays a lot of poker. Did you know that?"

Left unsaid was that a gambling problem made the player vulnerable to blackmail and other subversion. It was something they covered during hiring and orientation. But even if Hamilton had a problem with gambling, it still didn't *prove* anything. "Mostly we just insult each other and he tells me about a bunch of conspiracy theories. Maybe he's playing poker now."

I was realizing that I knew almost nothing about Hamilton. A week ago, I would have said he was the closest thing I had to a friend at work.

On the screen, Salt put down her pen and leaned back. "Why didn't you run? You must have been notified — there was a big enough leak that the Seattle agents escaped. But you still went to the opera."

"It was Attilio Pagano." Delia looked between her two interviewers and sighed at their lack of reaction. "You wouldn't understand. And I was told the finding spell had been temporarily neutralized." She looked straight at the camera. "To be clear, I knew nothing about the attempts to kill Jennifer Perkins and Simon Bowers until after the fact."

"She really seems to like you," Simon commented.

"Doesn't everyone?" My stomach growled. We'd left Silver Edge before the food arrived, and hunger was catching up with me. "I need to get something to eat. You want anything? Ha ha, just kidding."

"Hilarious. I can get something delivered, if you want. My treat."

"Nah." I shoved my shoes back on and stood. Accepting all the perks of Silver Edge while I was hiding from assassins was one thing. Having Simon pay for stuff when we were at work was another. It seemed like a bad precedent to set, especially now that the people trying to kill us had bigger problems. And I needed a few minutes alone to clear my head. "I'll just grab something from one of the carts on the square. Let me know if Delia says anything useful while I'm gone."

Except I was pretty sure she'd already given us the answer, at least as far as Hamilton was concerned. What else could she have meant about the spell being temporarily neutralized? I watched the floor indicator in the elevator count down as I wondered how I'd completely missed Hamilton's involvement.

It wasn't hard to find the answer. After planning my whole life around academia for so many years, this job had just been a stopgap to keep a roof over my head. I'd done the work, but I'd treated it as a temporary thing. I hadn't bothered to really get to know anyone here, not even Hamilton.

But it wasn't as if academia would suddenly welcome me back with open arms. And the longer I stayed away, the more I realized how messed up that environment had been. Maybe it was time to stop mourning my old life and start looking forward to what came next.

FORTY

After I went outside, I had to dodge commuters on bicycles, tourists taking pictures of the river lights, and a party bike holding six inebriated seniors in swimsuits and feather boas, but I finally made it to the falafel cart next to the river bus stop. That was one of the best parts of living in Floodmouth — no matter how late you stayed out at night, there was always someplace to eat.

The falafel wrap with yogurt sauce was overcooked, overpriced, and tasted like heaven. Long experience had taught me that walking while eating one of these would leave me trying to clean sauce from my shirt, so I leaned against the railing and watched the traffic on the river as I ate.

A private water taxi zipped by, well over the speed limit; I hoped their fare was willing to pay the fine. Based on the sirens, the river patrol had already been alerted. Then a rental paddleboat came into view, and I understood why the taxi hadn't been worried. Never meant to be on the river at night, the paddleboat had no lights. If the drunken idiots on board were lucky, the river patrol would pull them off the water before another boat crashed into them. I double-checked the location of the nearest orange lifebuoy, just in case.

But the show was over before I'd finished eating, concluding with the arrival of the river patrol, blue lights flashing. In five minutes, they'd taken custody of the laughing occupants and hitched the paddleboat in tow. When the revelers sobered up, they wouldn't be laughing. The city took river safety seriously, and unlit watercraft were major hazards. Plus, the paddleboat was almost certainly stolen. The culprits would be lucky to only lose a year of weekends to community service.

As soon as the patrol boat pulled away, paddleboat bobbing in its wake, the river bus drew up to the dock. There was the usual confusion of passengers attempting to board while others tried to leave and I waited for the crowds to move out of the way so I could get back to The Vault.

Then I saw Hamilton.

He was seated on the bow deck facing the opposite bank, arms around an overstuffed backpack on his lap. With his hood up over his ball cap, I might not have recognized him if I hadn't seen that sweatshirt and hat combo before.

On any other day, I would have assumed he was going home. But now I knew where he lived — he was headed in the wrong direction.

Calling Simon was the only thing I could think of doing. "Hamilton's here!" I whispered as soon as he answered. "He's on the bus going upriver." Shuffling behind the people waiting to board, I peeked around the man in front of me so I could keep my eyes on my colleague. "What do you want me to do?"

"He's not going towards home," Simon noted. "Has he seen you?"

"No."

"Okay." From the sound of things, Simon was running. "Follow him. I'll let Salt know what's going on. We'll get a team to pull him off in a few stops. Don't let him see you." He disconnected.

The river bus was only a quarter full when I followed everyone on, so I was able to find a spot to stand where I could see Hamilton, yet still be far enough away that he wouldn't notice me. My heart skipped every time he moved, which was ridiculous. It wasn't as if I was in any danger. This was a public place. We didn't even know for sure he was involved. And even if he was, he didn't know that *I* knew. There was no reason I couldn't sit next to him and strike up a conversation, aside from my face immediately giving everything away.

The river bus had spells for traction on the deck, hull strength, and general floatation. Running into the paddle-boat probably wouldn't have damaged it. As we cut through the night air, I studied the designs, looking for anything interesting, but they were standard commercial spells. Still, the practice soothed my raw nerves.

At the next stop, I tensed, ready to jump off at the last minute if Hamilton exited, but he stayed put. The backpack was interesting. It was the same one he brought to work when he rode his bicycle, but I'd never seen it more than half full. With anyone else, it would hold a change of clothes or a few books, but with Hamilton it was unlikely to be anything so mundane. It might be the spells against acci-dental teleportation that he'd been developing for the past five years. Or his life savings in small denominations. No, wait, if it was his life savings, it would probably be in gold bullion. Hamilton had expressed many thoughts about the dollar and the gold standard.

After loading more passengers, the boat crept away from the dock. A few people glanced at the water ahead to see if there were smaller craft we were trying to avoid. One man checked his watch impatiently. Our slower speed was probably the FBME buying time to get a team in place upriver. I rubbed my arms to stay warm and politely turned down the offer of a seat inside the covered area.

My phone rang. Simon. I stabbed the button so it would stop ringing before Hamilton turned to check. "Please tell me you're close. I'm freezing out here."

"We're setting up at the Carter Street stop. How's he acting?"

In another two blocks, this would be over. "He hasn't moved since I got on."

"Good. Stay alert."

Simon hung up before I could ask what that even meant. Surely he wasn't expecting me to *do* anything during the arrest. My skills in citing references and researching spell origins wouldn't be much use this evening. Maybe I would look into taking a self-defense class when all this was over, just in case I needed to wrestle with something smaller than a pterodactyl. Tonight, I planned to stand back and watch the professionals do their thing.

Then it all fell apart.

FORTY-ONE

The man who'd been glancing at his watch waved to catch the pilot's attention. "Hey! Is there a reason we're going so slow? I have an appointment."

"Come *on*," I muttered in disbelief. "This late at night?" But it didn't matter. Hamilton raised his head and looked at the pilot suspiciously. Then he slipped a hand into his coat pocket and removed a stack of small white rectangles — spells on cardstock.

"Crap." I redialed Simon, but my phone died before the call went through. Around me, I saw all the aimlessly scrolling people look up from their dark phones.

On the banks of the river, the lights shifted to purple. Except it wasn't the lights that had changed — a violet shell of magic surrounded the boat, rising from the hull and covering the space above us. Hamilton had triggered a Gaudin's shield, which would block almost everything. Nobody was boarding or leaving the vessel until the shield was destroyed, unless the FBME had a mage with them.

The only way to get FBME agents *through* a Gaudin's shield was to create a second shield around the agents. The two shields would merge, creating one contiguous space until the spells were separated again. That was one reason the spell wasn't often used for its original purpose — any protection was nullified during a collision with another similarly equipped vehicle.

The mutterings around me gained an edge of panic as even the least able to sense magic realized something strange was happening.

Hamilton stood, activated another card, and slapped it against the pilot's back. A web of silk erupted, enveloping the struggling pilot in a cocoon as I watched. The spell moved so quickly that if Hamilton hadn't pulled his hand back, he would have been incorporated. In twenty seconds, the pilot was no longer visible under the white mass and the shiny outside dried to a matte beige. Hamilton pushed, and the pilot tipped over, landing on the deck where he wriggled. His muffled yells told me he was still able to breathe, at least.

A passenger ran forward to help the pilot, but Hamilton raised his hand. "Stay back!" Then he stepped to the controls and opened the throttle.

With a roar, the boat accelerated to its top speed, and we were thrown backward. One woman would have gone overboard if the Gaudin's shield hadn't prevented it. Another passenger helped her to a seat.

At this rate, it would be a race between Hamilton killing us through his piloting or his spells. Eventually, he'd use the stack of cards in his hand. Then what? Maybe his backpack really was filled with spells. That was a nightmare image. My fellow passengers and I could be hostages for a long time. Without knowing Hamilton's endgame, I couldn't counter him.

Luckily, there were few small craft on the river at night,

and those scattered in front of us, then bobbed in our wake. Harbor patrol was probably already getting complaints from all the vessels moored along the river.

The Carter Street stop approached, and I saw Salt and Bowers standing on the dock. I put one hand to the side, palm up, in a 'what can I do?' gesture as we flew by without stopping.

Before we reached the bridge, the boat jolted, throwing everyone forward. Cries of alarm went up as people struggled to stay upright. I'd been hanging onto the railing, but it was almost torn from my grasp as a woman flew into me. We'd bumped into something, though it unfortunately hadn't slowed us down.

This couldn't go on.

After helping the woman gain her balance, I pulled myself along the rail toward the bow, looking down at the water. Bright yellow planks floated by. We'd run over the paddleboat, either the one the river patrol had towed or a second one. I hoped nobody had been aboard.

Moving along the side of the boat gave me a better look at the Gaudin's shield. It was a fairly solid piece of work, but I suspected there would be weak points where the shield met the hull. Unless Hamilton had taken pains to reinforce the shield from the inside, I could probably find a spot and force enough separation to get the other passengers through, as long as they had somewhere to go. But dropping unprepared into the murky waters of the Flood River after dark sounded like an awful way to die.

The first option had to be talking Hamilton into releasing everyone.

When I was within hearing range, I took one hand from the rail and waved to catch Hamilton's attention. "Hey!"

The rush of the water drowned out his words, but I could read his lips as he said, "What are *you* doing here?"

All the bad guys knew me, which *definitely* shouldn't have been a point of pride. But we had bigger problems at the moment.

"Slow down," I screamed. The boat skipped in the water, and I grabbed the railing next to the wheelhouse. Now I could talk without yelling. "Seriously, Hamilton, you're going to hit something at this rate."

"Relax," he replied, though he eased back a little on the throttle. "The spells on the hull are good, and the shield will protect the rest."

"I think you missed your physics class on the day they talked about momentum." When he frowned in confusion, I tried again. "If we hit something with its own spelled hull, the boats will be okay, but you and I and everyone else on board are going to splatter against the shield as we go from forty miles per hour to a dead stop."

Back when I'd been teaching the basics of spells, I'd had to cover the chapter on unintended consequences. Since physics wasn't required as a pre-requisite, I had an entire sequence of videos showing the bloody interiors of unscratched vehicles. I'd called that lecture *The importance of crumple zones*.

Protection spells weren't as simple as everyone assumed. Momentum was real. Gas diffusion was important if you wanted people to breathe for long. Heat could build up quickly. There were all sorts of ways to kill people while trying to keep them safe.

Hamilton had obviously forgotten the material in that chapter, but he slowed the vessel so we were going at almost the boat's normal speed. "Fine."

"Thank you." I pushed a strand of hair from my eyes. "What's the plan?"

"The *plan*," he echoed, "is to get out of here and not spend the rest of my life in prison."

That seemed like more of a goal than a plan, but he hadn't been paying attention to the career planning video we were supposed to watch before our quarterly reviews. We'd spent that morning making jokes about the idea of planning a career when there was no hope of advancement. It had been the one bright spot in my day, and I'd held onto that feeling when my boss had surprised me with complaints about my lack of communication skills.

"Okay, but how are you going to accomplish that?" I relaxed one hand from my death grip of the railing and pointed to the glow of blue lights staying a constant distance from us. Another pair kept pace behind us. "We already have an escort. At some point, the river won't be deep enough to keep going." Honestly, I'd never considered how far the Flood could be navigated by a river bus, but it had to be a shorter distance than for the smaller patrol boats. "Your best bet would be to stop at a dock near a public teleporter and run in before they catch up."

"As if I'd trust one of those." He shook his head. "The Wisconsin mage council invented the transporter spell. They own a lab that works on DNA sequencing of heritable diseases associated with mages. Coincidence? I don't think so. They're working on ways to change your DNA without anyone noticing."

This was a conspiracy theory I'd heard before. If I didn't head him off, next Hamilton would show me the map of Wisconsin and pictures of the renowned Wisconsin Center for Heritable Diseases.

"Okay, okay, but if not that, then what?"

"I'm going to get off this boat and get out of this damned vampire city, that's what." He yanked the wheel sideways to avoid something in the water, and people in the back cried out. "Did you know they never bothered to tell me it was time to leave? People were getting rounded up this evening, and the first I hear of it is a news alert about missing agents in Seattle. Two years I've been working for those assholes and they couldn't warn me? One text and I would have disappeared without anyone getting hurt." He took his eyes off the river to stare at me. "You're an idiot for trusting a vampire. Especially a vampire whose father is a senator. Do you know how they really select senators?"

Sometimes talking to Hamilton was like pressing buttons on a jukebox with fifteen different rants, all of which were about shadowy cabals who controlled the fate of humanity. All the while, he'd been taking money from a bunch of vampires who wanted to live forever. The irony was too much.

"Okay, but focus here, Hamilton. How are you going to get off the boat? You need to think about turning yourself in before this gets any worse."

His eyes cut to me, then back at the water, almost as if he felt guilty about something.

My stomach dropped. "What are you going to do?"

Instead of answering, he cut back on the throttle and spun the wheel, until we were facing the other direction, then opened the throttle and aimed directly for the two river patrol boats that had been following us. They cut to either side, skipping over our wash. When I looked back, they were turning, but Hamilton was already turning the wheel again and cutting the power.

The boat came to a stop perpendicular to the banks,

blocking part of the waterway. We bobbed in the suddenly quiet night.

Hamilton brushed by me. "Sorry about this, but they have to think I'm dead long enough for me to get out of the city. Witnesses would mess everything up."

He thumbed one of his cards to activate it and dropped it on the deck. When he triggered a second, the purple glow of a personal Gaudin's shield surrounded him. He gave me a quick salute. "It's been nice knowing you." Then he climbed over the rail, his shield merging with the one covering the boat, and dropped to the river. I ran to the side and saw that he'd activated two more spells, a walk-on-water and a see-me-not. The purple aura of the Gaudin's shield was just visible as he inched across the surface of the water toward the steel ladder attached to the bank.

With the patrol boats on the other side of the river bus, Hamilton couldn't be seen by anyone other than all my fellow passengers. *Witnesses would mess everything up*, he'd said. I turned away from the rail and scrabbled on the deck for the card he'd dropped.

FORTY-TWO

The card was laminated to a stiff rectangle of metal, something I'd only seen on spells that were intended to be kept for emergencies. The lamination would keep it from getting wet or torn, and the metal would protect it from folding. If the person who'd designed the bracelet that killed Evan had paid attention to folding issues, I'd never have been here.

But the spell on this card wasn't an eight-hour blanket or an emergency flare. I stared at it while the other passengers began cautiously moving toward the front of the boat. The spell was active, even if it didn't appear to be doing anything, but the modules all ran together. When I designed spells, I left in extra marks to make it easier to reverse engineer. Hamilton was either lazy or he'd aimed for obfuscation.

"Break it down," I muttered. The active section was a timer, of a type popular thirty years ago. The Floyd timer — as it was officially known — had been superseded by the Kwang timer, which was a little trickier to cast, but was more accurate than its predecessor. Internally, I shook my head at Hamilton's shoddy work — absolutely not important now, but still.

Attached to the timer was a module that I couldn't see because the lamination had bubbled up. I angled the card, trying to make out what was underneath. Giving that up for a lost cause, I moved to the last section.

High-temperature fire.

So... Either this had been meant to weld pieces together after assembly, which seemed unlikely, given our circumstances, or... "This is a bomb."

Right afterward, I realized I probably shouldn't have said it so loudly.

The nearest man drew back. "A *bomb?*" I heard the word echo across the deck as the other passengers repeated it. "We have to get out of here!" He ran to the other side of the boat and banged on the shield, yelling to the river patrollers, though I doubted they could hear him. "Help! There's a bomb!"

Hamilton had angled the boat so the authorities couldn't see when he went over the side. But it would only work if the passengers didn't report his escape. And the only way to ensure that was to kill all of us. I checked the timer and saw that it had progressed through half its delay. I had maybe two minutes before it went off, and that only if the delay remained linear. There was a reason nobody used Floyd timers anymore.

I raised my voice to be heard above the hubbub. "Does anyone have a lighter? Or a knife?" If I could get through the plastic, I could destroy the spell by tearing the card apart. "Is there a *mage* on board?"

I heard my questions being loudly repeated by the other passengers, but nobody came forward.

If Julie were still alive, she would have been the perfect

person to take care of this. Just a fraction of her magical ability would have solved this problem. But I'd never had even the smallest spark.

What I *did* have, though, was years of training telling me that the interface between two different spells — like the seam between the Gaudin's shield and the hull strengthener — was always a weak spot. We could probably push them far enough apart to slip through, but only one person at a time. With less than a minute to go, we could send two or three people into the water. Hamilton's secret getaway would be ruined, even if the rest of us died.

But... If I couldn't stop the spell from exploding and I couldn't get everyone off the boat in time, maybe I could keep everyone here and get this slim piece of cardstock *out*.

The port railing where Hamilton had gone through would be the weakest area, so I started there, running my hands over the shield where it touched the magic surrounding the hull. If Hamilton had intended to seal the spells together, he could have strengthened the bottom of the shield and used pressure on the outside to hold it in place. That's what *I* would have done if I'd been using a Gaudin's shield to protect something. Luckily, Hamilton hadn't bothered.

A glance at the card showed the timer was nearly done. If I didn't get the bomb off the boat in the next few seconds... Well, standing next to it would probably be best. Get it over with quickly instead of having a few minutes of panic trapped on the boat watching the fire get closer.

There! The spell warped where I pushed at it. Just a bit, but I didn't need much. Holding the card against that spot, I shoved as hard as I could until the laminated plastic slipped from my fingers.

The card fluttered down toward the water where

Hamilton had landed. I could still see him, a purple outline moving carefully along the thin plane that walk-on-water provided. It was a good spell, as escape spells went, but it had its limitations, requiring excellent balance and concentration. One wrong step and he would fall into the river. Hamilton's ultra-marathon training was helping him tonight.

Then the card slipped under the water, and the river exploded.

FORTY-THREE

The river bus jolted. An alarm went off, and the deck tilted ever so slightly as everyone — including me and the pilot still cocooned on the deck — screamed. The spell on the hull had been *good*, but not rated to withstand a bomb going off in the river next to it. Water rained down and pooled on the shield above us.

We were all trapped on the sinking river bus, the only person who might know how to patch the hull was trapped under a mass of webbing, and I couldn't disable the Gaudin's shield because Hamilton had taken the spell card with him. The boat shifted again. Yes, definitely taking on water. A knot of passengers stood on the stern bashing at the shield with makeshift weapons. It probably wouldn't help, but I couldn't blame them for trying.

I grabbed the nearest passenger, a middle-aged woman who looked less panicked than most. "We might be able to free the pilot by soaking his back in water. Maybe rub at it a little." Hamilton had slapped the spell card between the man's shoulder blades — as long as the paper wasn't laminated, dumping water on it should speed up the spell's disintegration. "Don't drown him."

She opened her backpack and pulled out a thermos. "All I have is tea."

"Even better." The tannins might help.

While she explained to the encased pilot what she was planning, I examined the railing and the adjacent spells. If the boat was taking on water, the hull spell might be weak enough to get through, but unless our evacuation involved swimming in the dark, we'd have to pierce the structure above the water line.

Behind me, loud swearing informed the world that the pilot had been freed and if he ever found out who had done that to him, their days were numbered. The deck tilted a little more.

I pushed at the edge of the two spells again. Maybe we really could get a person through the gap. The longer this went on, the more rescue boats would be in the water around us, so it wouldn't be all that dangerous and —

With a click, the Gaudin's shield disintegrated. The river water that had pooled on the shield after the blast rained down, soaking my hair and shirt. Suddenly, the distant lights were clearer and every phone around me buzzed or beeped as queued messages came through. I checked my phone, but it remained stubbornly dark. One of the spells Hamilton had been throwing around must have damaged it.

I looked over the railing at the water. Hamilton had been knocked sideways by the blast and all his cards had fallen into the river. Though it had taken a few minutes, eventually something in the water reacted with the ink he'd used and his spells fizzled.

With his ultra marathoner's build, Hamilton had negative buoyancy and apparently he'd never learned to swim. He bobbed in the choppy water, clutching an orange life preserver tightly. A river patrol boat with Salt and Bowers aboard pulled my erstwhile friend from the water and slapped null cuffs on him. When Bowers glanced over and saw me, his shoulders relaxed. He gave me a quick nod before turning back to Hamilton.

In a few minutes, our pilot finished slapping the remnants of webbing off and took the helm again. The water bus limped to the nearest dock, where we all rushed onto solid land. By that time, the mages who worked for the transport department had arrived, and they cast spells to plug the hole until it could be repaired. There was a general air of disappointment among the onlookers, who had been hoping for a more dramatic finale, but that wasn't my problem. I walked past them without stopping, letting my wet hair fall forward to shield my face from all the devices recording the scene.

"Miss? Miss, wait!" A police officer, a pale guy young enough to have been in one of my classes at the university, put a hand on my arm to stop me. "The Federal Bureau of Magic Enforcement doesn't want anyone to leave..."

My phone was still dead, the night air was chilly, and I just wanted to get warm and sit somewhere quiet and absorb the fact that two people I'd trusted had been involved in the conspiracy. Some of that must have shown on my face when I turned to face the police officer.

I held up my FBME identification in silence.

He let go of my arm as if burned and took half a step back. "Ah, sorry."

I let the hand holding the identification drop to my side and resumed walking without a word. He'd thought I was a vampire, I realized. No wonder Simon found it easier to socialize in a place like Silver Edge, where nobody drew back in fear.

A block away, I found an open coffeeshop, and bought a mug of tea, carrying it to the corner table so I could watch everything through the windows. A bomb blowing a hole in a river bus would be treated as a terrorist act. With magic involved, the FBME had jurisdiction. Probably I should have stayed there to help. Or not. The streets were overrun with emergency response vehicles and serious people in windbreakers with acronyms in large letters. My place was safe in the basement of The Vault, working with the other evidence technicians. Just not Hamilton.

Ugh. I really was the *worst* judge of character.

I saw a familiar figure walking along the pavement and tried to ignore the flutter in my chest. Had I not just been thinking about what a terrible judge of character I was? Falling for a coworker, especially one who wasn't yet comfortable in his own skin, was just another example.

But even though I might not be able to control my emotions, at least I could make sure Simon never knew about it. So I stayed in my seat, raising one hand to acknowledge him as he walked over.

He slid into the chair opposite me. "At the rate you keep saving people, the Bureau is going to have to give you a plaque or something." He took off his FBME jacket and handed it across the table.

I pulled it on, grateful for the heat. It smelled like vinyl and Simon. "Does that sort of thing come with a cash bonus?"

"Probably just a fancy mug, but it's the thought that counts. You ready to go? I have a car."

Getting to my feet took effort. As we walked, I said, "Do you think they give out staff awards at Silver Edge?

Amanda said she could get me a job there." The car was warm and comfortable and I stopped worrying about getting river water on the cushions when I saw the cleaning spell.

"No idea, but I can ask if you want me to." He bumped the temperature up another two degrees.

"You won't ask," I said around a yawn.

"Probably not," he agreed. We sat in comfortable silence all the way back to The Vault.

THE REST of the night was a blur of interviews and reports, but I got brief glimpses of the other things happening with the case. Hamilton remained far more angry about the vampires leaving him to be caught than he was about me foiling his escape, so he was telling everything he knew. That wasn't really all that much, since he'd been contacted anonymously and been paid in cash, but at least we knew which cases he'd tampered with. *That* was a legal nightmare all in itself, and I was glad I didn't have to handle the fallout.

Hamilton's information, combined with what Delia had given us, confirmed our theories. The vampire mages had created wearable spells meant to treat depression and anxiety, while at the same time harvesting power for vampires wearing the corresponding puzzle keys. Seattle had been the test site, and despite several cases of bracelet-wearing vampires succumbing to the dangerous hunger, they'd expanded to Floodmouth.

Because it worked.

Sick vampires, the ones who couldn't get enough of a boost from feeding on humans, were healthy again. "It doesn't scale, of course," Delia said, "but if you're one of the few benefitting..." She trailed off.

It was the morning after she'd been arrested, and she'd asked to see me. Since Salt thought Delia might let something slip while I was there, she'd had Simon fetch me from his office where I had fallen asleep while finishing my statement. Before I'd been allowed in the room, Salt had drilled in a set of rules which basically came down to one: no matter what happened, I wasn't to get near Delia. If I was worried for my safety, I was to hit the alarm strip that ran around the circumference of the room, and help would be there in seconds.

Delia looked older after a night without sleep. In the harsh lighting of the interview room, I could see all the lines of age that had been hidden at the opera last night. But despite her hands being shackled to the desk, she still had the bearing of the woman who had been a mentor to me.

Salt had given me a list of questions, but I wasn't a trained interviewer and Delia knew it. When I'd tried to direct the conversation, Delia had just smiled and ignored me, as if I was a puppy who wasn't behaving.

I folded my hands in front of me on the table. "Did the job at the Ferugia Project even exist?" The question wasn't on Salt's list, but I had to know.

Delia's eyes were kind. "Did they urgently need someone with your skills? No. When I complained that your life had been endangered, I was told to get you out of town. But you'd have had a place at the project if you'd taken the offer." She shook her head. "You'll see that as a sign that you don't deserve the position, but that's how things work. Some opportunities come along because you know the right person, other offers evaporate due to factors you can't control. And you'd have been brilliant there. You're wasted at the FBME, sitting at a desk and writing reports for court cases that half the time don't go to trial."

It stung to have my work so casually discarded, so I circled back to her. "It didn't bother you that people died?"

"Of course it bothered me. But at first, I didn't make the connection. And when I did..." Her smile was wistful. "Twenty years ago... Even *five* years ago, I would have said that I'd had a good life and when it was my time, I'd go gracefully. But you know, when it actually *is* your time, things look a little different. Cheating death becomes more important than anything or anyone, especially people you've never met. You can look down at me all you want and swear you'd never do the same, but just wait until it's you."

"So no regrets." Nothing she'd said would help us find the rest of the conspiracy, but her callousness offended me.

"Oh, my dear, of course I have regrets. Life is full of them. But I do wish I could solve this final puzzle before I die."

"Which puzzle is that?"

"You." She rested her forearms on the table and leaned forward. "Trust me when I say you would have been the perfect candidate to make the project really viable. And yet they balked at the last minute and you ended up at the FBME."

Eight months ago, I'd been expecting a formal offer when Delia had called to tell me it had all fallen through. Her regret had been so genuine that I hadn't thought twice when she'd begun inviting me for the occasional coffee and offering career advice. "You didn't need me to help develop spells for public applications."

"No. We had this problem, you see. Our special mages were untrained and they were making mistakes. But we couldn't just bring in someone with experience, because when trained magic users disappear, people notice."

"The Grenada Five," I said, to let her know I understood her reference.

In the early 1980s, five of the world's top mages had been recruited or coerced or kidnapped — there were many theories and nobody knew for sure. They had created a spell that could kill anyone from afar. Using the spell as a threat, the organization demanded cash and the release of four inmates in a Nevada federal prison. They'd proved their capabilities by killing a general deep in the Raven Rock Mountain Complex, the US command center built to take over in case of a nuclear attack.

Two days later, the Grenada facility and all five mages had been bombed from orbit. Nobody survived.

These days, mages above a certain level were monitored a lot more closely.

(According to Hamilton, the Grenada Five disaster had been a rogue CIA op. The inmates they'd been trying to free had been CIA operatives imprisoned by a clandestine left-wing paramilitary government that had taken over Area 51. He had aerial maps of the Grenada compound that supposedly showed American flags and a CIA seal on one door. But Hamilton also had photos of Bigfoot entering a Hawaiian rainforest at the head of a military convoy, so I questioned the veracity of *everything* he showed me.)

"Indeed," Delia agreed. "So I was tasked with bringing in someone to fill that gap. And it took three years, but I found you. Not a magic user, but with all the knowledge we needed. You were perfect."

Again, I felt a ridiculous surge of pride. "Someone didn't think so."

"No, they didn't, and I find that interesting. Don't you?

What about you scared them so much that they didn't accept my recommendation? And then they tried to kill you! Simon, I understand. His death would have been political — his father has enemies among the vampire elite. But you..." She shook her head, looking at me as if the answer would be clear if she just stared hard enough.

"I have no idea."

"Neither do I. And now, I suppose I never will." She sat back in her chair. "So that's my only regret at the moment. A puzzle I'll never put together." She looked ruefully at the camera near the ceiling. "Though I suppose it won't bother me for long." Her posture straightened. "The one who recruited me is — Ah..."

As I watched from across the table, she went limp.

I forgot all of Salt's warnings about keeping my distance. "Delia?" I threw myself across the table to keep her from falling off the chair. "Help! I need help in here! Somebody!"

In those ten seconds before the door opened, Delia could have ripped out my throat with her fingers, absorbing my life force while my blood splattered on the wall. But Delia was already dead; her heart stopped instantly when she attempted to reveal information about the conspiracy.

A team ran in the door and shoved me out of the way as they unshackled her so they could start CPR. Delia's head lolled to the side, a trickle of blood running from one nostril, and then they moved her to the ground and I couldn't see her anymore.

FORTY-FOUR

When Simon found me, I was in his office, shoving my belongings into my bag with shaky hands. "I just need to go home and sleep in my own bed and forget about everything for the rest of the day," I said.

"That wasn't your fault." He took my freezing hands between his and held them tight enough to stop the shaking. "She was ill. She had just a few days to live, and they wouldn't be easy days, either."

His words rang true. On one level, I'd known that. Delia wouldn't have needed to siphon energy from other vampires if feeding from humans had been enough to keep her going. And she'd said it herself — she'd had a good life. But to have it all happen in front of me... "I've never seen someone die before."

Then another thought struck me. "Salt's going to kill me." She'd sent me in with a list of questions, and not only had I not asked them, the person I was interviewing had dropped dead.

Simon shook his head. "She knew. Probably from the

minute Delia didn't ask for an attorney. It was only a matter of time."

He was right. *But damn you, Delia, for calling me into the room*, I thought. Now, all my memories of her were tainted with the image of her slack body with blood coming from her nose. Though I supposed all my memories of her were tainted by everything she'd done. Maybe it was better this way.

Simon was still holding my hands, and I pulled mine back before it could get weird. "I'm still going home. Trix and I are going to bake chocolate chip cookies and watch terrible movies while she grades assignments." I slung my bag over my shoulder. "Tell Salt..." I bit back the rest of the sentence because Supervisory Agent Salt was standing in the doorway.

Her gaze traveled over my bag to Simon and then back to me. "Nice job in there, Perkins. The bit about using untrained magic users is new, and that gives us a solid place to start."

I blinked and stared. Instead of the lambasting I'd been expecting, she had given me a genuine compliment. Nothing about the Bureau made sense. "Uh... thanks."

"The two of you should take the rest of the day off. Get some rest. You look terrible. I'll see you both in my office tomorrow morning at eight-thirty sharp."

A moment later she was gone again, striding toward her office at a speed that would leave me running to catch up. Everyone in her path shifted out of her way.

"Maybe we're getting those commendations tomorrow," I suggested.

Simon huffed a laugh. "Your optimism is a wonder to behold."

"Well." I made an awkward gesture with my hands that

could have been a wave. "It's been an experience working with you, but I think I'll stick with my real job. If you ever need evidence analyzed, give me a call."

"I'll do that."

And then I left, happier to put distance between me and The Vault than I ever had been before, and considering never coming back.

FORTY-FIVE

A good night's sleep, a double dose of sugar, and some quality time spent with my best friend put everything into perspective. Plus, our rent was due in two days. So I showed up for work the next morning. On the way in, I'd stopped by Silver Edge to drop off chocolate chip cookies for the staff there. Trix's family recipe couldn't be beat, and we'd made four batches.

At The Vault, I left another container in the basement break room, hoping that might make the rest of the technicians more favorably disposed toward me. Not everyone had loved Hamilton, but he'd been there a long time. Meanwhile, I'd been there less than six months and most people barely remembered my name. I didn't need a mentor to tell me how this would likely end.

Hamilton's workspace was already bare — everything had been collected as evidence in the case against him. The tiny plastic dinosaur he'd given me just a few days ago had been beheaded and left on my desk. Yeah, things were going to be beyond awkward in the basement for a while. But at least I could put that off for a few minutes, because it was time to meet with Salt.

I brought another container of cookies — smaller this time — up to the fourth floor with me and stopped by Simon's office. The floor was busier than I'd ever seen it, and I didn't recognize half the vampires crammed into the space. Apparently, outside help had been brought in.

Simon was seated behind his desk, typing on his laptop. Sleep had done him good. The tense lines around his eyes had faded, and he looked almost relaxed. One eyebrow went up when I put the container down. "For me?"

"Everyone should try one of Trix's chocolate chip cookies at least once before they die." I shrugged. "Or you can give them to your mom, I guess."

"Well, in that case..." He cracked the lid on the container, releasing the smells of sugar, chocolate, and vanilla into the office. To my surprise, he picked a cookie and bit into it, closing his eyes to savor the moment. "You're right," he said around a mouthful of confectionery. "These are pretty good." He herded me out of his office as he continued eating. "But you should try Che's. He uses caramel chips and he browns the butter."

From what Trix had told me about their weekend in Dublin, a recipe swap wouldn't be hard to arrange. "I'm open to judging a contest." Slowing my steps, I asked, "Do you know why Salt wants to see us?"

"Let's find out." He knocked on Salt's closed door.

It was opened by Deputy Director Bowdey.

Salt sat behind her desk, a slew of papers covering every surface. "Bowers. Perkins. There you are." She waved us in. "You know the deputy director?" Apparently, the question was rhetorical, because she ignored us as she talked to the other vampire. "The partnership worked better than I'd hoped."

Bowdey narrowed his eyes at Salt. "Someday, one of your gambles is going to blow up in your face," he said. "You got lucky."

"Probably." Salt didn't look worried. "I'd like to keep them together as a team. We won't always need someone with Perkins's skills out in the field, but it would be useful to have her available, especially for however long it takes us to unravel this mess. It's going to require some fiddling with the paperwork on your end."

Better than she'd hoped? That sounded like she'd deliberately sent us out together to draw out the conspiracy. Simon and I shared a glance. He'd had the same thought. And what did it mean she wanted to keep us together?

The deputy director shrugged. "You're allowed to make the decisions about your team."

Speaking while two powerful vampires stared at me wasn't easy. "Magical evidence technicians work in the basement," I forced out. "I'm a liability out in the field when Bowers needs backup." Though tempted, I didn't offer to show them the nearly pristine target from the shooting range.

"She brings up a good point," Bowdey said, and I relaxed just a little. Then he continued. "She'll need more training."

Surely they couldn't force me into a completely new job. I opened my mouth to protest, but Simon cleared his throat. He said, "I assume that would put her in a new pay grade?"

I closed my mouth again.

The deputy director had the faintest of smiles on his face, as if he knew I'd been about to protest until extra money came into play. "I assume it would."

Salt waved a hand toward the door. "Now that's cleared up, get back to work. I'm going to need the two of you at Delia Tarragona's place going over everything with a fine-tooth comb. We need to find out who she was talking to and where they are."

Simon and I were halfway back to his office when I finally felt safe enough to say anything. "Remind me to never make her angry. She'd probably send us on a hike through the forest to find all the bear traps."

"Hm. You okay with this?"

It was a good question. But Delia hadn't been the only one wondering why I'd been targeted. And what better way to find out than to be part of the investigation? "I'm okay with this."

He was quiet for a moment. Then he cleared his throat. "You realize you're going to have to pass a firearms test."

A week ago, I'd have thought he was being a serious asshole, but now I could hear the humor in his voice. "Maybe my problem was the teacher."

"Uh-huh. Or maybe you just need to keep your eyes open." He pulled on his jacket and picked up his duffle bag. "Ready?"

"Ready."

We were already arguing about whether it would be faster to get to Delia's home by subway or water bus by the time we left The Vault and went out into the bright sunny skies of Floodmouth.

EPILOGUE

We'd been looking through Delia's belongings for three weeks, and I was finally coming to terms with the fact that she was both a person I admired and also a person who looked the other way when terrible things happened.

Unlike most people I knew, Delia had kept physical photos, even in an age of digital photography. The closet in her home office had a shelf of thick albums that memorialized her trips around the world. Every photo had to be cataloged and described, with the location determined from cues within the picture. The work was tedious, and we were making our way through the albums between examining rooms that had already been searched.

The current album showed events from four years prior, mostly camping trips that Delia had taken with one friend or another. She'd hiked the entire Appalachian Trail in the previous album, and this time she was somewhere near a lake. Given the vegetation and wildlife, it was west of the Rockies.

Delia's kitchen table was starting to feel like home. I flipped to the next page in the album. "Is it irony or just sad that we're stuck inside examining photos of the great outdoors?"

"Just sad," Simon replied, his fingers on the keyboard not slowing. He stopped to take a photo from behind its plastic cover so he could angle it in the light. "Can you make out the writing on this sign?"

Taking the photo from him, I held it up. The left third showed a body of water with roped buoys. On the right was a cluster of faux-rustic cabins. Between the two was an open area with a fire pit. The sign Simon had mentioned was between two cabins, but the wood looked like something had chewed on it and the letters were indistinct. "Pine Ridge? Or maybe Fire Ridge? I can't tell."

He turned back to his computer and typed. "Let's hope it's Fire Ridge. That might be enough to identify the location."

I glanced over the photo again, looking for anything else that might help us. The only visible car, a minivan, had too much mud on the rear bumper for the plate to be visible.

Each cabin had a small sign hanging above the door, but the photo was too blurry to make anything out. Then I saw the woman standing on the porch, and my breath caught.

She was older, her hair darker, as if she hadn't been spending hours in the sun, but I knew that posture as well as I knew my own.

It was *impossible*.

Yet there she was.

"Jen?" Simon was leaning toward me, his tone worried, as if he'd been calling my name for a while. "What's wrong?"

Afraid that the photo would change if I looked away, I pointed to the woman.

He tried to take the photo so he could look more closely, but I was clutching it too tightly. "You know her?"

I had to be wrong about this, but I knew in my bones that I was right. And if this was true, it changed *everything*.

Delia had died with one question, and I suddenly knew the answer.

I forced enough breath out to say, "That's my sister."

In the sudden silence, the only noise was the hum of the refrigerator. Simon's voice was careful. "She's too old to be Maya."

Taking my eyes from the photo for the first time, I looked into the face of this vampire who had become one of the people I trusted most in the world. All I could see was concern for me. That would change as he worked out the implications. This was the last moment everything would be uncomplicated, that my loyalties would align with the FBME, but there was no way around it. I couldn't keep this a secret.

Looking back at the photo, the shock hit me again, more muted this time. It was her. I was sure of it.

"That's Julie."

READY FOR ANOTHER *Floodmouth adventure with Jen and Simon? My monthly newsletter has writing updates, foster kitten pictures, and other things you might enjoy. Plus you get free short stories, like* Floodmouth Cases: Dangerous Secrets, *when you sign up!* https://tmbaumgartner.com/subscribe/

ACKNOWLEDGMENTS

This book was inspired by a question posted in Reddit's r/NoStupidQuestions (and thereafter copied to all corners of the internet): "Could a vampire policeman enter my house if they had a warrant?" The original poster then commented: "This question has destroyed many of my friend groups." So I ought to start by thanking the user Snipper64. May your friends appreciate the chaos you bring to their lives!

My friends are all amazing and remain unfazed by vampire questions. Without them, I might never leave my house and the foster kittens would be *far* less socialized. So thank you!

As always, I need to thank my critique group for pointing out the parts of this novel that worked and also suggesting that the villain should show up before the book was almost done. When they're right, they're right, dangit.

With this novel I had a goal of improving my world building game, which led to things like maps of Floodmouth and a menu for the Little Bites Cafe. There's even an AITA post set in Floodmouth! A big thanks to my Patreon subscribers for supporting me as I produced tourism brochures that looked more PowerPoint presentations. You're very awesome people!

Finally, thank you to my brother Eric for proofreading the final draft. Our English teachers would be proud.

(Proud of you, that is — I think I'm still in the doghouse over my inability to diagram sentences.)

ABOUT THE AUTHOR

T. M. Baumgartner is a speculative fiction writer who has difficulty following directions. This probably explains why the IRS recalculates her tax refund after she files it every year. At various times she has been a veterinarian, Unix system administrator, software developer, and after-hours book-shelver in a medical library.

Theresa currently lives in Northern California in a house with too many animals. She knits hats for garden gnomes and fails to grow tomatoes despite living in the perfect climate.

She also writes cozy mysteries under the pen name Tess Baytree.

Want updates about new releases? Silly dog anecdotes? Free stories? Join the newsletter mailing list! Go to https://tmbaumgartner.com/subscribe/ or point your phone's camera at the QR code above.

The marketing department here at Speculative Turtle Press is great at tail wagging, but a little challenged by tasks that require thumbs.

If you enjoyed this book and would like to help other readers find it, please tell your friends and consider leaving a review at your favorite site.

ABOUT THE AUTHOR

ALSO BY T.M. BAUMGARTNER

As T.M. Baumgartner:

Shift Happens

The Chaos Job (Jackpot Drift #1)

The Chaos Connection (Jackpot Drift #2)

The Chaos Nexus (Jackpot Drift #3)

Dragon Freehold

All Gremlins Great & Small (The Portal Storms #0)

All Rocs Wise & Wonderful (The Portal Storms #1)

All Basilisks Wild & Sparking (The Portal Storms #2)

Theoretical Magic (The Floodmouth Files #1)

As Tess Baytree:

Death Walks a Dog (Penelope Standing #1)

Death Tracks the Scent (Penelope Standing #2)

Death Smells a Rose (Penelope Standing #3)

Death Trims the Tree (holiday novella)

Death Crashes a Wedding (Penelope Standing #4)

Death Paints a Picture (Penelope Standing #5)